HARDCASTLE'S ACTRESS

HARDCASTLE'S ACTRESS

Graham Ison

This first world edition published in Great Britain 2007 by
SEVERN HOUSE PUBLISHERS LTD of
9–15 High Street, Sutton, Surrey SM1 1DF.
This first world edition published in the USA 2007 by
SEVERN HOUSE PUBLISHERS INC of
595 Madison Avenue, New York, N.Y. 10022.

British Library Cataloguing in Publication Data

Ison, Graham
    Hardcastle's actress
    1.   Hardcastle, Detective Inspector (Fictitious character) - Fiction
    2.   Police - England - London - Fiction
    3.   Detective and mystery stories
    I.   Title
    823.9'14 [F]

    ISBN-13: 978-0-7278-6515-1   (cased)

All Severn House titles are printed on acid-free paper.

Typeset by Palimpsest Book Production Ltd.,
Grangemouth, Stirlingshire, Scotland.
Printed and bound in Great Britain by
MPG Books Ltd., Bodmin, Cornwall.

Glossary

APM: assistant provost marshal (a lieutenant colonel of the military police).

BAILEY, the: Central Criminal Court, London.
BAILIWICK: area of responsibility.
BEAK: magistrate.
BEF: British Expeditionary Force in France and Flanders.
BLUES, The: alternative name for the Royal Horse Guards.
BOB: shilling (now 5p).
BRADSHAW: timetable giving routes and times of British railway services.
BRIEF: warrant *or* police warrant card *or* lawyer.
BUCK HOUSE: Buckingham Palace.
BUN IN THE OVEN, to have a: to be pregnant.
BURGESS: citizen of a borough.
BUSY: detective.

CATS AND DOGS, to come down: to rain heavily.
CID: Criminal Investigation Department.
CIGS: Chief of the Imperial General Staff.
C-in-C: Commander-in-Chief
CIVVIES: civilians (i.e. not members of the armed forces).
COFFIN NAILS: cigarettes.
COSTERMONGER: fruit-seller.
CLYDE (*as in* D'YOU THINK I CAME UP THE CLYDE ON A BICYCLE?): to deny that the speaker is a fool.
COLDSTREAMER: soldier of the Coldstream Guards.

COMMISSIONER'S OFFICE: official title of New Scotland Yard, headquarters of the Metropolitan Police.
COPPER: policeman.
CULLY: alternative to calling a man 'mate'.

D: detective.
DABS: fingerprints.
DARTMOOR: remote prison on Dartmoor in Devon.
DDI: Divisional Detective Inspector.
DIGS or DIGGINGS: rented lodgings, usually short term.
DOGBERRY: policeman or watchman (*ex* Shakespeare).
DOG'S DINNER: mess.
DRUM: dwelling house.

EIGHT O'CLOCK WALK, to take the: to be hanged.

FARTHING: one quarter of an old penny.
FEEL THE COLLAR OF, to: to make an arrest.
FOURPENNY CANNON: steak and kidney pie.
FRONT, The: theatre of WWI operations in France and Flanders.

GAMAGES: a London department store.
GLIM, a: a look (a foreshortening of 'glimpse').
GODS: gallery of a theatre.
GREAT SCOTLAND YARD: location of an army recruiting office, not to be confused with New Scotland Yard.
GUV *or* GUV'NOR: informal alternative to 'sir'.

HORSE'S NECK: brandy and ginger ale; reputed to be a favourite drink among officers of the Royal Navy.

IRONCLAD, a: a warship.

JIG-A-JIG: sexual intercourse.
JILDI: quickly (*ex* Hindi).
JUDY: girl.

KATE CARNEY: army (rhyming slang: from Kate Carney, a music-hall comedienne of the late nineteenth and early twentieth centuries).

LINEN DRAPERS: newspapers (rhyming slang).
LORD CHAMBERLAIN: an officer of the Sovereign's Household, formerly responsible for licensing theatres in London and other places where the Sovereign may reside.

MAGSMAN: common thief.
MANOR: police area.
MARLBOROUGH: famous public school in Wiltshire.
MILLING: fighting.
MONS, to make a: to make a mess of things, as in the disastrous Battle of Mons in 1914.
MUFTI: army term for plain clothes.
NICK: police station or prison.
NICKED: arrested.

OFF ONE'S NUT: to be crazy.
OLD BAILEY: Central Criminal Court, London.

PAPER THE HOUSE, to: to give away free tickets for a theatre show.
PEACH, to: to inform to the police.
PICCADILLY WINDOW: monocle.
PLATES: feet (rhyming slang: plates of meat).
PLONK, the: the mud of no-man's-land.
POMPEY: Portsmouth.
PONY: £25 sterling.
PROVOST: military police.

QUID: £1 sterling.

ROYAL VICTORIAN ORDER: an order of chivalry within the personal gift of the Sovereign.

SAM BROWNE: military officer's belt with shoulder strap.
SANDRINGHAM: royal residence in Norfolk.

SCREWING: engaging in sexual intercourse with.

SELFRIDGES: a London department store.

SELL THE PUP: to attempt to deceive.

SHILLING: twelve pence, now 5p.

SKIN-AND-BLISTER: sister (rhyming slang).

SKIP *or* SKIPPER: informal police alternative to station-sergeant, clerk-sergeant and sergeant; also, a naval commander.

SMOKE, The: London.

SOVEREIGN, The: The King, or Queen regnant.

SOVEREIGN (or SOV): £1 sterling.

SPALPEEN: rascal; a worthless fellow.

SPIN A TWIST: to tell an unbelievable tale.

STAGE-DOOR JOHNNY: young man frequenting theatres in an attempt to make the acquaintance of actresses.

STIPE: stipendiary magistrate (a qualified barrister presiding alone in a petty sessional court).

STIR: prison.

SWADDY: soldier (*ex* Hindi.)

TOBY: police area.

TOMMY or TOMMY ATKINS: British soldier. The name 'Tommy Atkins' was used as an example on early army forms.

TOOLEY STREET TAILOR: conceitedly bumptious fellow.

TOPPED: murdered or hanged.

TOPPING: a murder or hanging.

TROUBLE-AND-STRIFE: wife (rhyming slang).

TUMBLE: sexual intercourse.

TUPPENNY-HA'PENNY: a contraction of twopence-half-penny, indicating something or someone of little worth.

UP THE SPOUT: pregnant.

WAR OFFICE: Department of State overseeing the army. (Now a part of the Ministry of Defence.)

One

Despite her father's warning about the fire risk, Kitty Hardcastle had lighted the candles on the Christmas tree that stood in one corner of the parlour at 27 Kennington Road, Lambeth. Intriguing brown-paper parcels of various shapes and sizes were piled beneath it; each bore a label indicating the particular member of the family for whom it was a gift.

Kitty and her younger sister Maud had collected sprigs of holly and spruce from the grounds of the nearby Bethlehem Royal Hospital, and arranged them tastefully around the pictures. Painstakingly prepared garlands had been strung from the corners of the room to the recently installed electric light fitting in the centre of the ceiling. And beneath the light, the mischievous Kitty had hung a sprig of mistletoe, but without much hope of benefiting from it. At least, not when her father was around.

This year, 1914, Christmas Day fell on a Friday and over the past twenty-one years, Ernest Hardcastle had always wound the eight-day mantel clock on a Friday, and he did so now.

In 1893, Hardcastle, then a young constable at Old Street police station, married Alice Roberts, who was nearly five years his junior. The rosewood chiming clock – a wedding present – had cost Alice's father, Battery Sergeant-Major Ted Roberts, twenty-nine shillings and sixpence, slightly more than a week's pay for a warrant officer.

'It's one o'clock, Alice,' said Hardcastle, taking his chromium-plated hunter from his waistcoat pocket and checking its time against that of the clock.

'The goose should be ready in about half an hour, Ernie,'

called Alice from the kitchen. She slipped off her apron and walked through to the parlour. 'And I hope it's worth it, the price I had to pay.'

'Good.' Hardcastle ignored his wife's comment about rising prices, and rubbed his hands together. 'Time for a drop of sherry, then.' He opened a cabinet and took out a bottle of Amontillado and five glasses. The glasses had been a wedding present too, and were only brought out on special occasions. Like Christmas.

'*Five* glasses, Ernie?' queried Alice.

'I reckon young Wally's old enough for a sherry, seeing as it's Christmas.' In view of what Alice had said about the cost of the goose, Hardcastle thought he had better not mention that the sherry had set him back four shillings.

'Well, I don't know,' said Alice doubtfully. 'He's only fourteen.' Even though she recognized that young Walter was growing up fast, she was not sure that he was yet ready for sherry.

'Won't do the lad any harm to learn how to drink properly,' muttered Hardcastle. But knowing that young Walter had been employed as a telegram boy since leaving school almost a year ago, his father was fairly certain that it would not be the lad's first taste of alcohol. 'Anyway, he'll be fifteen next month.'

Once the whole family had assembled, Hardcastle proposed a toast. 'A merry Christmas, and here's health and happiness to us all,' he said, raising his glass. 'And may this terrible war be over before *next* Christmas.' It proved to be unfulfilled optimism; the Great War, as it became known, was to last nearly another four years, and be responsible for the death and maiming of millions. And a change in the social order of the country that could not possibly have been visualized when it started.

But the Hardcastles' hopeful celebrations were interrupted by a knock at the door.

'Oh, no, I don't believe it,' said Alice. 'Not on Christmas Day.' Regrettably, she was all too accustomed to her husband being sent for to deal with some serious crime.

'Don't fuss yourself, Alice,' said Hardcastle. 'It'll most

likely be one of the neighbours dropping in to wish us the compliments of the season.' He placed his glass carefully on the mantelpiece beside the clock and made for the front door.

The young policeman saluted. 'Mr Hardcastle, sir?'

'What is it, lad?'

'There's a message for you, sir. You're wanted at Scotland Yard.' The PC pulled a flimsy message from his pocket and handed it to Hardcastle. 'Urgent it says, sir.'

Hardcastle quickly scanned the form. 'Oh bugger it!' he exclaimed loudly.

'*Ernest!*' cautioned Alice from the sitting room.

Hardcastle recognized his wife's use of his full name as a reproof for having sworn, but chose to ignore it.

'Come in, lad, and have a glass of sherry to warm yourself.'

'Thank you very much, sir.' The young policeman did not recall ever having been offered a drink by so senior an officer. Removing his helmet, he followed Hardcastle through to the sitting room.

Taking the sixth remaining glass from the cabinet, Hardcastle filled it. It was an unusual act of generosity on his part, but Christmas was different.

'A merry Christmas, sir,' said the PC, 'and you too, ma'am,' he added, glancing at Alice Hardcastle.

'I doubt it will be,' grumbled Hardcastle. As the divisional detective inspector in charge of the Criminal Investigation Department for the A or Whitehall Division of the Metropolitan Police, he was accustomed to being called out by a service that habitually set its corporate face against acknowledging the existence of high days and holidays.

'I'm afraid I've got to go out, Alice,' said Hardcastle. He glanced at the message form again and turned to the PC. 'Did they say what it was about, lad?'

'No, sir,' said the young policeman. 'All I know is what's on the message,' he added, and chanced a smile towards Kitty, the Hardcastles' eldest daughter.

Kitty, a winsome eighteen-year-old who rarely failed to

attract the attention of young men, smiled in return and lowered her eyes in what she believed to be a fetching way.

'Oh, it's too much,' complained Alice. 'What about Christmas dinner?'

'You go ahead and enjoy it,' said Hardcastle. 'But keep a few slices of cold goose for me. There's no telling when I'll be back. I don't even know what it's about. All it says here – ' he tapped the message form – 'is that I've to see Mr Ward immediately.'

New Scotland Yard was a grim, grey fortress of a building that overlooked the River Thames and the half-built County Hall on the opposite bank. The Yard, like Hardcastle's own police station facing it, had been built from granite that, fittingly, had been hewn by Dartmoor convicts.

Being Christmas Day, the main entrance to the building was closed and Hardcastle was obliged to enter by what was known as Back Hall, the black door to which was in the corner of the courtyard.

Nodding in response to the duty constable's salute, Hardcastle mounted the stairs to the tiled corridor where were to be found the offices of the Yard's most senior officers.

Detective Chief Inspector Alfred Ward, the officer in charge of the Central Office of the CID at Scotland Yard, had only recently returned from another bout of the persistent illness that was to bring about his death two years later. But Ward was a dedicated policeman and thought nothing of interrupting his Yuletide break when there was a duty to be undertaken.

'I'm sorry to have spoiled your Christmas Day, Mr Hardcastle,' Ward began, 'and I would have found another officer if I could have done so. Unfortunately all the Central Office detectives are otherwise engaged on duties of a various kind.'

'I see, sir.' Hardcastle was not convinced of that. The detectives of the Murder Squad at Scotland Yard regarded themselves as an elite, and tended to look down on divisional detectives. There was no point in arguing, but

Hardcastle would have been prepared to bet that they were all at home enjoying Christmas dinner with their families.

'Windsor,' said Ward with his customary brevity.

'Windsor, sir?' echoed Hardcastle.

'Seems there's been a murder, Mr Hardcastle. The body of a young woman was found in Windsor Great Park at four o'clock this morning. The Chief Constable of Windsor thinks that his detectives are not up to investigating a murder, and he's asked for assistance from the Yard. The Commissioner has acceded to the request and, as you are an officer skilled in the investigation of murder, I've picked you for the job.'

'Thank you, sir.' Hardcastle was, however, unimpressed by Ward's blandishments; he realized that his selection was an expedient rather than recognition of his ability.

'So get yourself down there as soon as you can, and let me know how you get on. I presume you'll take one of your own sergeants.'

'Yes, sir.' Hardcastle immediately decided that he would take Detective Sergeant Charles Marriott with him. Although he was loath to ruin Marriott's Christmas Day in the way his own had been marred, he did not intend to take an assistant unfamiliar with his ways. And Marriott knew his DDI's methods better than anyone else.

'Get on with it, then,' said Ward, and waved a hand of dismissal. He dipped his pen in the inkwell and began writing a minute in the file that lay open on his desk.

To put it mildly, Lorna Marriott had not been pleased when Hardcastle arrived at the Marriotts' Regency Street quarters to summon her husband for detached duty. Despite Marriott's attempts to quieten her, she had told the DDI, in no uncertain terms, what she thought about a police force that took their children's father away from his family on Christmas Day.

Hardcastle confined himself to commenting that it would be even worse when Marriott was a divisional detective inspector. Although it was meant to imply that Marriott would eventually reach that exalted rank, Lorna did not see it that way, and it did little to improve her mood. If anything, it worsened it.

As it was Christmas, the train service from Waterloo to Windsor was infrequent. Consequently, it was gone five o'clock by the time the two Metropolitan officers arrived at the police headquarters adjoining the police station in St Leonard's Road.

'I'm Divisional Detective Inspector Hardcastle of the Metropolitan Police, and this here's Detective Sergeant Marriott,' said Hardcastle to the sergeant manning the front office desk. 'I'm here to see the chief constable.'

The elderly sergeant pulled thoughtfully at his beard, apart from which he made no move to do Hardcastle's bidding. 'Bless you, sir,' he said, 'the chief constable's at home with his family, it being Christmas Day like.'

'I'm well aware what day it is, Sergeant,' snapped Hardcastle. 'However, your chief constable sent for me urgently, so you'd better tell me where I can find him. And a bit quick an' all.' He was in no mood to be thwarted by an individual whose attitude suggested that he was unlikely to do anything in a hurry.

'Perhaps I'd better get the inspector, sir.' This sort of dilemma was not one with which the sergeant was prepared to deal on Christmas Day. Or, for that matter, on any other day.

'Yes, perhaps you had,' said Hardcastle, and turned to his own sergeant. 'If it's like this when they've got a murder on their hands, Marriott, God alone knows what it's like when they haven't. It's no wonder the King insists on the Metropolitan Police guarding Windsor Castle.'

'Yes, sir.' Marriott had long ago learned that monosyllabic answers were the safest response to Hardcastle's tirades about the inefficiency of others. Apart from which he was fairly certain that the King neither knew nor cared which police force guarded his Berkshire residence.

A minute or two later, a uniformed inspector emerged from an office at the rear of the police station. Flicking the last of some crumbs from the front of his tunic, he stared at Hardcastle. 'My sergeant tells me you want to see the chief constable, sir,' he said in tones that implied Hardcastle had made a fatuous request.

'No,' said Hardcastle flatly. 'Your chief constable wants to see *me*.'

'Might I ask what it's about, sir?'

'God Almighty,' thundered Hardcastle. 'It's about a murder. I've been sent down here to deal with the death of some young woman who was found in Windsor Great Park at four o'clock this morning. And apparently you haven't got any detectives who are up to finding out who topped her. There, Inspector, now you know what it's all about.'

'Ah, yes,' said the Windsor inspector, 'I thought that's what it'd be, sir. In that case you'll need to see our detective inspector. He's in charge of our CID and is dealing with the matter. He's upstairs at the moment.'

Hardcastle glared at the uniformed sergeant, now sheltering behind his inspector. 'You could have said that to start with, Sergeant,' he snapped. 'I don't have time to waste, you know.'

'I'm sorry, sir, but I didn't know that's what you'd come about,' said the sergeant.

'Well, I haven't come down here to clear up a case of sheep-stealing, that's for sure,' said Hardcastle tersely. And with that he followed the local inspector up a flight of stairs at the rear of the building.

The man who greeted Hardcastle and Marriott was a tall, grey-haired man of about fifty years of age. His opening statement completely disarmed the London DDI, and did much to defuse the foul temper that had been building ever since the Kennington PC had knocked at Hardcastle's door earlier that day.

'I'm Detective Inspector Angus Struthers, Mr Hardcastle.' The Windsor DI spoke with a marked Aberdonian accent, and crossed his office with his hand outstretched. 'I can't tell you how sorry I am to have been instrumental in getting you sent down here on Christmas Day of all days. Do take a seat, and you too, er . . . ?'

'Detective Sergeant Marriott, sir.'

'Good. Well, I'm pleased to meet you both, and I'm sure I can persuade you gentlemen to take a dram while I tell you what we know.' Struthers opened a filing cabinet and took out a bottle of Scotch whisky and three tumblers. But then he turned. 'Which is not very much, I'm afraid. Apart from the young woman's identity, that is.' He finished pouring the whisky and handed the glasses to the London detectives. 'You'll not be wanting water, I take it, Mr Hardcastle?' To a Scotsman such dilution would have been tantamount to sacrilege.

'Indeed not.' Hardcastle took a swig of his whisky, noting at the same time that the Windsor DI's speech was a little slurred. But then it was Christmas. 'And who is the murder victim, Mr Struthers?'

'Her name's Victoria Hart.'

'How did you manage to identify her so quickly?'

'She's an actress of sorts who'd been appearing in a revue at the Windsor Empire,' said Struthers. 'Well, more of a song-and-dance artiste, I suppose you'd call her. Apparently, she's been likened to a younger version of Marie Lloyd, but a bit more risqué. Her body was found by a park ranger, name of Jenkins – Harry Jenkins – and he'd seen the show recently and recognized her.'

'Cause of death?' queried Hardcastle.

'Manual strangulation.'

'Are you certain of that, Mr Struthers?' Hardcastle was surprised that a post-mortem examination had been conducted so quickly. If it had.

The Windsor detective smiled. 'Aye, we managed to get a pathologist to do the PM this morning.'

'Must have cost a pretty penny, getting him out of bed on Christmas Day,' grunted Hardcastle, aware of the fees charged by London pathologists.

Struthers laughed. 'I reckon the rich burgesses of the Royal Borough can afford it,' he said, leaning across to top up Hardcastle's glass. 'It seems that the woman had been dead for some time before she was found. The pathologist estimates that she was probably killed at around seven o'clock on Christmas Eve.'

'So, what do you know about this woman?' asked Hardcastle.

'Not a great deal as yet,' said Struthers. 'But we did follow up on what the park ranger—'

'Is there a resident caretaker at this Windsor Empire?' asked Hardcastle, cutting across what Struthers was saying.

'Yes. I was about to mention him. Joseph Sharples is his name, and he also acts as stage-door keeper.'

'Well, in that case,' said Hardcastle, 'we'd better pay him a visit and see what we can find out.' He intended to waste no more time in Windsor than was necessary.

'Been done already, Mr Hardcastle.' Struthers reached across his desk and picked up several sheets of paper. 'I've got his statement here, but to save you reading it straight away I'll summarize what he had to say.' He put on a pair of horn-rimmed spectacles. 'Victoria Hart's been appearing in a revue at the Windsor Empire for the past two weeks.' He looked up. 'It was called *Beaux Belles*. Daft sort of title, if you ask me. However, it closed yesterday, Christmas Eve. They've a pantomime starting there tomorrow, apparently. The only interesting thing to come out of that – ' he put down the statement and pushed it to one side – 'is that she had several admirers.'

'Did she take up with any of these admirers, do we know?' asked Hardcastle.

'That I don't know, but it shouldn't be too difficult to track them down. According to Sharples there were one or two army officers who took an interest in her – Household Cavalry swells by all accounts – from up the road at Combermere Barracks.'

'Anything else?'

'It seems that her performance was a bit, well, daring, I suppose you'd call it. We took a statement from the park ranger who found her. As I said, he'd seen the show, and he told me that she appeared in top hat, a basque – that's a corset-like affair, apparently – black silk tights and shoes with high heels.' He laughed. 'And nothing else but a silver-topped cane. Did a bit of an exotic dance, by all accounts. Didn't go down too well with the matriarchs of Windsor, I can tell you, but it was very popular with the male members of the audience. Particularly when she belted out her final song: *"We don't want to lose you, but we think you ought to go"*. Real patriotic stuff that brought the house down, and I'm told she succeeded in persuading quite a few to join up.'

'Not surprising,' commented Hardcastle. 'Was she helping with recruiting, then?'

'She certainly was, and there was a recruiting sergeant waiting in the wings,' Struthers continued. 'He'd appear on stage with her at the end of the show and wait for these youngsters to rush up and take the King's shilling. Probably because they got a kiss from Miss Hart when they signed on,' he added with a chuckle. 'But they'll likely live to regret it once they get to Aldershot.'

'Or die regretting it when they get to France,' said Hardcastle cynically. He was all too aware of the rout suffered by the British Army at Mons the previous August. 'Apart from these army officers, was there anyone else who called regularly at the stage door?'

'Quite a few, it seems.' Struthers paused as though unwilling to express an opinion. 'I suppose that because of the revealing costume she was dressed in on stage there were one or two young bloods who fancied their chances with her. Thought she was easy game, maybe. I have to say that a lot of actresses are.'

'And do *you* think she was, sir?' asked Marriott, looking up from the notes he had been making.

'I don't really know, Sergeant,' said Struthers. 'But an actress who appears half naked gets that sort of reputation, I suppose. Whether it's justified or not.' He paused, and chuckled. 'I doubt she'd ever appeared north of the border. The elders of the Kirk of Scotland would have had a few choice words to say about that, I can tell you.'

'You referred to her just now as *Miss* Hart, Mr Struthers,' said Hardcastle. 'Does that mean she's unmarried?'

'We've not discovered that yet. But I do have the address of the actor-manager who put the show together. His name's Percy Savage. I'm hoping he can tell us more, but he may not know much about the girl's private life.'

This sort of lackadaisical approach to a murder investigation did not suit Hardcastle. 'Does this Savage live locally?' he demanded.

Struthers flicked back a page in his action book. 'He's in theatrical diggings in Alma Road.'

'Well, in that case, why don't we go and see him? On the other hand, he might already have gone, seeing as how the show's closed.'

Struthers looked doubtful. 'I'm not sure we'll get a cab, seeing that it's Christmas,' he said. 'The only motor car here is the chief constable's, and we daren't take that.'

Hardcastle shook his head in bewilderment. 'Then we'll walk.' On the way down, he had familiarized himself with a map of Windsor that he had purchased from the station bookstall – surprisingly open on Christmas Day – and knew that Alma Road was less than half a mile from the headquarters. 'I could do with a breath of fresh air.' He stood up and put on his hat and coat.

'There's not really much point in my coming with you, Mr Hardcastle. The chief constable was adamant that it's to be your enquiry. We just don't have the resources or the experience to deal with a murder here.'

Hardcastle was surprised at Struthers's unusual candour, but decided that the DI had had a little too much to drink to make any valuable contribution to the enquiry. 'Talking of the chief constable, I'll need to speak to him at some time. When d'you reckon he'll be coming to work?'

'Not before Monday, Mr Hardcastle,' said Struthers after consulting a calendar. 'If then.'

'Good grief,' said Hardcastle.

Two

The man who answered the door of the Victorian house in Alma Road had a glass in his hand, was wearing a paper hat and appeared slightly the worse for drink. He had abandoned his jacket, collar and tie, and his waistcoat was undone. For a moment or two he gazed closely at the two detectives.

'Yes, what is it?' he demanded brusquely, his surly manner a contrast with his festive appearance.

'Mr Savage?' asked Hardcastle.

'No. I'm Mr Armitage. What d'you want?'

'Is there a Mr Savage here?' asked Hardcastle patiently.

'Who wants him?'

'Police,' said Hardcastle.

The surliness disappeared, and Armitage laughed. 'About time, too.' Still holding on to the door – probably for support – he leaned back. 'Percy, the busies have come for you.' He faced the policemen again. 'You'd better come in, I suppose. Will you join us in a drink?'

'No, thank you,' said Hardcastle.

Four people were seated around a comforting coal fire in the parlour. In the centre of this group a small, low table was filled with glasses and a variety of bottles. Clearly the little party had been enjoying itself.

In addition to a middle-aged woman in an armchair – who proved to be Armitage's wife – two much younger women and a young man were seated on a large sofa. The man was between the two girls, his arms around their shoulders.

'Are you Mr Savage?' asked Hardcastle.

'Yes, that's me. Savage by name, but a pussy cat by

nature.' The speaker laughed and squeezed the two girls. A man of about thirty, he was dressed in a colourful striped blazer, cream flannel trousers and an open-necked white shirt; attire that Hardcastle thought more suitable for the cricket field than Christmas Day. Savage's black hair was pomaded flat to his head and he had a neatly trimmed moustache.

'I'm Divisional Detective Inspector Hardcastle of Scotland Yard.' Hardcastle decided that mention of the Yard sounded more impressive than Cannon Row police station, apart from which he was, in a sense, temporarily attached to Commissioner's Office. Furthermore, he thought that the young dandy lounging on the settee was not taking the arrival of the police seriously.

It had the required effect: the levity vanished. Savage relinquished his hold on the two girls and stood up. 'Whatever is it?' he asked, his face taking on a grave expression.

'It's about Victoria Hart,' said Hardcastle.

'What about her?'

'She's been murdered. Her body was found in Windsor Great Park in the early hours of this morning.'

'Oh good God Almighty!' Savage's face went white. 'I don't believe it. On a Christmas Day too. What a terrible thing to have happened. She was top of the bill.'

Hardcastle glanced at the two girls. Their expressions and their pallor showed that they were deeply shocked by the news. 'Are these young ladies part of the show that Miss Hart was in?' he asked.

'Er, yes, they are. This is Vera Cobb and that's Fanny Morris,' said Savage, waving a hand at each of his two companions in turn. 'They're mainly dancers, but they sing a bit.' It did not sound too complimentary.

'I see. So obviously you would both have known Miss Hart,' Hardcastle said, addressing the two women.

'Yes,' said the older one, whom Savage had indicated was Vera Cobb. The other girl, white-faced and clearly still in shock at the news of the leading lady's death, merely nodded. 'We dance with Vicky,' added Vera, 'sort of in the background, when she does her final act.'

The woman in the armchair looked at Hardcastle. 'Oh, what a terrible thing to have happened,' she said in an abstract way, before lapsing into silence once more.

'When did you last see Miss Hart, Mr Savage?'

'At the matinée performance yesterday. We'd decided from the outset not to have an evening show so that the boys and girls could get home for Christmas.'

'Why are you still here, then?'

Savage smiled and indicated the two girls. 'I'm rather enjoying the company, Inspector, and Mr and Mrs Armitage here invited us to stay on and join in their festivities.'

'How well did you know Miss Hart?' asked Marriott.

'I knew her very well. We're a travelling company, you see. We've been a troupe for about eighteen months now.'

'How many of you are there?'

'We've got four acrobats, a vent—'

'A what?' queried Hardcastle.

'A ventriloquist,' said Savage, 'and there's a burlesque character comedian, a female impersonator, an escapologist and one or two others. As I said, Vicky was top of the bill. But it's mainly the girls – all ten of them are dancers – that bring in the audience. Hence the name of the show: the *Beaux Belles*. They're all very good, but not particularly well known.'

'Did you all leave the theatre together? After the show, I mean.'

'Not immediately. We had a party on stage to mark the end of the run, and to celebrate Christmas,' said Savage. 'That went on till about half-past six, I suppose. Then a few of us went across to the Bull. That's the pub opposite the theatre. Just for a few final drinks.'

'And did Miss Hart go with you?'

'No, she didn't, Inspector. She received a telegram, not long after the party on stage had started.'

'Oh? What was that about?'

'I've no idea, but round about five o'clock, Joe Sharples – he's the stage-door keeper – came in with a telegram for Vicky. She read it, clapped her hands and said she had to go. And with that she rushed off, presumably to her dressing room.' Savage regarded Hardcastle sadly. 'And that was the last time I saw her.'

'What happened to this telegram, Mr Savage?'

'I don't know. I think she might have taken it with her. On the other hand she might have given it back to Sharples. You'll have to ask him.'

'Did Miss Hart say what was in the telegram, Mr Savage?'

'No. But she seemed pleased with whatever it said.'

'And you went with Mr Savage to the pub, did you, miss?' asked Marriott, turning to Vera Cobb.

'Yes, that's right.'

'What time did you leave the Bull, Mr Savage?' asked Hardcastle.

'About seven, I think.' Savage looked at Vera for confirmation. The girl hesitated, but then nodded. 'Then we came back here to Alma Road and had supper with Mr and Mrs Armitage. Me, Vera and Fanny Morris. And I went to bed at about half-past eleven.'

Hardcastle glanced at Mr Armitage. 'And you can confirm that, can you?'

Armitage paused briefly. 'Oh, yes. That's right.'

'Did Miss Hart have any romantic attachments that you knew of, Mr Savage?' asked Hardcastle.

'Actually it's *Mrs* Hart, Inspector,' said Savage. 'She was married, so she said.'

'Is Hart her married name? Or was Victoria Hart her stage name?'

'No, I'm sure it was her real name,' said Savage. He glanced at Vera and Fanny. 'I think that's right, isn't it, darlings?'

It was Fanny Morris who answered. 'Yes, I think so,' she said.

'I'm sure it was,' agreed Vera.

'I've never met him, but I understand that he's in the navy,' volunteered Savage. 'A commander, I think Vicky said he was.'

'I'll bet Mr Struthers didn't know that,' said Hardcastle in an aside to Marriott. 'We'll have to make sure the commander's informed. Wherever he is.'

'Yes, sir.' Marriott made a note in his pocket book.

'Even though Mrs Hart was married, Mr Savage, d'you know if she had any admirers? Any gentlemen friends who might have taken her out to dinner, for example?'

'I doubt it. In fact, she was a very proper sort of girl. I know she appeared on stage in a saucy costume, but a lot of actresses dress like that these days. It didn't mean she was free with her favours. As far as I know she was very loyal to her husband, and often mentioned him. As a matter of fact I think she was quite worried about him, on account of him being at sea in one of those ironclads.'

'I've heard that there were several army officers who made a habit of pestering her. Sharples, the stage-door keeper, told local officers that there were quite a few who called at the theatre for her.'

'It happens with attractive showgirls, I'm afraid,' said Savage. 'Everywhere we go there are stage-door johnnies who think they can have their way with them. That's right, isn't it, girls?'

'Rather,' said Vera, a little too keenly, and she and Fanny Morris giggled.

'Where are you going when you leave here, Mr Savage?' asked Marriott.

'Back to London. To the Playhouse Theatre in Northumberland Avenue. We've got a show starting there on the fourth of January.'

'And what address will you be staying at?'

'We've got digs in Pimlico, me and Fanny and Vera. It's where we always stay when we're in Town.'

'That's handy,' said Hardcastle. Pimlico was close to his own divisional boundary. 'Perhaps you'd give my sergeant here the exact address.'

'Certainly, but I'm not sure we'll be able to put the show on without Vicky.' Savage was obviously concerned that the loss of his star performer would affect the future of the revue that he managed.

'I could take her part, Percy,' Vera Cobb put in quickly.

Savage looked thoughtful. 'Well, maybe.' He was aware that Vera did not possess the magnetism that Victoria Hart

had displayed so admirably. And although she had occasionally deputized for Victoria, he was by no means certain
that she could fill the role on a permanent basis.

'Where was Mrs Hart in lodgings here in Windsor?' asked
Hardcastle.

'Not far from here. In Clarence Road, as a matter of fact.
I'd sometimes walk her home after the show, particularly
if there were any men hanging about at the stage door. I
think she was a bit worried by them.'

'Anyone in particular?'

'I don't think any of them made a nuisance of themselves, although I did warn one persistent cavalry officer
to clear off.'

'When was this?'

'A few days ago. Last week, perhaps. We were coming
out of the theatre after the last performance and this fellow
asked her to join him for supper.'

'Any idea who he was?'

'No, I'm afraid not.' Savage laughed. 'I didn't ask for
his name.'

In retrospect it seemed to Hardcastle that Victoria Hart
had had good reason to be concerned. And that interested
him. 'I see. Well, I think that's all for the moment, Mr
Savage,' he said. 'But I will need you, and these two ladies,
to come down to police headquarters to make statements
before you leave. And I shall doubtless be seeing you again
in London.'

On their way back to St Leonard's Road, Marriott asked,
'D'you think Savage had anything to do with it, sir? Bit
too full of himself in my opinion.'

'Maybe he did, maybe he didn't,' said Hardcastle enig-
matically, 'but I reckon he's got his hands full with those
two. However, if the pathologist is right in his assessment
that the girl died at about seven o'clock, then Savage has
a lot of witnesses who'll be prepared to say he was in this
here Bull public house. We'll have to put it to the test, but
rest assured I'll have the right man in the dock before I'm
done.'

And of that, Marriott was in no doubt. 'Savage seems to

be doing all right for himself, sir,' he said. 'Those two girls were quite lookers.'

'Yes, they were,' said Hardcastle, 'but I thought that that young Vera Cobb jumped in there a bit *tout de suite* when she realized there was a vacancy for Mrs Hart's role. Especially as the Hart girl topped the bill.'

'Are you thinking Vera might have murdered her, sir, just to get the part?'

'You know me, Marriott,' said Hardcastle. 'I never jump to conclusions, and I never dismiss anyone from my list of suspects till they rule themselves out, or I do. But strangling's not usually a woman's game. They ain't usually strong enough for it.'

It was close to eight o'clock by the time Hardcastle and Marriott got back to the Windsor police headquarters. Struthers was still in his office, poring over reports, a glass of whisky close to his right hand.

'How did you get on, Mr Hardcastle?'

'Apparently Victoria Hart was a married woman,' said Hardcastle, 'so there's the question of informing her husband.'

'I didn't know that.' Struthers was clearly a little perturbed by this further complication. 'Do we know where he can be found?' he asked.

'According to Savage, he's a commander in the Royal Navy. Mrs Hart told him that he's at sea in an ironclad. But God knows where. Could be anywhere.'

Struthers made a note on his pad. 'I suppose the Admiralty's the place to start,' he said.

'You can leave that to me,' said Hardcastle. 'The Admiralty's less than a quarter of a mile down the road from my nick in London.' He turned to Marriott. 'Get a telegraph off to DS Wood and tell him to speak to someone there.'

'Yes, sir,' said Marriott, 'but I doubt he'll find anyone there on Christmas Day.'

'God Almighty, Marriott, there's a war on. There must be a duty officer or someone of the sort.'

'Is there a telegraph here I can use, sir?' Marriott asked Struthers.

'If you see the duty inspector downstairs, Sergeant, he'll arrange it for you.'

'And the best of luck,' said Hardcastle drily as Marriott left the office. He had not been impressed by the duty inspector's lack of industry. 'Well now, we need to make a call on this here Combermere Barracks, Mr Struthers. I'll have to speak to someone about these young officers who've been plaguing the life out of Mrs Hart.'

'I doubt if there'll be anyone at the barracks at the moment,' said Struthers. 'I suspect that most of them have been granted furlough over Christmas.'

'I just hope that there's not an invasion, then,' said Hardcastle caustically. 'Now, perhaps you could advise me of a half-decent boarding house hereabouts. And not too expensive, neither. The Commissioner's not very generous when it comes to forking out for detective officers working out of Town.'

'All arranged, Mr Hardcastle,' said Struthers, surprising the London DDI yet again. 'I've booked rooms for you and the sergeant at the Horse and Groom. It's an inn on Oxford Road. Very comfortable, and they serve a decent ale.'

'Well, that's something, I suppose,' murmured Hardcastle. What he had learned so far of the death of Victoria Hart had resigned him to a lengthy stay in Windsor, and good ale would go some way to making it tolerable.

Hardcastle and Marriott arrived at police headquarters at half-past eight on Boxing Day morning. Although the threatened snow had not materialized, there was a chill wind in the air and Hardcastle had turned up the collar of his Chesterfield overcoat.

There was a different sergeant on duty at the counter. 'Good morning, sir,' he said. 'You'll be the London officers, I take it. Mr Struthers says you're to go straight up.'

Angus Struthers was seated behind his desk, a pile of paperwork in front of him. 'There's a telegraph here for you, Mr Hardcastle,' he said, taking a sheet of paper from the top of the pile. 'Arrived about ten minutes ago. From a Detective Sergeant Wood in London.'

Hardcastle skimmed through the message form. 'Ah, that's something, I suppose,' he said. 'The navy's got off its arse and located Commander Hart for us.'

'Is he at sea, sir?' asked Marriott.

'No. As luck would have it, his ship – HMS *Dauntless* – is docked at Portsmouth and he's coming here this morning. Should arrive about midday.'

Commander Kenneth Hart, a man of about thirty, was short and stocky, and not unlike a young Rear-Admiral David Beatty in appearance. High on the left shoulder of his uniform jacket was the blue-and-white ribbon of the Distinguished Service Cross.

'What exactly happened to my wife, Inspector?' asked Hart, once introductions had been effected. There was no sign of grief on the man's face, nor sound of it in his voice, and Hardcastle wondered whether his relationship with the late Victoria had been less than perfect. If that were the case, he might not be too concerned about his wife's demise. On the other hand, perhaps he had become so inured to sudden death that he had schooled himself not to display any emotion.

'At the present time, Commander, there is little I can tell you,' said Hardcastle bluntly. 'Her body was found by a park ranger in Windsor Great Park at four o'clock yesterday morning. However, the medical evidence indicates that she had been strangled at about seven o'clock the previous evening.'

'Had she been . . . ?' But Hart did not complete the sentence. Even so down-to-earth a naval officer as he, could not bring himself to put the question into words.

'According to the pathologist's report, Commander, she had not been interfered with sexually, if that's what you were going to ask.'

'Thank you, Inspector. There's some comfort in that.' Hart toyed with a button on his jacket before looking at Hardcastle again.

'I'm afraid I have to ask you some rather delicate questions, Commander,' continued the DDI.

'Carry on.' Hart spoke brusquely, much as Hardcastle imagined he might have addressed a petty officer.

'Was your relationship with your wife an amicable one?'

'If you mean did we get on, the answer's yes, extremely well. Given that I was in the navy and she was part of a touring theatrical company, we really didn't have much time to get on each other's nerves.' The commander was obviously not a man to mince his words. 'D'you mind if I smoke?' he asked, producing a short-stemmed pipe from somewhere within his jacket.

'Not at all.' Hardcastle took out his own pipe, but before filling it with his favourite St Bruno, he offered his pouch to Hart.

'I'll smoke my own if you don't mind, Inspector,' said Hart, and spent a few moments rubbing a leaf of navy-cut tobacco in the palm of his hand.

Hardcastle decided that there was little to be gained by being less than straight with this bereaved sailor. 'Do you know if your wife had any men friends?' he asked.

'She may have done.' It was a realistic reply, almost as if Hart was acknowledging that such things did occasionally happen, even in his own marriage. 'It's not much fun for a vivacious young woman like Victoria being married to the navy. Apart from anything else, she was an actress, and a damned good one. They have a different perception of life, you know. But I don't think she was unfaithful, if that's what you're driving at.' He hesitated briefly. 'Not that I'd've known, mind you, being stuck at sea in my tin coffin.'

'Are you likely to be in Portsmouth for much longer?' asked Hardcastle.

Hart gave a cynical laugh. 'I'm afraid that John Fisher's the only person who can tell you that, Inspector. He's the First Sea Lord.' He paused to relight his pipe. 'When is my wife's body likely to be released for burial?' He waved the match in the air to extinguish it, and dropped it in the ashtray.

'Almost immediately, I imagine, Commander,' said Hardcastle, 'but it's a matter for the coroner, you see.'

Hart nodded. 'Perhaps you'll let me know.'

'How long have you been in Portsmouth, sir?' asked Marriott, knowing that if he did not ask the question Hardcastle would.

'Since the twenty-first of December. Why?'

'I wondered if you'd seen your wife since you docked.'

'No. Unfortunately, we don't all go home when a ship comes into port, you know, Sergeant. Someone has to stay on duty and I happened to draw the short straw. My wife was supposed to be coming back to London on Christmas Eve, and we were going to spend a few days together.' For a moment Hart looked immeasurably sad. 'I suppose I'll have to find something else to do now.'

'I learned from Savage—' Hardcastle began.

'Who's Savage?' interrupted Hart.

'He's the actor-manager who runs the show your wife was in.'

'Yes, of course. I'm sorry. Do go on, Inspector.'

'He told me that your wife received a telegram at about five o'clock on Christmas Eve, during a party the cast were having at the theatre. Apparently, she left almost immediately, but no one seems to know where she went. I wondered, Commander, if you had sent that telegram.'

'No, I didn't. You don't know what it said, do you?'

'I'm afraid not, but enquiries are in hand to discover its contents,' said Hardcastle and, leaving the subject of the mysterious telegram, asked, 'Will you be staying in London, Commander?'

'In all probability, yes. We have a house in Chelsea, but I'm not sure I could face those empty rooms in the circumstances. I'll probably stay at the Army and Navy Club while I sort out the funeral.'

'Even so, perhaps you'd let my sergeant have your Chelsea address,' said Hardcastle. 'We may need to get in touch with you again.'

Hart handed Marriott a card and stood up. 'You will let me know of any developments, Inspector, won't you?' he said.

'Certainly, Commander,' said Hardcastle, and shook hands.

'Rum sort of cove, sir,' said Marriott, when Hart had left the police headquarters. 'Didn't seem terribly cut up about his wife's murder.'

'I suppose it's part of being a naval officer, Marriott,' said Hardcastle. 'Stiff upper lip and all that sort of thing. On the other hand, it seems a bit odd that he should have been in Portsmouth since the twenty-first, but apparently made no attempt to see his wife. I don't necessarily accept that he was on duty for the whole time since his ship docked.'

'D'you think he and his wife did get on, sir, or was he just putting on a bold front? They do say that sailors have a girl in every port. What's good for the goose, and all that.'

'I don't know,' said Hardcastle thoughtfully. 'But seeing as how he's been in the country since the twenty-first, he certainly had time to come up here and top her, duty or no duty. He can't have been on watch, or whatever the navy calls it, for twenty-four hours a day. But time will tell, Marriott. Time will tell.'

'What d'you propose to do next, Mr Hardcastle?' asked Struthers.

'Given that we'd probably be wasting our time trying to get any sense out of the army before tomorrow, Mr Struthers, I'd like to have a look at where Mrs Hart's body was found. Then I intend to visit her theatrical digs in Clarence Road. See if that throws up anything.'

'I had officers examine the area thoroughly when the body was found,' said Struthers, 'but I can quite understand you wanting to see it for yourself.'

'It's always been my practice, Mr Struthers.'

'As you're in charge of this enquiry,' continued Struthers, 'I think the best idea is for me to stay out of your way. We're not really up to investigating murders here in Windsor.' He seemed intent on hammering the point home, and held up a hand before Hardcastle could disagree; not that he was likely to. 'What I mean is that I'm here to give you any assistance you need, but the chief constable was adamant that I wasn't to interfere in any way.' He paused. 'Other than to give you support and advice about local matters, that is. And we'll do everything possible in that regard.'

'Very commendable,' said Hardcastle. 'Perhaps, then, you'd make arrangements for me to see the commanding officer at Combermere Barracks some time on Monday. Oh, and I need to see the chief constable,' he reminded Struthers. 'As a matter of courtesy, you understand.'

'Leave it to me, Mr Hardcastle.' Struthers produced his bottle of whisky once more. 'Before you set off again, perhaps you'd take a dram on the successful outcome to this dreadful business, eh?' And with that he poured three measures of Scotch.

'I'm obliged, Mr Struthers,' said Hardcastle as he raised his glass. But he had come rapidly to the view that the head of Windsor's CID was something of a toper.

Three

Much to Marriott's chagrin, Hardcastle decided to forgo lunch. 'We need to examine the ground before the light fades,' the DDI had said.

Struthers had sent one of his detective sergeants, a man called Stone, with the two London detectives, and they arrived at Windsor Great Park at about two o'clock on Boxing Day afternoon.

Harry Jenkins, the park ranger who had discovered Victoria Hart's body, was on duty again and escorted the policemen to where he had found her. 'If you're wondering why I'm doing a double shift, sir, I offered to stand in for a mate of mine on the Christmas Eve night duty,' he said as they walked to the spot. 'He's got a family and I've no one. Christmas don't mean much to me.'

'I understand from Mr Struthers that you knew Mrs Hart, Mr Jenkins.' Hardcastle was not at all interested in Jenkins's duty arrangements.

'I didn't know her as such, sir,' said the ranger, 'but I'd seen the show she was in. And very good she was too. It was a terrible shock, finding that young girl lying there dead.'

'What time was it that you found her?' Hardcastle knew what Struthers had said, but it was his practice always to question witnesses himself. Whether they had already made a formal statement or not.

'Must've been about four in the morning, sir. I was having a ride round. The mare likes a bit of exercise, and this time of year you sometimes find revellers in here getting up to all sorts of things. The soldiers is the worst, sir, but then they always was.' Jenkins gave a sly smile. 'An' I should know. Find 'em in here with some tart they've picked up. Well, I'm sure you know what they gets up to. Being a policeman from London an' all.'

'Yes, I do.' Hardcastle was well aware of the carnal activities of guardsmen in St James's Park, an area of greenery and trees adjacent to Wellington Barracks. 'Tell me what you saw.'

'I was just approaching the ridge there – ' Jenkins used his riding crop to indicate the slight rise in the ground beyond which lay King's Road – 'when I saw a bundle of clothing under this oak tree. Well, that's what it looked like. Hello, I thought to meself, and what's this here? So I dismounted and walked across. It was then I saw it was a woman. I guessed straight away she wouldn't be sleeping natural like, not in this weather.'

'How cold was it, Mr Jenkins?'

'Enough to freeze the balls off of a brass monkey it were, sir. I thought she might be tipsy; you get a lot of that, especially over Christmas. It's not uncommon to find a drunken prostitute in here of a night, and we've got a few in respectable Windsor. Still, you'll always find 'em wherever you find Tommy Atkins. Anyhow, I give her a bit of a shake, but she never moved. It was then I saw she was dead. I've seen a few stiffs in me time when I was fighting the Boers, sir. Third Hussars, King's Own, I was. But I'd never seen a pretty young thing like that as cold as mutton.'

'Had you ridden round the park previously, Mr Jenkins?'

'No, sir. I know what I said about the shenanigans of swaddies with a few jars inside 'em, but it was Christmas, so I thought I'd leave 'em be. They can cut up a bit rough when they've had a few wets, an' they'd likely have had a few more than usual over the Yuletide. Mind you, I've had a few fistfights in the wet canteen over the years, but I'm getting a bit past it now. And you don't go looking for trouble, do you, sir?'

'So what did you do next?'

'I put me spurs into Bessie – she's me mare, sir – and galloped across to King's Road. I found a copper straight off and brought him back here. George Harper it were. I know most of the coppers in Windsor.'

'Did you see anyone else at that time, Mr Jenkins? Or hear anything unusual? A motor car for instance.'

'No, sir. It was as quiet as the grave.' Jenkins gave Hardcastle a guilty glance. 'Begging your pardon, sir. Not exactly the right word to use in the circumstances, is it?'

'And how far is King's Road from here?'

'Just the other side of the ridge, sir,' put in Detective Sergeant Stone. 'No more than five minutes' walk.'

'So whoever murdered this young woman could have gone straight across there and disappeared into the town,' mused Hardcastle.

'It's possible, sir,' said Stone, 'but I had a word with Harper, the constable who was called by Mr Jenkins here, and he never saw nor heard anything untoward. He reckoned he hadn't seen a soul for all of an hour. I have to say it was a bit surprising, being Christmas night an' all. But as Mr Jenkins said, it was a fearful cold night, so I suppose they was all tucked up at home, or in a tavern somewhere.'

'Kindly arrange for me to see this PC Harper, Stone.' Hardcastle spoke sharply, annoyed at not having been told when first he arrived in Windsor about the exact circumstances of the body's discovery. He turned back to the ranger. 'When did you see Victoria Hart in this show, Mr Jenkins?'

'Last Saturday, sir. That'd be the nineteenth. A real beauty she was.' Jenkins shook his head. 'A shocking terrible waste. She was a good dancer, that girl, and I wouldn't mind betting she turned a few heads, what with that outfit she wore.'

'Was there a recruiting sergeant there, the night you saw the show?'

'Oh yes, sir. Miss Hart sang that song . . . ' Jenkins paused. 'How does it go? Yes, I've got it. "We don't want to lose you, but we think you ought to go". Fair brought tears to your eyes did that, the way she sang it. Anyhow, a good half-dozen young fellows couldn't wait to go rushing up on to the stage and sign on. Course, the attraction was that

they all got a kiss from her for taking the King's shilling.'
He shook his head. 'But the way things is going across the
water, they'll regret it when the bullets start flying.'

Hardcastle nodded, and started to wander around the area
where Victoria Hart had been found, occasionally poking
at leaves and twigs and clumps of grass with the ferrule of
his umbrella.

'We did a thorough search of the area, sir,' volunteered
DS Stone. 'Didn't find a thing.'

'So Mr Struthers told me, Stone,' said Hardcastle without
either looking up or interrupting his perambulations. 'What
about footprints, tyre marks? Find anything like that, did
you?'

'A few indentations, sir, but nothing that could be identified. The ground was a bit hard, like it is now. It'll be the
frost most likely.'

'I dare say,' commented Hardcastle drily as he continued
to examine the ground around the oak tree. Finally aban-
doning his search, he said, 'Well, Marriott, there are only
two possibilities: either Mrs Hart was killed here, or she
was killed somewhere else and carried here.'

'Yes, sir,' agreed Marriott wearily. He was always puzzled
that his chief so often found it necessary to state the obvious.

'If the last was the case,' Hardcastle continued, 'the
murderer must've been a strong bugger. And now, Stone,
we'll go and have a look at the lodgings where she was
staying. Clarence Road, I believe.'

'Yes, sir.' Stone took out his pocket watch and looked at
it. 'Er, now, sir?'

Hardcastle stared at the detective. Stone must be at least
fifty years of age, possibly older, and gave the impression
that he was coasting gently towards his pension without
having to exert himself too much. 'I've often worked past
midnight on a murder case, Stone, and sometimes all night,'
he said. 'You ask Sergeant Marriott. And if I have to do
the same here, I will. Even on Boxing Day.'

The implication, that anyone else involved in the investigation would also work late if necessary, was not lost on
Detective Sergeant Stone.

Standing behind Hardcastle, Marriott smiled wryly.

'Good afternoon to you, Mr Jenkins, and thank you for your assistance,' said Hardcastle, turning to the park ranger.

Jenkins doffed his cap. 'I can't say as how it's been a pleasure, sir.'

The house in Clarence Road was similar to the one at which Hardcastle and Marriott had interviewed Percy Savage, the actor-manager.

'We came here yesterday morning, sir,' said Stone as they approached the front door. 'Me and Mr Struthers.'

'And what did you do when you got here?'

'We spoke to Mrs Seymour, sir. Mrs Matilda Seymour, that is. A widow lady. She's the landlady, and well known to police.'

'D'you mean this woman's got a criminal record?' snapped Hardcastle, turning on Stone accusingly.

'Oh no, sir,' said Stone hurriedly. 'But we've one or two young policemen who put up here from time to time.' The Windsor detective was rapidly realizing that he would have to be very careful how he phrased any information he passed on to Hardcastle.

'Are any of them still living here?'

'Yes, sir. A young PC called Gilbert Taylor.'

'So presumably he was here at the same time as Mrs Hart.'

'Yes, sir, I suppose he was.'

'I shall look forward to speaking to PC Taylor,' said Hardcastle. 'It would have been useful if I'd been told at the outset that there was an officer living in the same house as the victim.'

'I'm sorry, sir,' said Stone. 'I thought the inspector would have mentioned it.'

'If he knew,' muttered Hardcastle. 'And in future don't assume that Mr Struthers has told me anything. Anything you know about, I want to know about. Is that clear?'

'Yes, sir.'

'Very well. I want to see Taylor tomorrow morning at nine o'clock sharp, Stone.'

'He might not be on duty, sir,' ventured Stone unwisely.

'Nine o'clock, Stone. Is that understood?'

'Yes, sir,' said Stone. Things had never been like this when he was working with DI Struthers, but then he had never been involved in a murder enquiry before.

The Windsor detective knocked loudly on the door and eventually a woman opened it. Best described as 'prim and proper', she put a hand to her mouth at the sight of the three men on her doorstep. 'Oh, it's you, Mr Stone,' she said, fluttering her eyelashes. It was a ridiculous gesture for a middle-aged woman to make, and Hardcastle imagined that she was possibly a retired actress, or even a failed one.

'Yes, it's me, Mrs Seymour. This is Mr Hardcastle, an inspector from Scotland Yard.'

'Pleased to meet you I'm sure, Inspector. I s'pose you've come about poor Victoria. It's a crying shame, a young girl like that being murdered in the prime of her life. And on Christmas Day an' all.'

'When did you last see Mrs Hart?' asked Hardcastle as the three officers were shown into a chintzy sitting room cluttered with bric-a-brac. The room was made gloomier than it needed to have been by the brown velour curtains and brown wallpaper and paintwork.

'It was when she went off to do the matinée. That'd be about two o'clock the day before yesterday, Christmas Eve.'

'Did she seem all right? I mean did she seem to be worrying about anything?'

'No, quite the opposite. She was full of the joys of spring. Said she was going back up London straight after the performance. Meeting her husband, she said. Apparently he's in the navy. An officer, he is.'

'Did she take her things with her then, Mrs Seymour?' asked Marriott. 'A suitcase? Anything of that sort?'

'No, come to think of it, she never.' It was apparent that this oversight had not previously occurred to Matilda Seymour. 'I s'pose she was meaning to come back here to pick 'em up. I never thought to ask.'

'But she didn't come back?'

'No, I never saw her again, the poor little mite.'

'I'd like to have a look at her room, Mrs Seymour,' said Hardcastle.

'Yes, of course.' Matilda Seymour paused. 'What shall I do with her things, Inspector? There's a few bits of clothing and personal stuff up there.'

'Sergeant Stone will arrange to have them returned to Commander Hart,' said Hardcastle, a statement that appeared to disconcert the sergeant.

The three detectives followed Mrs Seymour upstairs and were shown into a large room on the front of the house. Apart from the double-sized iron bedstead, there was a table upon which rested a china washbowl, a large ewer and an old copy of *The Stage*. An upright chair, its cane back broken in places, was tucked into a corner next to a mahogany wardrobe. The only indication that the room was usually let to members of the theatrical profession was an unframed and yellowing bill of a years-old show at the Windsor Empire.

'Get searching, Marriott. And don't get in the way, Stone.' Hardcastle turned to the landlady. 'Did Mrs Hart have any callers during the time she was here, ma'am?' he asked. 'Gentlemen callers in particular.'

'Not that I recall, no. Oh, just a minute, though, I do remember that young Mr Savage popped in once or twice. Said he wanted to talk to her about the show. Victoria told me afterwards that they were making some changes to her routine.'

'Did he speak to her in this room, or downstairs in the sitting room?'

Matilda Seymour seemed puzzled by the question. 'No, he came up here. Twice, I think he came. Yes, I'm sure it was twice. He stayed for about an hour each time.'

'And what time of the day would that have been?'

'Late on in the morning, both times.'

'Are you sure about the time?' Hardcastle wondered why Savage had found it necessary to call on Victoria Hart at her digs rather than discussing her 'routine' when they were both at the theatre. And to spend an hour in her bedroom. But he thought he knew.

'Yes. I offered him a bite of lunch both times, but he said he had to get back to the theatre.'

Marriott finished his search of the room. 'These are the only things that might be important, sir,' he said to Hardcastle, and handed him a few letters tied with a pink ribbon. 'The rest of the stuff is clothing and make-up and scent. That sort of thing.'

Hardcastle put the letters in his pocket. 'We'll have a look at those later,' he said. He had no wish to examine them in the presence of Mrs Seymour. If they were from a lover, rather than Commander Hart, he did not want the landlady gossiping about it all round Windsor. And she looked the sort who might enjoy a good gossip.

'One other thing, Mrs Seymour,' he said. 'What was Mrs Hart wearing when she left here to go to the theatre the day before yesterday?'

Mrs Seymour did not hesitate. 'She had a high-necked white blouse and a black skirt. A bit daring, I thought, coming that much above the ankle, but she *was* an actress. They're always different, aren't they? And before she left, she put on her black cloak and her favourite hat with the turned-up brim. She always dressed beautifully, and I told her how nice she looked.'

'When she was found, sir—' began Stone.

But he was silenced by a critical look from Hardcastle. 'Not now, Stone,' he said sharply.

'What's in those letters, Marriott?' asked Hardcastle, once the two were ensconced in the office that had been allo-cated them at police headquarters. 'Anything that might help?'

'Difficult to say, sir.' Marriott plucked one of the missives out of the small pile he had spread about on the desk. 'There's seven of them, and they're all unsigned. Well, what he's actually written at the end is "Your admirer".'

'Interesting,' mused Hardcastle. 'Addresses?'

'Only the places to which they were sent, sir. They're all addressed to theatres in and around London.' Marriott looked up. 'Obviously theatres where she was appearing at the time. But there aren't any to her Chelsea address – the one Commander Hart gave us – and there's no sender's address on the letters themselves.'

'What about dates? Are there dates on them?'

'Yes, sir. This is the earliest one, dated the thirteenth of November nineteen-thirteen.' Marriott held up one letter, and then set it aside before riffling quickly through the remaining ones. 'And this, the last, is dated the twelfth of May this year.'

'What's in 'em, Marriott?' Hardcastle asked again.

'They're love letters of a sort, sir. Whoever he is says how much he admires her, her talent and her singing. And how he can't wait to look into her eyes again. In one of them, he even asks her to marry him. And they all finish off the same.' Marriott selected another letter at random. '"Love and kisses and hugs" is what it says in this one, and they're all silly stuff like that. And there are always a few crosses at the end, but as I said, there's no signature. I suppose her husband might've sent them, before they were married. Whenever that was.'

'Why not sign them, then?'

'Perhaps it's something to do with the war, sir. You know, Defence of the Realm Act, and all that sort of thing. Wasn't allowed to say which ship he was in, or where he was.'

'I think you're getting a bit carried away there, Marriott. There wasn't a war on in May nineteen-fourteen when that last letter was sent. It's a shame we can't get fingerprints off paper,' Hardcastle added gloomily. 'No, a pound to an olive it's a secret admirer what wrote them, and somehow or other we've got to find out who he is. But I wonder why they stopped in May,' he mused.

'We could ask Commander Hart, sir,' suggested Marriott.

'He'd probably go off his nut.' But then Hardcastle said, 'On the other hand, he might know about 'em. Their marriage could've been a bit of a sham. Always a bit risky getting wed to an actress, I'd've thought. And I should think the navy frowns on divorce.'

'He could have solved that problem by topping her, sir,' said Marriott. 'Especially if he'd got a lady-love of his own somewhere.'

'Yes, he could do that, Marriott, and he was in Portsmouth from the twenty-first of December. Like I said, that would have given him plenty of time to get across here, do the deed and get back to his ship, or to London.'

'Will you be wanting to see him again, sir?'

'Yes, Marriott, I will. We'll go to London tomorrow, straight after I've seen this PC Taylor that's been kept a secret from us. I'll need to see Harper, the copper that Jenkins called, too. And I suppose I'd better see the chief constable at some time. If he can be bothered to put in an appearance. But that can wait, as far as I'm concerned.'

On the Sunday morning, Hardcastle and Marriott arrived at the Windsor police headquarters as usual at half-past eight.

The bearded sergeant who had been on duty on Christmas Day was on duty again.

'Good morning, sir,' he said deferentially.

Hardcastle grunted an acknowledgement and made for the stairs.

But there was a surprise awaiting him. Seated behind Detective Inspector Struthers's desk was DS Stone.

'Good morning, sir,' said Stone, rapidly standing up.

'Where's Mr Struthers, Stone?' asked Hardcastle.

'He's had an accident, sir.'

'Accident? What sort of accident?'

'He fell down the stairs and broke a leg, sir. Late last night. He's in the King Edward the Seventh Hospital in St Leonard's Road.'

Given Struthers's propensity for whisky, Hardcastle believed he knew how the inspector had come to fall down the stairs, but he chose not to comment on it. At least, not to Stone.

'So you're in charge, are you, Stone?'

'Yes, sir.'

Hardcastle frowned. The prospect of DS Stone acting as liaison between him and the Windsor force did not please him. He had earlier come to the conclusion that Stone was loath to do anything that demanded either the meanest show of initiative or the slightest effort.

'You were going to say something yesterday about what Mrs Hart was wearing when she was found.'

'Yes, sir.'

'There's one thing I want you to bear in mind, Stone: don't ever interrupt me when I'm interviewing a witness. For all you knew, what Mrs Hart was wearing might have been relevant, and you didn't know if Mrs Seymour was the killer.'

'D'you think so, sir?'

'I don't know. Do you?'

'Er, no, sir.' Stone failed to see what Hardcastle was driving at, but as Struthers had repeatedly said, the Windsor force was not accustomed to investigating murders.

'Well, what *was* she wearing when she was found?' demanded Hardcastle, only just keeping his exasperation under control.

'A black fur coat, sir. Full-length. Mr Struthers reckoned it was musquash, whatever that is.'

'It's the fur of the musquash, Stone, a vole from North America, and it'll have cost her at least a pony.'

'A pony, sir?' Stone looked puzzled. He failed to see the connection between voles and ponies.

'Twenty-five pounds,' said Hardcastle with a sigh. 'What else was she wearing?'

'Just that black corset thing she wears for her act, and them black tights that stage people wear. Oh, and black shoes, sir.'

'Well, we know she left the theatre during the party they were having because Savage said she got a telegram,' mused Hardcastle. 'Either she was in a tearing hurry, or she wore it deliberate like, because whoever she was meeting asked her to.' But then he decided there was little point in discussing this line of enquiry any further. At least, not with Stone. 'Is PC Taylor here?'

'Downstairs, sir. Along with PC Harper. Shall I get them up here?'

'No, I'll talk to them in that interview room of yours. Taylor first.'

'Very good, sir. Want me to come with you?'

'No thanks,' said Hardcastle. 'I think I can manage on my own. With the help of Sergeant Marriott here.'

But Hardcastle's sarcasm was lost on Stone who promptly sat down, relieved that his assistance was not required.

Police Constable Gilbert Taylor was probably no more than twenty-two years of age. He was a clean-cut young man who carried his uniform well.

'I'm DDI Hardcastle, lad, and this is DS Marriott. Sit down.'

'Sir.' Taylor perched rigidly on one of the hard, upright chairs with which the spartan interview room was furnished, and placed his hands firmly on his knees. It was the nearest he could get to sitting to attention.

'And for God's sake relax, lad. I'm not going to eat you. Smoke if you want to.'

'Sir.' Taylor smiled, fingered his moustache and adopted a more comfortable posture. But he declined to smoke.

'Now then, DS Stone tells me that you're in digs at the same Clarence Road house where Victoria Hart was staying.'

'Yes, sir.'

'You know of course that she's been murdered.'

'Yes, sir.'

'How well did you know her?'

'Not very well, sir. What with her being at the theatre and me being on shift work, our paths didn't cross all that much. I'd sometimes run into her in the kitchen about midday. I suppose she'd just got up, and I was going on late turn, like.'

'What sort of woman was she, Taylor?'

'Very pleasant, sir.' The PC paused, as if wondering whether to go on, but then he said, 'And very pretty, sir.'

'So I've been told,' said Hardcastle.

'She was a friendly girl, too, sir. Always laughing.'

Hardcastle frowned. 'How friendly?'

'She'd always have a chat if I met her in the kitchen or on the way in or out. She told me to call her Vicky.'

'And did she ever flirt with you, lad?'

'No, sir. She was just friendly.' Taylor reddened slightly at the suggestion.

Hardcastle concluded that the young policeman had not been a policeman very long. 'To your knowledge did she have any gentlemen callers?'

'As far as I know, sir, only the chap who played the lead in the show she was in. I met him one morning when I was going out.'

'Percy Savage?'

'I believe that was his name, sir. Anyway, he offered me a couple of free tickets for the show. *Beaux Belles*, it was called.'

'And did you go to see it?'

'Certainly not, sir.'

Hardcastle smiled. 'Oh? And why was that?'

'Well, sir, it was like a bribe, wasn't it? So I refused and reported the matter to my sergeant.'

'Good gracious!' exclaimed Hardcastle. 'Which sergeant was that?'

'Sergeant Miller, sir. He's the sergeant on duty at the desk this morning.'

'And what did he say?'

PC Taylor paused. 'He said I should've gone to see the show, sir.'

'Thought he might have.' Hardcastle smiled. 'Did Victoria ever mention her husband?'

'No, sir,' said Taylor. 'I didn't know she was married.'

'Well, she was, to a naval commander.'

Taylor shook his head. 'I never knew that,' he said.

'All right, lad, that'll do. If you think of anything else that might help, come and see me. And don't bother going through your own people.' From what he had seen of the strict hierarchy of the Windsor force, Hardcastle could imagine that some incompetent fool would take it upon himself to decide whether a piece of information was important or urgent. And it might not reach him in time. Or, worse still, not at all.

Four

Police Constable George Harper was a much older and more mature man than PC Taylor.

'You were called to the body of Victoria Hart by Mr Jenkins, the park ranger, Harper. Is that correct?'

'That's correct, sir.' Harper flicked open his pocket book and referred to it. 'On Friday the twenty-fifth of December at four-ten a.m. in King's Road, Windsor, sir, I was patrolling my beat in a north-westerly direction when I was approached by Park Ranger Harry Jenkins. He informed me that he had found the dead body of a young woman who he identified as Victoria Hart, an actress currently appearing at the Windsor Empire. I accompanied him to the scene and examined the body, satisfying myself that she was indeed deceased. I told Jenkins to remain with the body and I proceeded to St Leonard's Road police station and informed the inspector.' The PC looked up. 'That was Inspector Richardson, sir. The inspector and I returned to the scene and Mr Richardson arranged for the attendance of the divisional surgeon and then the removal of the body to the mortuary attached to the King Edward the Seventh Hospital.'

'According to the pathologist, it appears that Mrs Hart was killed at about seven o'clock the previous evening.'

'So I understand, sir.' Harper closed his pocket book.

'Did you see or hear anything during your tour of duty that was likely to have been connected with this murder?'

'Nothing untoward, sir. In fact the last person I'd seen was a man staggering along the road, obviously three sheets to the wind, sir. But he took one look at me, straightened up and disappeared. That was about an hour before Jenkins reported finding the body, sir.'

'Did you see anyone in a motor vehicle, or a man with a woman who could have been Mrs Hart?'

'No, sir. It was very quiet. I later rendered a full written report regarding the matter, sir.'

'Seems to be a rare example of an efficient officer,' said Hardcastle, once Harper had left them.

'Indeed, sir,' said Marriott.

'Right then, we'll go to London,' said Hardcastle. 'There are a few more questions I want to put to Commander Hart, mainly about them letters you found.'

'We'll try this club of Hart's first, Marriott,' said Hardcastle as they boarded the train at Windsor's Riverside station. 'Like he said, I doubt he'll be able to face his house in Chelsea, not after losing his wife. But if he's not at the club, the Chelsea address is where we'll go.'

It was a tiresome and slow journey to Waterloo, but once there, the two detectives took a cab to the Army and Navy Club in Pall Mall.

'I understand that Commander Kenneth Hart is staying here,' said Hardcastle to the hall porter.

'He won't be *staying* here, sir. We don't have any bedrooms, you see. However, the commander is in the club. Am I to take it you wish to see him?'

'Yes,' said Hardcastle, biting back a sarcastic response to the man's punctiliousness.

'And who may I say is enquiring, sir?'

'Divisional Detective Inspector Hardcastle of the Metropolitan Police.'

'Very good, sir. If you'll be so good as to wait one moment.' The hall porter crossed the huge, echoing lobby and went through a door on the far side.

'Pompous arse,' muttered Hardcastle at the porter's retreating back. 'How come the commander didn't know there wasn't any sleeping accommodation here, I wonder, Marriott?' he mused while they were waiting. 'Bit suspicious, that.'

But before Marriott could suggest that Hart probably had not had the time to find out, the hall porter returned. 'If you'll follow me, gentlemen, the commander is in the smoking room. There's hardly anyone here today, being a Sunday,' he added, 'particularly being the Sunday after Christmas. All away at their country houses most likely.'

As Hardcastle and Marriott approached Hart, he stood up and extended a hand. 'Inspector, do you have news for me?' Although he was now wearing civilian clothing, he could not have been mistaken for anyone but a naval officer.

'Not yet, Commander, I'm afraid. These enquiries do take time. But rest assured, I shall find whoever was responsible for your wife's death.'

'I have to say that that's comforting, Inspector,' said Hart as the trio sat down in the far corner of the room. 'May I offer you gentlemen a drink?'

'Very kind, I'm sure,' murmured Hardcastle. 'A whisky, if I may.'

'And you, Sergeant?'

'The same, sir, please,' said Marriott.

Once the drinks had been served, Hardcastle broached the delicate subject of the letters that had been found in Victoria Hart's room at Clarence Road.

'I'm sorry to have to put this to you, Commander, but during the course of our enquiries a quantity of correspondence came into our possession.' Hardcastle produced the seven letters and proffered them to the naval officer. 'I was wondering if you knew anything about them.'

Hart riffled through them, as if trying to identify the writing on the envelopes. But his frown deepened as he read the first two or three letters. 'But what do they mean, Inspector?' he asked, finally tossing the letters on to the occasional table that separated him from the detectives.

'I was hoping you might be able to tell me, Commander,' said Hardcastle. 'In fact, I was wondering if it was you what wrote 'em.'

'Certainly not, Inspector. It's not the sort of sloppy stuff I'd write to my wife, although it seems to be an educated hand. They don't mean a thing to me. Of course, you have to bear in mind that my wife was an actress, and that her profession tends to attract admirers. And, I have to say, a few cranks at times. I remember once that she received a string of letters from some religious madman who took exception to her costume, and what he described as her provocative and sinful dancing.' Hart gave a grim smile at the recollection. 'But Victoria always laughed it off. She was quite accustomed to receiving missives of that nature, but only two or three at most, and they usually ceased when the show moved on.' He waved a hand towards the letters. 'May I ask where you found them?'

'At Windsor, in her digs at Clarence Road. They were tied up with pink ribbon, and the first one is dated the thirteenth of November nineteen-thirteen.'

'Good God!' Hart's chin sank on to his chest as it dawned upon him that one does not keep letters from a crank and tie them up in pink ribbon. The awful conclusion was that for over a year Victoria had been conducting a clandestine affair while he was at sea. *After their marriage.*

'Was your relationship with your wife an amicable one?' asked Hardcastle.

'Yes. I said so when I saw you yesterday,' Hart responded sharply.

'I know that's what you said, Commander, but I wondered if you wanted to revise your answer.'

'What the devil d'you mean by that?' Hart's temper began to shorten, but Hardcastle attributed that to the letters he had just read.

'I'm sorry, but if I'm to find your wife's murderer, I have to ask questions that can sometimes be painful.'

'Mmm, I suppose so,' mumbled Hart. 'I'm sorry, Inspector, but those – ' he gestured at the letters – 'have come as something of a shock. And in answer to your question, I'd always believed that our marriage was idyllic, given the constraints that the navy and, I suppose, the stage, places on married life. Mind you, my parents weren't particularly overjoyed at the match. And my mother definitely didn't like the idea of my marrying an actress.'

'How long *have* you been married, sir?' asked Marriott.

Hart switched his gaze to the sergeant. 'About eighteen months.' He thought for a moment or two. 'Yes, we were married on the seventh of June nineteen-thirteen. In Portsmouth.'

Marriott scribbled the date in his pocket book. 'And how did you meet, sir?'

'Look, is all this really necessary? I really don't see—'

'I'm afraid it is, Commander.' Hardcastle interrupted Hart's protestations. 'The more information we can discover about your wife, the better chance we have of arresting her killer.'

'I suppose so,' said Hart, but not being a detective, he could not quite see how. 'A group of us from the ship went to see this show at the Theatre Royal in Pompey. And there was this marvellous girl wearing a sort of black tight-fitting corset affair and black tights. She had lovely legs and danced . . . well, erotically, I suppose you'd call it.' Hart looked embarrassed. 'I was quite smitten with her, as a matter of fact.' He paused for a moment, savouring the memory. 'I sent flowers to the stage door three nights running and eventually plucked up the courage to ask her out to dinner. That was in April, I suppose. April of nineteen-thirteen. When my ship was next back in Portsmouth, a fortnight later, the show had moved on, but I tracked her down to a theatre in Southampton. To cut a long story short, I pursued her relentlessly and she eventually agreed to marry me. She was called Victoria Lester then, but insisted on using her married name after the wedding. I suggested it would damage her career, but she said that she was proud to be married to me and was going to use the name Victoria Hart from then on. She said that people in her profession often changed their name. In any case she was joining the company of *Beaux Belles*, so it wouldn't matter.'

'Where were you married?' asked Hardcastle.

'In London, at All Saints in Cheyne Walk, Chelsea. Victoria was thrilled with the wedding. I must say her parents did it all rather splendidly. And a group of my brother officers formed an arch with their swords as we came out of the church. But then, I'm sure you're familiar with that sort of thing.'

Hardcastle nodded, although that type of ceremonial had

certainly not featured at his own wedding. The prospect of a corridor of policemen with raised truncheons horrified him.

'Mind you, it was overshadowed a little,' continued Hart.

'Oh?'

'I had taken Victoria to the Derby on the Wednesday before the wedding, and she was terribly upset when that wretched suffragette Emily Davison threw herself in front of the King's horse. She died while we were on our honeymoon.'

Hardcastle recalled the event quite clearly, and had been wryly amused that the DDI of V Division had been landed with it. Usually it was A Division that bore the brunt of such Votes-for-Women fanaticism.

'Did you have any rivals for your wife's hand, Commander?'

'I dare say I did, Inspector,' said Hart, smiling. 'As I said, Victoria was a very attractive girl, and I'm sure she had many admirers.' But then the smile vanished and he suddenly became extremely sad. 'God, who would want to do such a thing?'

'I presume you've been at sea for most of your married life, Commander?'

'One of the penalties of being a naval officer, Inspector. I went to the Naval College at Osborne at the age of thirteen, and I've been in the navy ever since.'

'I meant at sea as opposed to being ashore,' said Hardcastle.

'I see. Yes. Most of my service has been afloat, thank God. Sailors are not terribly keen on stone frigates, you know, Inspector.'

'Stone frigates?' Hardcastle raised his eyebrows.

Hart smiled. 'It's what the Royal Navy calls its shore establishments,' he said.

'Oh!' Hardcastle always had great difficulty in understanding the armed forces. 'One other thing, Commander: I presume your solicitor will be handling Mrs Hart's will.'

'Good God! I'd never thought about that. Yes, of course.' Hart paused. 'I suppose she made a will,' he said, half to himself.

'And his name, sir?'

Hart frowned. 'What can my solicitor's name possibly have to do with the murder of my wife, Inspector?'

Hardcastle smiled disarmingly. 'I don't know, Commander, but you never can tell when such bits and pieces of information will come in handy.'

From his expression, it was apparent that Hart was not convinced that this stolid detective was up to the task of finding Victoria's killer. Nevertheless, he imparted the information. 'His name is Courtney and he has offices in Chancery Lane somewhere. I'm afraid I can't remember the number, and it's an age since I've called there.' He paused to apply a match to his pipe. 'Have you discovered who sent the telegram to Victoria that you mentioned the other day, Inspector?'

'Not as yet, Commander, but enquiries are being pursued. What makes you ask?'

'I was wondering if whoever sent it could have been the chap who wrote those,' suggested Hart, gesturing at the letters.

'I've no idea,' said Hardcastle, as he and Marriott rose to their feet, 'but I'm determined to find out. Thank you for the drink, Commander,' he added, and waited while Marriott gathered up the letters.

'What's going to happen to those, Inspector?'

'I'm going to find whoever wrote them, Commander.'

'D'you think he might have been responsible for Victoria's death?'

'Everyone's a suspect until I'm satisfied they had nothing to do with it, Commander. Doubtless we'll be in touch again. I presume you're staying at the Chelsea address you gave me, as there's no accommodation here.'

'Yes, I am. When we spoke at Windsor, I didn't realize that there weren't any rooms here. I've not been a member that long. In fact, my captain only put me up for membership six months ago.'

'Should you need to, Commander, you can always leave a message for me at Cannon Row police station. It's opposite Scotland Yard, just off Whitehall. In fact, it's not far from the Admiralty, which is just down the road.'

Hart smiled. 'I do know where the Admiralty is, Inspector,' he said. 'Although I do try not to call there too often.'

'We'll call in at the nick just in case that ace detective Stone has got off his arse and sent us a telegraph about something or another,' said Hardcastle as they left the club. Hailing a taxi, he said, 'Scotland Yard, cabbie,' and turning to Marriott, added, 'Tell 'em Cannon Row and half the time you'll finish up at Cannon Street in the city.'

'Yes, I know, sir,' said Marriott, who had heard this piece of advice at least a thousand times.

But there were no messages from DS Stone of the Windsor force.

Hardcastle pulled out his chromium-plated hunter and flicked open the cover. 'Five o'clock, Marriott. There's no point in rushing back to the sticks tonight. Go home and spend the night with your family. I'll see you tomorrow morning at eight o'clock at the nick. And my respects to Mrs Marriott.'

'Thank you very much, sir,' said the delighted Marriott.

Hardcastle's first call on the Monday morning was to the Admiralty in Whitehall.

He was surprised to find that the provost marshal of the Royal Navy was a lieutenant commander, several ranks lower than his army equivalent, who was a brigadier general. And he made the mistake of commenting on it.

'The navy's different from the army, Inspector,' said the provost marshal, who had introduced himself as Hillman. 'Ship's captains are responsible for discipline, together with the master-at-arms, the ship's corporal and the shore patrols. As a consequence, it doesn't need any more than a lieutenant commander to do what little I have to do. Anyway, what can I do to help you?'

Hardcastle wished he had not queried Hillman's rank. 'I'm conducting an investigation into the murder of a naval officer's wife at Windsor, Commander,' Hardcastle began.

'Really?' Hillman drew a writing pad across the desk and took out his fountain pen. 'Who was the officer?'

'A Commander Hart, who's on HMS *Dauntless.*'

'In *Dauntless,*' commented Hillman. 'In the navy we say that someone is *in* a ship, not *on* it.'

Hardcastle got the impression that he was being treated to a lecture on the terminology and structure of the Royal Navy, but he struggled on. 'Commander Hart's ship docked at Portsmouth on the twenty-first of December, but he claimed to have been on duty from then until Christmas Day. His wife, an actress who was appearing in a show at Windsor, was murdered at about seven o'clock on the twenty-fourth and her body was left in Windsor Great Park.'

Hillman busily wrote all this down before looking up. 'What's your query, then?' he asked. 'Were you perhaps thinking that this Commander Hart was in some way responsible for his wife's death?'

'I don't know who killed her, Commander, that's why I'm making enquiries.' Hardcastle was beginning to get a little irritated by Hillman.

The provost marshal put down his pen and adopted an air of exasperation. 'What exactly d'you want to know, Inspector?'

'If Commander Hart's claim that he was on duty for the whole of that time is a valid one. He actually said that he'd drawn the short straw.'

'Ah, I see. I imagine that Hart and his captain tossed up for which of them would remain on duty. I dare say that Hart fell for the stint up to and including Christmas Day, and the skipper took over for the rest of the time. Does that answer your query?'

'Not exactly. Would Commander Hart have been able to leave the ship at any time during the period he was on duty?'

'Just wait for a moment, if you would, Inspector,' said Hillman, and left the room.

'This is a rum set-up, Marriott,' said Hardcastle while they were waiting for the provost marshal to return. 'Seems a funny way to run a navy.'

Minutes later, Hillman came back. 'I've just spoken to a colleague, Inspector, and I gather that enquiries were made of the Admiralty about Commander Hart at some time over Christmas.'

'That's so, Commander. We had to contact him to tell him of his wife's murder.'

'Ah, I see. Well, I've also learned that the skipper of *Dauntless* is a four-ringer, and Hart's the number one.'

'Would you mind explaining that in English, Commander?' asked Hardcastle acidly.

Hillman grinned. 'The captain has four rings on his sleeve – a full-blown captain, in other words – and Hart is his first lieutenant.'

'But Hart's a commander,' said Hardcastle, 'not a lieutenant.'

'Don't worry about it, Inspector. The navy's a strange organization.'

'I'm beginning to see that,' grunted Hardcastle.

'But to answer your question, Commander Hart was acting captain in the absence of the skipper, and there is no way in which he would have left his ship. In time of war that would have been regarded as the gravest of offences.'

'Thank you, Commander, that's all I wanted to know.' Hardcastle stood up.

'Perhaps you'd keep me posted on developments, Inspector,' said Hillman as Hardcastle reached the door.

'It's usually quite some time before we feel someone's collar for a topping, Commander, and even longer before he takes the eight o'clock walk.' Hardcastle, determined to repay Hillman for his pedantry about naval argot, was delighted to see an expression of bewilderment cross the provost marshal's face.

Hardcastle and Marriott arrived back at the Windsor police headquarters at just after eleven o'clock.

'Anything happened, Stone?'

'No, sir,' said Stone, hurriedly standing up.

'Thought as much,' said Hardcastle. 'Right then, you can

show me and Sergeant Marriott the way to the theatre where
this here *Beaux Belles* was showing. I want a word with
the stage-door keeper. See if he can shed any light on the
swells who were plaguing the life out of Mrs Hart.'

'The chief constable's here this morning, sir,' Stone said.
'Mr Struthers said you wanted to see him.'

'Not really,' said Hardcastle, 'but he probably wants to
see me. Very well, you can show me to his office.'

'Ah! Hardcastle is it?' The chief constable was wearing a
well-cut three-piece Harris tweed suit, probably made for
him by any one of several local tailors prepared to give him
a substantial discount. He twitched briefly at his moustache
– identical to that sported by Lord Kitchener – leaned
forward to link his hands together on his desk, and peered
closely at the two Metropolitan Police officers.

'Yes, sir, and this is Detective Sergeant Marriott.'

Almost as if acknowledging a mere sergeant was beneath
his dignity, the chief constable nodded briefly in Marriott's
direction before returning his gaze to Hardcastle. 'I'm most
grateful to Sir Edward Henry for sending you here, Inspector.'
He spoke in such a way as to imply that he and the
Commissioner of the Metropolitan Police were bosom friends,
but in truth the Chief Constable of Windsor only rated the
equivalent of a superintendent in the London force. 'The fact
is that we have little experience of investigating murder here.
Apart from anything else we have Windsor Castle in our area
which, you'll appreciate, is a great responsibility.'

'But only its perimeter, sir,' said Hardcastle with a
disarming smile. He knew that officers of his own division
of the Metropolitan Police were responsible for guarding
Windsor Castle and its grounds. He also felt like mentioning
that A Division – known in the force as Royal A – encom-
passed Buckingham Palace, St James's Palace, 10 Downing
Street, Parliament and the seat of government, but that its
officers still managed to investigate the occasional murder.

'Quite so.' The chief constable moved quickly away from
the subject of Windsor Castle. 'I'm told that Struthers is in
hospital. Most unfortunate,' he murmured. 'However, Stone

is a most capable officer and I'm sure he'll be of great assistance to you.'

'I'm sure he will, sir.' Hardcastle spoke the lie smoothly. Even on so brief an acquaintance, he had concluded that Detective Sergeant Stone was lazy and incompetent, but that little would be gained by saying so to the chief.

'Well, Inspector, I'll let you get on.' And with that the chief constable returned to studying the file on his desk.

'Strange that the chief didn't ask how the enquiry was going, sir,' said Marriott, once they were back in their own office.

'He doesn't have to worry now that we're here, Marriott,' said Hardcastle. 'Washed his hands of it. Mind you if the King happens to ask him how it's going, he'll seek me out a bit *tout de suite*. I doubt that His Majesty takes too kindly to dead bodies being found in his back garden, so to speak. But right now, we'll get the ace detective Stone to lead us to the Windsor Empire.'

It was some minutes before Marriott's knocking on the stage door of the Windsor Empire in Peascod Street brought a result, but eventually the shuffling figure of Joseph Sharples appeared. He was at least sixty, and what little hair he still had was snow white.

'What's all the bleedin' racket, eh?' he demanded, but then caught sight of DS Stone. 'Oh, it's you lot, is it?' He turned and walked slowly towards his office, leaving the police officers to close the door and follow.

Sharples was exactly the sort of man whose surly attitude Hardcastle took a delight in crushing.

'This is Detective Inspector Hardcastle of Scotland Yard, Joe,' said Stone. 'He's investigating the murder of Victoria Hart.'

'*Divisional* Detective Inspector,' snapped Hardcastle, irritated that the indolent Windsor sergeant could never seem to get his rank right.

'Sorry, sir,' mumbled Stone. 'This is Joseph Sharples, sir, the stage-door keeper and caretaker.'

'Well, Sharples, if you think I'm standing in there while

you answer my questions, you've got another think coming.' Hardcastle nodded towards the cramped cubicle from which Sharples controlled the side entrance to the theatre. 'So find me somewhere decent where I can sit down. And get a move on because I don't have time to waste messing about with tuppenny-ha'penny stage-door keepers.'

Sharples blinked at Hardcastle's blunt instructions and took a deep breath. The Windsor policemen were far more amenable, but then they were always cadging free tickets. And Sharples could be relied upon to find them. Despite his abrasive manner, he was never averse to currying favour with the local constabulary. But this Scotland Yard officer was clearly someone to be reckoned with.

'I s'pose the auditorium's the best place, sir,' said Sharples, with uncharacteristic servility. Without another word, he led the detectives through a labyrinth of passage-ways until eventually the quartet arrived in the auditorium. 'Them's the four-tails,' he announced, by which, Hardcastle assumed, he meant 'fauteuils', and gestured at the front row of seats. 'Cost you four bob to sit in them, they do.'

'I'm not interested in a guided tour of this fleapit or the prices you charge,' said Hardcastle sharply. 'Just sit down and listen.'

It was not the best of places to conduct an interview, but was an improvement on the cubbyhole near the stage door. Hardcastle and Sharples sat on the end of the front row of seats, half turned to face each other, while Marriott and Stone sat in the row immediately behind.

'Now then, for a start I want to know what time Mrs Hart left the theatre on Christmas Eve.'

'I told that Inspector Struthers all that,' complained Sharples, glancing back at Stone as if seeking an ally.

'Well, now you're going to tell me,' barked Hardcastle, leaning closer to the stage-door keeper. 'And to begin with you can tell me the time the matinée usually finished.'

'Same as always,' said Sharples churlishly. 'Curtain up at half-past two, and down again about half-past four. Interval's twenty minutes.'

'And what time did Mrs Hart leave the theatre on Christmas Eve?'

Sharples took a battered tin from his pocket and began to roll a cigarette.

'Take your time,' said Hardcastle acidly.

'I'm thinking.' Sharples ran his tongue along the gummed edge of the cigarette paper. 'Oh yeah, I remember now,' he said. 'Must've been about five o'clock. Seeing as how it were the last performance, they had a bit of a party on stage. After the audience had gone home, of course,' he added with a chuckle. But the chuckle was stilled by a stern look from Hardcastle. 'It was about then the telegram arrived for Mrs Hart.'

'Telegram? What telegram are you talking about?' demanded Hardcastle, as though he knew nothing of it. Although Savage had told him that a telegram had been delivered, all he knew so far was that Commander Hart had denied sending it. 'Did you tell Detective Inspector Struthers about it?'

'I can't remember. I might've done. I'm not sure.' Sharples began to look very shifty.

'And it was addressed to Mrs Hart, was it?' asked Hardcastle, as usual double-checking the facts.

'Yes, it were. So I took it to her where the party was being held like. Up on stage.'

'What happened next?'

'Well, she read it, of course. Then she clapped her hands and told everyone that she'd got to leave. And she handed the telegram back to me. "Throw that away for me, Joe," she says, "because I haven't got any pockets." And then she laughed.'

'What did she mean by that?'

'Well,' said Sharples, 'she was still wearing that costume what she always wore on stage, and there weren't no pockets in it.'

'And I suppose you read this telegram?' said Hardcastle accusingly.

'Well, I did have a glim at it.' Sharples looked away and concentrated on stubbing out his half-finished cigarette in the ashtray on the armrest.

'What did it say?' demanded Hardcastle, the menace in his voice demonstrating that his temper was rapidly shortening.

'It said something about asking her to meet him in the lounge of the White Hart Hotel in the High Street as soon as possible as he had a surprise for her.'

'Who was this "him" you're talking about, Sharples?'

'I dunno, sir. There weren't no name at the end of the message, just the letter "K". I remembered the name of the hotel because it was the same as Victoria's, being Hart like. And I remember the bit about meeting this here "K" as soon as possible because I heard her say to Mr Savage that she hadn't got time to change. The next thing I knows is that she rushes off and puts her coat on over that costume of hers and disappears out of the stage door like a dose of salts.'

'Did she say anything about coming back, Mr Sharples?' asked Marriott, leaning forward.

The stage-door keeper turned in surprise at a question coming from behind him. 'Come to think of it, sir, she did. As she went out of the door, she said, "I'll be back for my things later, Joe." But she never did. I wondered whether it was her husband what had sent the telegram. It crossed me mind that he might've got one of them new-fangled motor cars and had whisked her off to London, that being the surprise like, what was mentioned in the telegram. Any road, I thought to meself, never mind, she'll be back for her stuff. Not that there was much of it. Just her make-up box and her cloak and hat, and a few other bits and pieces.'

'Have you still got this telegram?'

'I might have,' said Sharples, with a grin.

Hardcastle seized the stage-door keeper by the lapels of his grey overall coat and drew the unfortunate man closer to him. 'I'm hoping for your sake you have, cully,' he said in low, threatening tones. 'And I'll tell you what you did with it. You stuck it in your pocket, and when you heard that Mrs Hart had been murdered you thought you'd make a few bob by flogging it to a newspaper. Well, I hope you haven't, because you'll fetch up in front of the beak. And

I'll be the one putting you there. What's more, if I find out that you never mentioned this telegram to Inspector Struthers, I'll probably nick you for obstructing the police. Got that, have you?'

The alarmed Sharples attempted to move back, but Hardcastle held him securely. 'It's here, guv'nor,' he whimpered, removing the telegram from his pocket with a trembling hand and passing it to the DDI.

Hardcastle took the slip of paper from its envelope and read the brief message.

GOT LEAVE + MEET ME SOON AS POSSIBLE WHITE HART HOTEL HIGH STREET + HAVE SURPRISE FOR YOU + LOVE K + STOP

'Have a look at that, Stone,' said Hardcastle, passing the telegram back to the local sergeant. 'It says it was sent from Windsor. Which post office d'you reckon that would have been?'

'Almost certainly the General Post Office in the High Street, sir.'

Hardcastle grunted. He was briefly tempted to tell Stone to make enquiries of the clerk in the hope that he might remember who had sent the telegram, but then decided that he would do it himself. He was none too sanguine about Stone's detective ability.

'I shall be seeing you again, Sharples.' Hardcastle stood up and started towards the rear of the auditorium and the main entrance to the theatre.

'You can't get out that way, sir,' said the stage-door keeper. 'It's locked.'

Hardcastle stopped and turned. 'Well, unlock it,' he snapped. 'By the way, I've heard that some army officers were making a nuisance of themselves enquiring after Mrs Hart.'

'They weren't no trouble, sir. There was only two of 'em. Nice young gents. They give their cards in and asked me to give 'em to Victoria.'

'And what were their names?'

'I've still got the cards in me office, sir.' Sharples now seemed desperate to assist.

'Go and fetch them, then.' Hardcastle let out an exasperated sigh and pulled out his pipe.

Sharples returned a few minutes later and handed the DDI two pieces of engraved pasteboard. On one was the name of Captain Sir Anthony Braden, and on the other Mr John Fry. Each included the officer's regiment – the Royal Horse Guards – and the address of Combermere Barracks, Windsor.

'Another thing,' said Marriott. 'Was the recruiting sergeant at this party that was held on the stage on Christmas Eve?'

'No, he wasn't, guv'nor,' said Sharples, 'but I have a few wets with him from time to time. Sid Phillips he's called.'

'Where's he stationed?'

'Don't know, 'cept to say it must be somewhere in Windsor. He's always in the pub right opposite here. The Bull, it's called. When he's not on stage talking youngsters into joining the army, stupid little sods.'

'If you see him before I do, tell him to call at the police station in St Leonard's Road and ask for me,' said Hardcastle.

Sharples shot a malevolent glance at the departing detectives. It was a glance that convinced Detective Sergeant Stone that it would be some time before the local police benefited from free tickets for the Windsor Empire again.

Five

Following a belated lunch that consisted of a pork pie and a pint of beer, Hardcastle and Marriott made their way to Combermere Barracks. Once Hardcastle had stated his business to the guard commander, a runner was sent to the orderly room. When the soldier returned, he escorted the two detectives to the office of Lieutenant Colonel Charles Winstanley, the commanding officer of the Royal Horse Guards.

The colonel was, in Hardcastle's opinion, rather tall for a cavalry officer. But then Hardcastle knew more about jockeys than he did about those regiments that the rest of the army referred to as 'donkey-wallopers'.

Thanks to the war, the ceremonial uniform of the Royal Horse Guards had, in common with the rest of the army, given way to khaki. But it was obvious from the colonel's appearance that no expense had been spared in the tailoring of his service-dress tunic and sand-coloured breeches. And it was apparent that his orderly had spent hours polishing the colonel's Sam Browne belt and riding boots.

Hardcastle introduced himself and explained, as succinctly as possible, about the murder of Victoria Hart.

'First I've heard of it,' said Winstanley in strident tones. 'D'you mean to say that Scotland Yard has sent someone all the way down here to investigate the murder of some common showgirl, Inspector?' He looked down his nose, something approaching a sneer on his face. 'And how does that affect the Blues, may I ask?'

'Victoria Hart was a talented leading actress, Colonel, rather than a common showgirl,' said Hardcastle, ignoring the colonel's question.

'Really? Not what I've heard.'

'And what have you heard, Colonel?'

'I understand that she appeared half naked, cavorting around the stage like some whore. Heaven knows why the Lord Chamberlain didn't intervene.' The implication in Winstanley's comment was that any ill fortune that had befallen the woman had been of her own making.

'You've seen the show, then, have you?' Hardcastle had taken an immediate dislike to Winstanley on account of his supercilious manner. He wondered briefly whether the colonel was yet another cavalry officer who had pestered Victoria Hart, and was already moving to the defensive.

'Certainly not, Inspector.' Winstanley bridled at the suggestion, and brushed at his moustache. 'I wouldn't dream of dignifying such performances with my patronage.'

'I suppose not,' said Hardcastle, who was beginning to enjoy himself. Despite Winstanley's denial he was convinced that the colonel *had* seen the show, but in mufti. 'Bit of Shakespeare more to your liking, I imagine.'

'As a matter of fact, I prefer Sheridan or Oscar Wilde. Anyway, what can I do to assist you?'

'I understand that at least two officers from here were making a nuisance of themselves by calling at the stage door and asking for Mrs Hart.'

'Who told you that?' demanded Winstanley fiercely, his frown implying that a Guards officer would never demean himself by such behaviour.

But with Wellington Barracks on his division, Hardcastle knew differently. In fact, he had heard, from what the police call 'a reliable source', that newly commissioned officers in the Foot Guards were required to prove their virility with a prostitute on the dining table of the officers' mess before an audience of their contemporaries. 'The police are not in the habit of disclosing their sources of information, Colonel,' he said smugly, 'but I am satisfied as to the reliability of that information.'

'Did you say *Mrs* Hart?' Winstanley, who had remained standing, and had not invited the detectives to take a seat, raised an eyebrow.

'I did,' said Hardcastle. 'She was the wife of a naval officer.'

'Good God!' The way in which Winstanley uttered those two words seemed to indicate a jaundiced view of naval officers and the sort of women they married. He removed his monocle and spent several seconds polishing it.

'It will, of course, be necessary for me to interview those officers,' said Hardcastle.

'Damn m'breeches! What a preposterous notion. Out of the question. The mere suggestion that any of my officers could possibly have been concerned in this sordid matter is an insult to the regiment.' Winstanley was almost apoplectic at the very idea. 'I shall speak to the chief constable.'

'You can speak to who you like, Colonel, but I'm a Scotland Yard officer and when I'm investigating a murder, I will interview whoever I want to. But if I'm faced with any interference, it'll be a simple matter for my Commissioner to speak to the Chief of the Imperial General Staff. I mean I wouldn't want to go to the trouble of actually *arresting* you for obstructing me in the execution of my duty, would I, Colonel? We might as well take the gentlemanly route, so to speak.'

Winstanley had not expected so robust a response to his objections. Certainly the Chief Constable of Windsor was far more deferential, even though he was a Member of the Royal Victorian Order, an order to which Winstanley had yet to be appointed. On the rare occasions that the chief constable was invited to a regimental dinner – usually along with the mayor and aldermen of Windsor – he was obsequious and clearly impressed by the uniforms, the mess silver and the superior attitude of the regiment's officers. 'Well, I suppose it could be arranged,' said the colonel grudgingly, 'but I don't want you interrupting the routine of the regiment.'

Hardcastle ignored that caveat, and changed the subject. 'I understand that a recruiting sergeant was always present at the Windsor Empire where Mrs Hart was appearing, Colonel. Would he have been from here?'

Winstanley gave a condescending laugh. 'We do not have sergeants in the Household Cavalry, Inspector,' he said. 'They're all corporals.'

'Really? Don't you have any sergeant-majors, then?'

'Corporal-majors, Inspector. They're called corporal-majors. And you can thank Queen Victoria for that. The term "sergeant" means servant, d'you see? And Her Majesty decreed that none of her personal cavalry were to be regarded as servants, so they are all corporals.'

Once again the customs of the armed forces had bemused Hardcastle. First a ship that had a corporal, and now an army unit with no sergeants. 'Have you any idea where this sergeant might have come from, then?' he asked.

'Not the faintest, Inspector,' said Winstanley.

Hardcastle took his hunter from his waistcoat pocket, glanced at it, wound it briefly and returned it. 'Perhaps you'd have a room made available where I could interview—' He broke off. 'What are those names, Marriott?'

'Captain Braden and Mr Fry, sir.'

'Yes, they're the ones, Colonel,' said Hardcastle. 'As soon as possible would be helpful.'

'Now look here, Inspector. I don't just—'

'I'm much obliged, Colonel.'

'Oh very well.' Despite his own perceived superior social standing, Winstanley was worried that this ill-bred inspector would keep his promise of arranging for Sir Edward Henry to talk to Lieutenant-General Sir Archibald Murray, the CIGS, and he was not prepared to take the risk. The last thing he wanted was an uncomfortable interview with the general officer commanding the Household Brigade to whom, undoubtedly, the CIGS would have sent a sharp note.

The adjutant of the regiment had been deputed to arrange a suitable office and to locate the two officers whom Hardcastle was intent upon interviewing.

'Which of these officers would you like to see first, Inspector?' enquired the adjutant.

'Don't make no difference to me, Captain. You can send either of the young buggers in.'

The adjutant's jaw dropped in amazement at hearing two Royal Horse Guards officers described as 'young buggers', but he quickly disappeared to do Hardcastle's bidding. He had doubtless been warned by his colonel to treat the fractious Hardcastle with some care.

A few moments later, a languid young officer appeared in the doorway of the office. Probably no more than twenty years of age, he had the pale beginnings of a moustache. It was an adornment that Hardcastle imagined to be obligatory in the Household Cavalry.

'Who are you?' demanded Hardcastle gruffly.

'Er, Cornet Fry.'

'Cornet?' Hardcastle put down his pen and stared at the soldier. 'That's a damn' funny name.'

'It's a rank, not a name. Lesser regiments call it second lieutenant.' Fry emitted a high-pitched braying laugh. 'Or "ensign" in the Foot Guards, I believe.'

'Good God!' Hardcastle had already come to the conclusion that he would never understand the military, and this was further evidence of it. 'Sit down and tell me why you were plaguing the life out of Victoria Hart, Mr Fry.'

'I was not plaguing the life out of her, as you put it. She's an attractive young woman and I saw nothing wrong in offering to take her out to supper.'

'What did she say to that?'

'She refused. Damned if I know why.' Fry sounded hurt, as though he could genuinely not understand any woman refusing an invitation from him.

'Probably because she was married,' said Hardcastle. 'To a commander in the Royal Navy.'

'Oh gosh, I say! Really?' Fry's face took on a reddish hue of embarrassment. 'She never said.'

'Probably thought it was none of your damn' business, lad,' said Hardcastle. 'So what exactly did she say?'

'She didn't actually say anything. Not to me, anyway. Not then. The first night I saw the show, I sent in my card with a note on it asking her out to supper.'

'What happened?'

'Nothing. She sent a message back with the stage-door

keeper. He said she wasn't interested, but I'm not sure he ever showed it to her. Anyhow, I saw the show again the next night and after it was over, I waited outside the stage door. When Victoria came out, at the end of the show, I spoke to her. I told her I'd sent in my card the previous evening and I asked her if she'd have supper with me.'

'What did she say?'

For a moment or two, Fry said nothing. He looked down and fiddled with the cross strap of his Sam Browne. 'She laughed, and said she didn't go out to supper with boys.' He spoke in a whisper, clearly embarrassed by the admission Hardcastle had forced out of him.

'I hope you're telling me the truth, young man,' said Hardcastle, 'because I'm investigating her murder. And whoever's responsible for it'll be standing on the hangman's trapdoor early one morning. You can be sure of that.'

Fry stared open-mouthed and white-faced at Hardcastle. 'Murdered! Good God! I didn't know that,' he said, clearly taken aback by this news.

'Are you telling me you knew nothing about it, Mr Fry?'

'No, nothing. I only came back from Christmas furlough this morning. Most of us did. We're off again in a day or two.'

Hardcastle was satisfied that this callow youth was incapable of faking the shock with which he had received the news of Victoria Hart's murder. 'Marriott,' he said, glancing beyond the young cavalryman, 'nip out and fetch that other fellow in here. Then Cornet Fry here can push off. Don't want him and his mate colluding, do we?'

The second officer to enter the room wore the rank badges of a captain and was about ten years older than Cornet Fry.

'And who are you?' asked Hardcastle, even though he knew perfectly well that this must be Braden.

'Captain Sir Anthony Braden . . . baronet.' Braden spoke with an air of insufferable superiority, sat down and crossed his legs, and without the courtesy of seeking Hardcastle's permission, lit a cigarette.

'Are you really?' said Hardcastle, leaning back in his

chair with an amused expression on his face. 'Well, Captain Sir Anthony Braden, baronet, tell me why you were making a nuisance of yourself badgering Victoria Hart at the Windsor Empire from time to time.'

'Since when have the police been taking an interest in the social activities of officers of the Royal Horse Guards?' It was obvious from Braden's arrogant demeanour, and his carefully cultivated drawl, that he resented being interrogated by a common policeman.

'Ever since the object of their attentions was murdered,' said Hardcastle mildly.

'*What?*' Braden shot forward in his chair. 'What d'you mean, murdered?'

'It's plain enough,' said Hardcastle. 'Victoria Hart was murdered.'

'But when did this happen?'

'When did you last see Mrs Hart, Captain Braden?'

'*Mrs* Hart?' Braden's reaction was similar to that of both Colonel Winstanley and Cornet Fry. 'Did you say *Mrs* Hart?'

Hardcastle sighed. 'Yes, she was married to a naval commander, and if I were in your boots, young man, I'd avoid him like the bloody plague if you happen to see him in the Army and Navy Club. And as for me, I'm wondering which of her so-called admirers killed her.'

'I say, now look here, none of us would have harmed a hair of that girl's head. Mind you, we didn't know she was married. I mean, you don't expect it, do you?'

'Don't expect what?'

'Well, one don't expect a girl like that to be married, eh what?'

'A girl like what?' It was a rhetorical question that Hardcastle posed. 'I suppose you thought that because she appeared on stage in a flimsy costume, and you'd got a title and a fancy uniform, she just couldn't wait to get on her back so's you could screw the arse off her, eh?'

Shocked by Hardcastle's earthy language, Braden blinked several times. 'No, that wasn't the case at all. She seemed a delightful girl, and I thought that if she—'

Hardcastle laughed. 'You might as well save your breath,

Captain Braden, because I don't believe a bloody word of it. You were out for a quick tumble, and you were sure that the girl you thought was a common tart wouldn't be able to resist you. Well, my lad, she wasn't a common tart. Not by any means. Now, let's get back to my question. When did you last see her?'

'I hope that you're not suggesting that I had anything to do with this unfortunate girl's death, Inspector.' Braden still maintained his lofty attitude, but now it was more of a barrier behind which he sought to hide.

'I'd be more inclined to agree with you if you didn't keep avoiding the question.' Hardcastle took out his pipe and began filling it with tobacco.

'It was the twenty-second of December, a Tuesday,' admitted Braden finally. 'I remember that because I was off on furlough the following day for the Christmas break.'

'You wouldn't think there was a war on,' muttered Hardcastle in an aside to Marriott.

'It was more of an embarkation leave,' said Braden. 'The regiment's off to France next week.'

'Go on, Captain Braden. You remembered that it was the Tuesday.'

'Yes. I'd seen the show on the Monday, the day before, and I saw this absolutely smashing girl singing and dancing. So I thought to myself, Braden, old boy, how about taking her out to supper.'

'And so you hung about at the stage door,' observed Hardcastle drily.

'How did you know that?' asked Braden, raising his eyebrows.

'Because there's always a crowd of conceited toffs hanging around the stage door of every theatre in the country,' said Hardcastle. 'Don't usually get 'em anywhere. But go on.'

Braden did not much care for being classified as a 'conceited toff'. 'She came out at about eleven o'clock, I suppose it must have been. I introduced myself and invited her to supper.'

'And what did she say to that?'

'*She* didn't say anything. But the smarmy chap who was with her – he was in the show – had the audacity to tell me to sheer off. I tell you, Inspector, if there hadn't been a lady there, I'd've knocked the cad down.'

'But that wasn't the only time you approached her, was it?'

'Well, I, er—' mumbled Braden, preparing to lie.

'How d'you think I found out that you'd been calling on Mrs Hart, eh, Captain?' Hardcastle held up a hand as Braden was about to speak. 'It's because you sent your card in. And Mrs Hart very sensibly ignored it, but the stage-door keeper hung on to it. I dare say she was sick and tired of every Tom, Dick and Harry trying it on just because she wore a revealing outfit. Well, the stage-door keeper took a note of everyone who did, and your name was on his list.'

Braden placed his hands on the table that separated him from Hardcastle and spent a few moments studying his fingernails before looking up. 'Well, you don't blame me, do you?'

'We'll start again. How many times did you call at the theatre?'

'Four.'

'And did you get to speak to her at all?'

'I told you. I tried, but that fellow who was in the show told me to sheer off.'

'And that was the only time you approached her personally, was it?'

'Yes.'

Hardcastle nodded slowly. 'What with there being a war on, I'd've thought you people would've had more to do than hang around a stage door making a nuisance of yourselves with a pretty girl. Still,' he added, 'you won't have much time for any of that, once you and your horse get across to France and the Hun starts taking pot-shots at you.'

'Now look here, Inspector—'

'Incidentally, d'you know of any other officer who hung about on the off-chance of bedding Mrs Hart?'

'No, I certainly do not, and that was not the—'

'You can go, Captain Braden, but I'll likely want to speak to you again.'

'What d'you think about those two, sir?' asked Marriott, once Braden had departed.

'Tooley Street tailors, the pair of 'em.' Hardcastle dismissed the two officers with a derogatory wave of his hand. 'All piss and importance. Still, Marriott, I don't intend to cross 'em off my list just yet. What interests me, though, is whether there were any other officers from here who might have taken an interest in our Mrs Hart.'

'D'you think she *was* free with her favours, sir?'

'Anyone's guess, Marriott, and I still have a fancy for that Percy Savage,' said Hardcastle, lighting his pipe and filling the room with tobacco smoke. 'But she certainly didn't have any truck with the cavalry, that's for sure. But being married to a sailor, she might not have fancied these horse soldiers. And from what I've seen of 'em, I don't blame her, neither.'

Convinced that the interrogation of the two Royal Horse Guards officers had been a waste of time, Hardcastle returned to the Windsor headquarters in less than an equable mood.

'There's a telegraph message for you, sir,' said Stone. 'From Cannon Row, wherever that is.'

'That, Stone, is my divisional headquarters. And I reckon we have more to deal with in a day than you do in a month.'

Stone remained silent and proffered the message form.

'It's from DS Wood,' said Hardcastle, and then he tutted. 'He shouldn't have sent this by telegraph. I reckon it's secret. Anyway, it's done now. He says that Commander Hart called in at Cannon Row this morning and wanted me to know that he's setting sail this evening in HMS *Dauntless*.' To Stone's surprise, Hardcastle struck a match and applied the flame to the message form. When it was all but destroyed, he dropped it in the ashtray. 'I don't want you saying a word about that message to anyone, Stone. And make sure that no one else talks about it. Otherwise you might be in trouble with Dora. To say nothing of the Official Secrets Act. Understood?'

'Who's Dora?' asked the bemused Windsor detective.

'The Defence of the Realm Act, Stone, an' it don't make an exception of coppers.'

Six

On the morning following Hardcastle's questioning of the Royal Horse Guards officers, a soldier appeared on the threshold of the room occupied by the London detectives. He had the appearance of a man fast approaching sixty years of age, and his waist must have measured a good fifty inches in circumference. That, and his suffused cheeks, testified to an excessive intake of beer over a considerable period of time. Using both hands, he pulled at the ends of his drooping, nicotine-stained moustache and coughed deferentially.

'Sergeant Sidney Phillips, Sixty-Sixth of Foot, Princess Charlotte of Wales's Royal Berkshire Regiment, at your service, gents.' He paused to give his moustache another tug. 'I understand you wanted to see me. According to Joe Sharples, any road.'

Concealing a smile at the theatrical demeanour of this character, Hardcastle invited him to take a seat.

'I'm told you're the recruiting sergeant who appeared on stage at the Windsor Empire with Victoria Hart and signed up anyone willing to join the Colours, Sergeant.'

'That I did, sir.'

'Better than being at the Front, I suppose.'

Phillips stroked his bulbous nose. 'Reward for long service in hard stations, sir. Any road, they reckon I'm too old for active service, but I'll tell you this much, guv'nor, I could still show these youngsters a thing or two. Blimey, when I think of the battle honours of my lot . . .' He paused and looked wistfully at the window behind Hardcastle before starting to reel off the names. 'Egmont-op-Zee, Copenhagen, Peninsular Wars, Douro, Talavera—'

'I'm sure your regiment has a commendable fighting history, Sergeant Phillips, but it's what happened late on Christmas Eve and early on Christmas Day that interests me, not what occurred last century.'

'Ah, yes, I s'pose so, guv'nor.' Phillips produced a pipe and a pouch of tobacco. 'Mind if I light up?'

'Go ahead,' said Hardcastle, and began to fill his own pipe. 'Now then,' he continued, when both men had their pipes well alight, 'how often were you at the theatre with Victoria Hart?'

Phillips replied without hesitation. 'Every night the show was on. Ten days not counting the Sunday. Theatre was closed Sundays. I never done the matinées, though.'

'And it was your part to come on stage at the end of the show when Victoria was singing her final song, and recruit as many volunteers as possible. Is that right?'

Phillips grinned broadly. 'That's right, guv'nor, and I caught a fair few, I can tell you. Nearly all for the Royal Berkshires an' all. Apart from a couple of young idiots who wanted to be donkey-wallopers, so I signed 'em up and sent 'em down Combermere Barracks. That'll teach 'em.' He shook his head. 'It's hard enough looking after your own kit without having to worry about a nag an' all the riding gear what goes with it.'

'How many d'you reckon you recruited?'

Phillips ran a hand round his chin. 'Well, now, let me see. Since the war started it must be—'

'No,' interrupted Hardcastle. 'During the time this last show was on.'

'I don't know offhand.' Phillips stared at the ceiling. 'All the records is down me office, see.'

'And where is your office, Sergeant Phillips?'

'The drill hall. That's where me office is.'

Hardcastle let out a sigh. 'And where is the drill hall?' he enquired with a patience that surprised Marriott.

'Bolton Road, guv'nor. And I reckon I must have recruited nigh on sixty. Well, me and Vicky.'

'At last,' muttered Hardcastle.

'Did you know of anyone who was bothering Mrs Hart,

Sergeant?' asked Marriott, looking up from the notes he had been making.

Phillips switched his gaze to Marriott, an expression of surprise on his face. '*Mrs* Hart did you say, guv'nor? Blimey, I never knew that. Are you sure?'

'She was married to a Royal Navy commander,' said Marriott wearily. He was beginning to tire of this oft-expressed surprise on the part of those whom he and Hardcastle had interviewed.

'Gawd blimey! If I'd've known that, I'd've been a bit more respectful. You'd never have known she was spliced to an officer. Always ready for a laugh and a joke was Vicky.'

'Well? Did she?' persisted Marriott.

'Did she what?'

Now it was Marriott's turn to sigh with exasperation. 'Did she have anyone pestering her?'

'There was always a few what was trying their luck with her. I s'pose it was that outfit what she used to wear on stage. She always got a round of applause and cheering when she come on.' Phillips paused to relight his pipe. 'I remember Joe Sharples telling me as how there was always a few stage-door johnnies hanging about,' he continued. 'Some of 'em was them dandified officers from up Combermere. Got a good opinion of themselves has that silver-spoon lot, but it'll be a different story when they're looking across the plonk. If it's anything like Bloemfontein was, they'll wish they'd never been born, I can tell you that, guv'nor. Anyhow, our Vicky never had no truck with any of 'em. But now I knows she was married, I ain't surprised.'

'And what about you?' asked Hardcastle. 'Did you ever try it on with her?'

Phillips let out a throaty laugh. 'What, with my trouble-and-strife living not ten minutes away? No, guv'nor, I ain't that stupid. Any road, Vicky was young enough to be me daughter. Mind you, I reckon that that Percy Savage might have been sniffing around, but I don't think he'd've had any more luck than the rest of 'em. Course, he was screwing that Vera Cobb most of the time.'

'Who's Vera Cobb?' asked Hardcastle with feigned innocence. It was his inveterate practice to pretend that he was little more than a bumbling Dogberry. But he recalled both the name and the fact that Vera Cobb had offered herself for Victoria Hart's part within minutes of learning of her death.

'One of them song-and-dance girls,' said Phillips. 'Pretty young kid, she is.'

'You seem to know a lot about what was going on at the theatre,' said Hardcastle.

'Well, guv'nor,' said Phillips, tapping the side of his large nose with the stem of his pipe, 'I was there every night, and I was always one to keep me eyes and ears open and me mouth shut.'

'Had you been recruiting at the theatre at other times, Sergeant Phillips?' asked Marriott. 'Before Mrs Hart's show was put on.'

'Yes, but I didn't get so many them times. It was Vicky what was the draw, see, guv'nor. Everyone what signed on the dotted line got a kiss from her. Well, they was practically falling over themselves to get up on the stage.' Phillips chuckled, a chuckle that developed into a rasping cough. 'They'll regret it, though.'

'Did she mention having done this sort of thing at other theatres, Sergeant Phillips?' asked Marriott.

'Oh yeah. She said she'd done it at two or three shows since the war started. She certainly mentioned she'd been in London and . . . ' Phillips paused in thought. 'Brighton and Pompey was a couple of the others, I think. Brighton for sure, but I think she said she was in Pompey before the war broke out, so she wouldn't have done no recruiting there.'

'What are you doing now the show's finished?' asked Hardcastle. 'You won't be recruiting at the theatre while they're running a pantomime, will you?'

'Don't see why not, guv'nor,' said Phillips with a laugh. 'You take it from me, the whole army's a bit of a pantomime. D'you know, I heard tell that on Christmas Day the Seaforth Highlanders and old Fritz even knocked off milling it to play football down near Houplines. That's in Belgium, that is. I think.' His face took on a mournful expression. 'An' from what I heard, Fritz beat the Jocks three–two.'

'You were saying about recruiting,' prompted Hardcastle impatiently. It seemed that all Phillips wanted to do was reminisce.

'So I was. Now Vicky's show's over, you'll find me wandering about the town most days. Castle Hill's a big favourite when these youngsters is watching them toy soldiers changing the guard at Windsor Castle.'

'Toy soldiers?' queried Hardcastle.

'Brigade of Guards, guv'nor,' said Phillips. 'Never see their arses east of Suez,' he added scornfully. 'Anyhow, these lads is standing there watching, all glassy-eyed, and they can see the girls is practically swooning. That's when I catch 'em. And all the better if they're walking out with some young judy. A fit young fellow like you ought to be at the Front doing yer bit, I tell 'em. Half the time his lady friend gives him a nudge and says something like "Go on, Fred." And before he knows what's happened he's down Aldershot getting his hair cut.'

'There was a party on stage after the matinée on Christmas Eve. Were you there?'

'Not me, guv'nor. That ain't my scene. No, I was round the town trying to get a few more to join up before I knocked off for Christmas. Catch 'em in the pubs when they're half pissed, and they'll sign anything.'

'Victoria Hart left the theatre at about five o'clock,' said Marriott, 'and went to the White Hart Hotel.'

'Is that a fact?'

'Did you see anyone with her while you were around the town?'

Phillips scratched at his moustache with the stem of his pipe. 'No, guv'nor, not as I recall. Mind you, I'd had a few jars meself by that time,' he admitted, 'and I wasn't exactly seeing straight.'

'Thank you, Sergeant Phillips,' said Hardcastle, cutting short the loquacious soldier's monologue. 'I might have to see you again. The drill hall in Bolton Road, you said?'

'I ain't often there, guv'nor, but Joe Sharples always knows where to find me.' Phillips laughed. 'Usually in the Bull in Peascod Street of an evening. It's right opposite the theatre.'

Although keeping an open mind, Hardcastle had more or less dismissed the two army officers as likely candidates for the murder of Victoria Hart. But there may well have been other, as yet undiscovered, admirers at Windsor, or even elsewhere. Apart from the writer of the letters found in Victoria's lodgings.

'It's the writer of those we need to track down, Marriott,' Hardcastle said, tapping the small pile.

'Bit difficult, sir, seeing that they've no sender's address and only "Your admirer" as a signature.'

'But we do have the addresses of the theatres he sent the letters to,' Hardcastle said thoughtfully. 'Have you read all of them, Marriott?'

'Yes, sir. Like I said the other day, they start in November nineteen-thirteen and continue at the rate of about one a month.' Marriott took a letter from the envelope. 'This one's the first and was sent to Daly's Theatre in Cranbourn Street. That's a turning off the Charing Cross Road on C Division's manor.'

'I do know where Cranbourn Street is, Marriott,' said Hardcastle patiently. 'I was a sergeant at Vine Street. Anyway, what's it say?' Although he was familiar with the contents of the letter, he saw no harm in hearing them again.

'This one starts off by proposing marriage, sir.' Marriott glanced up. 'Incidentally, all the letters are addressed to *Miss* Victoria Hart. Some of them don't have a stamp or postmark on them, so it's possible he handed those in at the stage door in person.'

'Which have stamps and which don't?'

'Those sent to the London theatres don't have a stamp or postmark, but the ones to out-of-town addresses were sent by post.'

'What's the postmark on 'em, Marriott?'

'Three of them had been posted, sir. And all of them have a Kingston upon Thames postmark.'

'I don't know how he expects her to accept his proposal
if he don't say who he is or where he lives,' muttered
Hardcastle with crushing logic. 'Do they all contain that
same sort of stuff?'

'More or less, sir, but it seems that somewhere along the
line, somebody told the writer that Victoria Hart was
married; probably one of the stage-door keepers. In the later
letters he says he doesn't believe it, and keeps on proposing.'
Marriott sifted through the letters until he found the one he
was looking for. 'This one, sir, was sent to the Empire
Theatre, Leicester Square. In it, the writer says that her
claim to be married is merely an attempt to put him off,
and that he doesn't believe it. He goes on to say that her
pretence is to no avail, and that he will pursue her to the
ends of the earth if necessary.'

'Sounds an educated sort of cove,' said Hardcastle. 'Any
indication that he's given up?'

'Only that the letters ceased in May this year, sir. But
she might have destroyed any others, and forgot to destroy
these.' Marriott tied the pink ribbon around the small
bundle. 'They're probably from another one of the cranks
Commander Hart mentioned.'

'Maybe. Maybe not.' Hardcastle thought about that
possibility for a moment or two before making one of his
mercurial decisions. 'Very well, Marriott, we'll go back up
the Smoke, and start by having another chat with Master
Percy Savage at the Playhouse Theatre. And if he ain't there,
we'll try his digs in Pimlico.' On the way out, he looked into
Detective Inspector Struthers's office and told Stone that he
and Marriott were returning to London. 'If you need me, you
can pass a message to Cannon Row police station,' he said.

Detective Sergeant Stone looked immensely relieved at
the departure of the London officers. So much so that he
filched a glass of DI Struthers's Scotch.

'I've got a feeling in my bones that most of the enquiries
into Victoria Hart's murder will be up here in London,' said
Hardcastle, as he and Marriott alighted from the train at
Waterloo station.

Marriott failed to understand how Hardcastle had arrived at that conclusion, but hoped that he was right. A prolonged stay in London would afford him the chance of seeing something of his wife and children. Lorna Marriott was less tolerant of the demands of the Metropolitan Police than was Hardcastle's wife Alice. But she had not had as long to grow accustomed to the exigencies of the Criminal Investigation Department.

Before going to the Playhouse Theatre, Hardcastle called into Cannon Row police station. 'Catto,' he bellowed as he passed the open door of the CID office.

'I thought you were in Windsor, sir.' Detective Constable Henry Catto struggled into his jacket, and rushed into the corridor as he recognized the DDI's voice.

'That's just where you were wrong, my lad. Always keep your movements secret. In that way you'll catch the villains unawares. That's what thief-taking's all about.'

'Yes, sir.' As usual, Catto was bewildered by Hardcastle's latest homily on criminal investigation. Whenever he had failed to let the DDI know where he had gone, he had been rebuked on his return. And on one occasion accused of being absent without leave.

'I've got a job for you, Catto, and that new chap.' Hardcastle turned to Marriott. 'What's his name?'

'D'you mean Watkins, sir?' Marriott had known Hardcastle describe some of his detectives as 'new chaps' when they had been on the division for more than a year.

'I don't know. If that's his name, I want him in here. Go and fetch him, Catto.'

'Er, he's out on an enquiry, sir.'

'Out? Doing what? I hope he left word where he's gone. I don't want people disappearing without leaving word.'

In view of what Hardcastle had just said about keeping one's movements secret, Catto was now more confused than ever. 'I understand he's looking into the theft of a wallet at the Royal Automobile Club, sir. It's in Pall Mall, sir.'

'God damn it, boy, I know where the Royal Automobile Club is. This is my bailiwick,' thundered Hardcastle. 'Well, he'd better not be too long doing it. Sergeant Marriott will

give you a list of four theatres. I want the pair of you to
get round 'em as quick as you can. They was where Victoria
Hart was appearing and where she received letters from
some cove who wanted to marry her.'

'Who was he, sir?' asked Catto unwisely.

'If I knew that, I wouldn't be sending you out, would I,
lad?'

'No, sir.' Catto was even more perplexed by this latest
exchange with his DDI.

'These theatres had letters handed in for Mrs Hart, probably to the stage-door keeper. Find out if he or anyone else
at the theatre remembers him.'

'What d'you want me to do if they do remember, sir?
Shall I arrest him?'

'Arrest him? You won't know where to find him, Catto.
If you can find the writer of anonymous letters who don't
put his address on 'em, you're a better detective than me.
And are you a better detective than me?'

'No, sir,' said Catto earnestly.

'Thought not. If I knew where he was, I'd've felt his
collar days ago. No, my lad, you don't do anything, because
I'll need to go out there and have a chat with whoever
remembers this individual. Got that, have you?'

'Yes, sir,' said Catto uncertainly.

'Well, don't stand there, lad. As soon as young what's-
his-name is back, get going. And start with Daly's.'
Hardcastle turned to his sergeant. 'We'll have a bite to eat
at the Ship and Shovel in Craven Passage, Marriott. It's just
round the corner from the Playhouse.'

Although the public house known as the Ship and Shovel
was just off Hardcastle's division, he knew it well and often
called in there for a drink on his way back from Bow Street
police court. As a consequence, the licensee greeted him
like an old friend.

'Haven't seen you in here for a bit, guv'nor.'

'Been a touch busy,' said Hardcastle tersely, and took a
long draught of his pint of bitter.

'Well, a Happy New Year to you,' said the publican, 'and

to you, Charlie,' he added, turning to Marriott. He pushed two hot steak and kidney pies across the counter. 'There you are, guv'nor. A couple of fourpenny cannons, straight out the oven. On the house.'

'A bit of Charing Cross railway station fell on this place back in nineteen-oh-five, Marriott,' said Hardcastle as they approached the Playhouse Theatre.

'Really, sir?' Marriott was always surprised by the historical snippets that his DDI revealed from time to time.

'Killed six people,' continued Hardcastle in matter-of-fact tones. 'Gave E Division something to think about, I s'pose.' As they reached the theatre, he pointed at a billboard. 'I see young Vera got the lead after all, then,' he said. 'There, see that, Marriott? Vera Cobb in Percy Savage's *Beaux Belles.*'

'I suppose Savage changed his mind, sir,' said Marriott. 'He seemed very doubtful about letting Vera take over Victoria's part when we spoke to him on Christmas Day.'

Hardcastle uttered a coarse laugh. 'If what Sergeant Phillips said about Vera and Savage is true, I reckon she must have threatened the bold Percy that he'd be going short of a bit of jig-a-jig unless she got the role. I reckon she's a conniving little bitch, that one.'

The stage door was open and Hardcastle rapped on the window of the keeper's cubbyhole. 'I'm looking for Percy Savage,' he said.

'You from the press?'

'No, police,' said Hardcastle sharply. He did not care for being mistaken for a reporter.

'Ah!' The stage-door keeper emerged from his tiny office. 'We've been getting a lot of them Fleet Street hacks round here ever since that Victoria Hart was done in. You dealing with that, guv'nor?'

'Just get hold of Savage for me, cully, because I don't have time to waste.'

'He's in his dressing room, sir. I'll show you the way.'

The stage-door keeper led the two detectives through a maze of subterranean passages. Eventually he stopped at a door bearing a piece of dog-eared card upon which Percy Savage's name had been scrawled.

'He's in here, guv'nor,' said the stage-door keeper, pointing at the card.

'I'd worked that out for myself,' said Hardcastle, and without knocking, pushed open the door.

'What the blazes . . . ?' Percy Savage was seated on a threadbare chaise-longue. On his lap, in an intimate embrace, was Vera Cobb. The young showgirl let out a shrill scream at the arrival of Hardcastle and Marriott, and, hastily moving from Savage's lap, quickly buttoned up the front of her frock.

'I want a word with you, Mr Savage.' Hardcastle placed his bowler hat and umbrella on a hatstand that had seen better days. 'And you too, miss,' he added, as Vera stood up as if to leave. With a sigh of resignation, she sat down again.

'Can I offer you a drink, Inspector?' Savage, recovering from the surprise of a visit from the police, indicated a half-bottle of gin on a shelf over a small wash-hand basin.

'No, thanks.' Hardcastle took the chair from in front of the dressing table and sat down. 'I've been making some enquiries about the death of Victoria Hart.'

'Oh, yes, I suppose you would have done,' said Savage, a little nervously.

'And I've found that she had quite a few admirers.'

'Yes, well, as I said when you came to see me on Christmas Day, she was an attractive girl, and actresses are always being bothered by men.'

'I've spoken to one or two,' continued Hardcastle, 'but I'm sure you know about some more. And not only in Windsor.'

'It was always happening, Inspector. Wherever we went. Some – usually the better mannered – would send in their cards or a bouquet of flowers, but Vicky always sent them back. She was married, you see.'

'So you said previously, and I've spoken to her husband.' Hardcastle suddenly changed his line of questioning. 'I also discovered that you tried it on with her, too.'

'I don't know where you got that from,' said Savage hurriedly, and then laughed nervously.

'I have received information from a reliable source that on at least two occasions you called on her at her digs in Clarence Road. Furthermore, you spent at least an hour with her in her bedroom. So, what've you got to say about that? Bit of a tumble on her bed, was it?'

Savage looked embarrassed, and Vera Cobb scowled at him, a look registering both suspicion and betrayal on her face, and pointedly moved further away from him. 'We were discussing a new routine for the show, Inspector.' He shot Vera a pleading look. 'Honestly, Vee.' It did not sound convincing.

'Why not hold those discussions in the theatre?' asked Hardcastle.

'I don't know how much you know about theatres, Inspector, but there's never a quiet moment. It's impossible to hold a conversation anywhere in a place like this.'

Hardcastle was doubtful about that claim. After all, here he was talking to Savage in his quiet dressing room, but he let it pass. For the moment. 'Where were you between, say, three o'clock on Christmas Eve and five o'clock on Christmas morning?'

'Surely you don't think I had anything to do with that terrible business, do you, Inspector?' Savage's face took on an expression of great concern.

'I suspect everyone until it's proved to my satisfaction that they weren't involved,' said Hardcastle mildly. 'I was thinking that maybe you tried it on with her, what with her old man being at sea, but that she spurned you, and you couldn't take it.' It was a comment that only served to heighten Savage's apprehension.

'Good God! Of course I didn't kill her.'

Hardcastle's accusation had struck fear into Savage, as he had meant it to. But it was one of Hardcastle's devices to concentrate the minds of witnesses.

'I told you all this before, Inspector,' Savage protested. 'We had a party on stage and after Victoria had left, we went to the Bull for a few drinks at about half-past six, I think it was.' Savage glanced at Vera and she nodded. 'Then we – Vera, Fanny and I – went back to the Armitages for supper, had a few more drinks and we all went to bed at about half-past eleven.'

'What d'you know about letters that Mrs Hart received, Mr Savage?' asked Marriott.

'Letters?' Savage looked blank. 'What sort of letters?'

'Letters proposing marriage.'

'But she was married,' put in Vera.

'I know she was,' said Marriott patiently. 'These were letters that arrived about once a month from November last year until May this year. Always at the theatre where she was appearing. Even when she moved theatres, this man found out where she was, and sent them there.'

Savage shook his head. 'As I said earlier, she was always being asked out to dinner or supper, and sometimes she'd get a bunch of flowers, but she never mentioned proposals of marriage. In fact, she said nothing about getting any letters.' He glanced at Vera. 'Did she ever say anything to you, Vee?'

'No, nothing.'

'When did Victoria Hart begin her recruiting, Mr Savage?' asked Hardcastle.

'Almost as soon as the war broke out. We were at the Palladium in Argyll Street. The management had agreed to allow a sergeant to come on stage at the end of the perform-ance and appeal for recruits. It was then that Vicky decided to join in. She was wearing that rather provocative outfit she always wore—' Savage broke off. 'It was very similar to the one that Vera wears now. Anyway, she said that any man who signed up would get a kiss from her.' He laughed. 'She nearly got killed in the rush.' He paused again. 'Oh, that wasn't a very clever thing to say, was it? Anyway, it seemed such a good idea that she did it at every theatre we went to after that. She must have recruited hundreds.'

'And what about you, Miss Cobb? Do you do any recruiting?'

'I've been doing my bit,' said the actress coyly.

'Of course she does,' said Savage. 'I expect the King'll

give her a medal.' There was a pause before the actor-manager made a suggestion. 'Why don't you and Sergeant Marriott drop in and see the show this evening, Inspector? I'll leave a couple of tickets for you at the box office.'

'I hope you're not trying to bribe me,' said Hardcastle sternly.

'I doubt I'd succeed,' said Savage sincerely. 'To tell you the truth, Mr Hardcastle, we've been half empty ever since we started the run. We've been papering the house every night.'

'I'll think about it.' But Hardcastle fully intended to take advantage of Savage's offer, for no better reason than that he might learn something that would assist his enquiries.

'That Vera Cobb didn't seem too happy at our arrival, did she?' said Hardcastle as the two of them left the Playhouse Theatre. For a change, he had decided against taking a taxi and he and Marriott were walking back to Cannon Row through Embankment Gardens.

Marriott laughed. 'If we'd been a minute or two later, sir, I reckon we'd've found 'em well at it in his dressing room.'

'Yes, and I doubt it would've been the first time. At least, from what Sergeant Phillips told us.'

Seven

When the two detectives arrived at the theatre for the eight o'clock performance, they were met in the foyer by Savage, and were escorted to a box close to the stage.

'I thought it would be better for you if you were away from the hoi polloi,' he said.

From the very first act, Hardcastle could understand why the theatre was only half full. An overweight comedian rode on to the stage on a unicycle and promptly fell off, losing his battered top hat in the process. From the way he swore, both to himself and at the baying crowd in the sparsely filled auditorium, it was not meant to be part of his performance. Once he had recovered himself, he began to tell a few jokes that fell as flat as he himself had been moments earlier. He finished by singing a comic song that was neither comic nor tuneful, and certainly did not keep pace with the orchestra. He departed to a chorus of booing from the gallery.

And so it went on. After a less than determined effort to get out of his straitjacket, the escapologist, still wearing it, was carried off by a couple of stagehands. The juggler dropped his Indian clubs, not once but five times, and the ventriloquist's sketch was greeted by shouts of 'You're moving your lips.'

By the time Vera Cobb took the stage, the audience was in an extremely ugly and combative mood, and it was apparent that nothing would satisfy it. Except, perhaps, the return of its money.

Wearing a revealing outfit, she danced – badly – and twirled her cane, twice dropping it so that it slithered across the stage. But worse was to come.

Presumably as a preamble to recruiting, she embarked on her finale by attempting to sing 'Jolly good luck to the girl who loves a soldier', a song made popular by the famous Vesta Tilley back in 1906. But the mob in the 'Gods' was having none of it, and drowned her out with catcalls. Several tomatoes struck the backcloth, and even before she had finished her song, Vera fled the stage in tears.

During this embarrassing performance, a recruiting sergeant peeped out from the wings, but the hostility of the crowd convinced him that he was unlikely to recruit anyone. He disappeared to the Northumberland Arms public house and sank three pints of mild and bitter in quick succession.

'If that lasts the week, it'll be a bloody miracle,' said Hardcastle as he and Marriott made their way back to Cannon Row.

On the Wednesday morning, Detective Constables Catto and Watkins reported the results of their enquiries into Victoria Hart's mystery letter-writer.

'You two took your bloody time,' barked Hardcastle. 'There was only four theatres in all. What did you do, stop and see the show at each of 'em?'

'No, sir, but I did have three of them to do,' said Catto, lamely attempting to excuse the delay. At least, that which constituted a delay in Hardcastle's eyes. 'I let Cecil do the one at Stratford, and I did the rest on account of them being near each other. In central London like.'

'I don't want chapter and verse on who did what and where,' snapped Hardcastle. 'Who the hell's Cecil, anyway?' he demanded as an afterthought.

'I am, sir,' said DC Watkins nervously.

'Good grief,' said Hardcastle.

'I thought I'd give him just the one, sir,' Catto repeated, 'on account of him being new to the department.'

'Very charitable of you, I'm sure, Catto. Had nothing to do with Stratford being seven miles away, I suppose? So, what did you find out?'

'DC Watkins went to—'

Hardcastle slapped the top of his desk with the flat of

his hand. 'He's got a tongue in his head, hasn't he?' Turning to the unfortunate Watkins, he said, 'Well, boy, what did you find out?'

'Er, nothing, sir.'

'Nothing?' Hardcastle peered at the ceiling. 'What d'you mean by nothing? Catto here will tell you that I don't stand for sloppy reporting.'

Somewhat belatedly, Watkins extracted his pocket book from somewhere inside his blue serge suit, a suit he had purchased – for the exorbitant price of thirty shillings – on his recent appointment to the CID. 'I visited the Theatre Royal Stratford East, sir,' he began. 'It's in Gerry Raffles Square—'

'I don't care if it's on the bloody moon, Watson.'

'It's Watkins, sir.' The young DC corrected the DDI nervously. 'Anyway, sir, I spoke to the stage-door keeper and he doesn't recall anyone leaving a letter for Victoria Hart when *Beaux Belles* was on at that theatre. But he did point out that it was nearly a year ago.'

'*Nearly* a year? What were the exact dates?'

'He wasn't sure, sir.'

Hardcastle grunted and switched his gaze to Catto. 'And what did you discover, lad?'

'Out of the three theatres I visited, sir, two of the stage-door keepers remembered someone handing in a letter for Mrs Hart. That was Daly's and the Holborn Empire.'

'Description?' demanded Hardcastle.

Catto referred to his pocket book. 'Same at both theatres, sir. The man was aged about thirty-five to forty. Around five foot eight tall. Black hair and a black goatee beard.'

'Well, what was he dressed in, Catto? I haven't got all day.'

'He turned up at the stage door in evening dress, sir, with a Chesterfield overcoat, a cane and a gibus.'

'A what?' roared Hardcastle. 'I hope you're not trying to get clever with me, lad.'

Catto looked hurt. 'It's what the stage-door keeper at the Empire called it, sir. I didn't know what it was, but he explained.'

'Well, perhaps you'd better explain it to me, lad,' said Hardcastle icily.

'It's an opera hat, sir.'

'Is it now? Then why the bloody hell didn't you say so?'

'Apparently a gibus is a bit different, sir,' said Catto, attempting to justify his use of the word. 'The stage-door keeper said it was named after its inventor, a Monsieur Gibus. He said he was French, sir.'

'Would be, I suppose,' commented Hardcastle.

'And it collapses flat, sir, so it's easier to carry, or to put on a shelf in a cloakroom.'

'A positive mine of information, aren't you, Catto? I don't suppose he gave a name, did he, this man with the gibus?'

'No, sir. But the stage-door keepers at both Daly's and the Holborn Empire reckoned that he must've seen the performance and then walked round to the stage door afterwards.'

'Quite the little detectives, aren't they?' muttered Hardcastle sarcastically. 'That means this cove must have written the letters in advance. Can't see him sitting in the orchestra stalls writing a letter, can you, Catto?'

'Not really, sir.' Catto risked a grin in the hope that the DDI was making a joke.

'Right, you can go,' said Hardcastle and waved a hand of dismissal. 'And well done, lad.'

Catto, delighted at receiving a rare word of praise from the DDI, left the office with Watkins.

'You'll have to get hold of that new man Wilson, Marriott,' said Hardcastle. 'Needs to learn how to report properly.'

'His name's Watkins, sir. I'll have a word with him.' But Marriott knew that Hardcastle was being his usual perverse self, probably because the enquiry into Victoria Hart's murder was not proceeding as quickly as he had hoped. The irascible DDI was always impatient, which was why he sometimes worked late into the night and at weekends, and expected all his detectives to do the same.

'If he ever has to give evidence up the Bailey he'll get eaten alive by any half-awake defence brief,' continued Hardcastle, refusing to give up on the shortcomings of his

most junior detective. He took out his pipe and began filling
it with tobacco. 'What were the names of the theatres that
our mystery man *posted* letters to?' He waved at a chair.
'Sit down, m'boy. Smoke if you want to.'

Having lit a cigarette, Marriott glanced at his pocket book.
'The Kingston Empire, the Aldershot Hippodrome and the
Wimbledon Theatre, guv'nor.' Recognizing that Hardcastle
was in a more relaxed mood, he lapsed into a less formal
mode of address.

Hardcastle waved away Marriott's cigarette smoke. 'God
almighty, m'boy, what's them coffin nails you're smoking?'

'Gold Flake, sir.'

'Dreadful. You ought to smoke a pipe, Marriott,' said the
DDI before continuing his comments about the letters. 'Not
much point in making enquiries at any of those theatres, at
least not yet. But why, I wonder, didn't he personally deliver
the one to the Kingston Empire? Couldn't have been far
from where he posted the others that are postmarked
Kingston upon Thames.'

'D'you think we'll learn any more by going back to the
two theatres that gave Catto a description of the man,
guv'nor?'

'Maybe,' said Hardcastle thoughtfully. 'What was in the
linen drapers about the murder, m'boy?'

'The locals in Berkshire ran it on Boxing Day, and the
nationals picked it up the next morning, and again on the
Monday.'

'I've got an idea.' The DDI relit his pipe and puffed
clouds of smoke into the air.

'You have, guv'nor?' Marriott sat up and took notice.
Hardcastle had had ideas in the past, many of them bizarre.
The irony was that they had often brought a complex case
to closure.

'Supposing we put it out that Victoria Hart wasn't
murdered, and is still alive? That it was some other actress.'

'What good would that do?' asked an incredulous
Marriott.

'It might flush out this bloody man who's been sending
her proposals of marriage, m'boy, that's what.'

'I don't think it would work, guv'nor.'

'Oh, and why's that, Marriott?' asked Hardcastle sharply. He was never happy when a subordinate argued with him. Even when that subordinate was Marriott.

Marriott knew this, but felt that, on occasion, it was his duty to dissuade his chief from attempting the impossible. He also recognized that the informality was over. 'I don't think Fleet Street would go along with it, sir.'

'Maybe you're right,' said Hardcastle grudgingly.

'On the other hand, sir, if we were to put out a story that Victoria had left something in her will for her secret admirer, that might run him to earth.'

Hardcastle eased himself back in his chair, and for some time said nothing. Then he leaned forward and put his pipe in the ashtray. 'You could just be right, Marriott. If we have a word with her solicitor, he might be game to play along. If I remember correctly, you took a note of his name when we talked to Commander Hart at the Army and Navy Club.'

'Yes, sir.' Marriott thumbed through the pages of his pocket book. 'He's Arthur Courtney, sir, with offices in Chancery Lane.'

'Good. He's bound to have a telephone, Marriott, being in the law. Give him a call, and make an appointment for us to see him.'

Minutes later, Marriott reported that Mr Courtney was prepared to see them at half-past eleven the following morning, New Year's Eve.

'Good,' said Hardcastle. 'That'll give us time to go back to Windsor and see what we can learn about this appointment Mrs Hart rushed off to keep at the White Hart Hotel.'

John Davis, the manager of the White Hart, a courtly middle-aged man impeccable in morning dress, peered at Hardcastle over his half-moon spectacles. 'From Scotland Yard, you say?'

'Yes, and I'm investigating the murder of Victoria Hart.'

'Yes, I heard about that. Terrible thing to have happened. Terrible. Perhaps it would be as well if you came into my office,' said the manager, and showed the detectives into a room just off the entrance hall.

Hardcastle explained, without giving too much away, that Mrs Hart had received a telegram asking her to keep an appointment at the hotel.

'And when was this, Inspector?'

'On Christmas Eve, at about five o'clock. The telegram asked her to meet the sender at this hotel.' Hardcastle turned to Marriott. 'Give Mr Davis the description of what she was wearing at the time.'

'An attractive woman with brown hair, aged twenty-five,' said Marriott. 'Wearing a black coat, believed to be musquash, and black shoes.'

Davis raised his eyebrows. 'No hat?'

'No, no hat,' said Marriott. 'At least, that's what we've been told.'

'Well, I'm sure that my staff would have remembered a woman coming in here without a hat. We don't normally see women in here without a hat. I would suggest that you speak to Granger, the hall porter, and the restaurant head waiter. There would be little point in talking to the barman because ladies are not allowed in the bar.' Davis rose from his chair and conducted the two officers back to the entrance hall. 'Granger,' he said, addressing the hall porter, 'this is Inspector Hardcastle of Scotland Yard. He has some questions to ask you.'

'How can I help you, sir?' Granger brushed briefly at the lapels of his gold-braided green tailcoat.

'I believe that a woman called Mrs Hart came in here shortly after five o'clock on Christmas Eve, Mr Granger.'

'Would that be the actress who was murdered, sir?'

'Yes, it would. Did you happen to see the show she was appearing in, Mr Granger?'

'No, sir.'

'So you wouldn't have recognized her.'

'No, sir, I'm afraid not.'

'Marriott, tell Mr Granger what she looked like,' said Hardcastle.

'Ah yes, I do remember such a lady, sir,' said Granger,

once Marriott had repeated the description. 'She came into the entrance hall at about a quarter past five, maybe half past, and took a seat. I particularly noticed how unusual it was that she wasn't wearing a hat. I assumed that she was waiting for someone, but I had to deal with another matter, and when I returned to my desk, the lady had gone.'

'Did she make a reservation for a room?'

'No, sir.'

'Did you see anyone with her?' asked Hardcastle.

'No, sir, no one.'

'Did you see, at about that time, a man aged some thirty-five to forty years old, five foot eight, with a black goatee beard?'

'No, sir, I don't recall such a gentleman.' Granger paused before adding, 'A tragic business, that young lady being murdered, sir. It's the talk of the town.'

'I dare say it is,' said Hardcastle. 'Thank you for your assistance, Mr Granger.' He turned to Marriott. 'Well, at least we can be fairly sure she was here, Marriott. It's just our luck that the cove with the beard must've arrived while the porter was away from his desk.'

'If it was him and not someone else, sir.'

'As you say, Marriott.' But Hardcastle was loath to abandon his theory that the letter-writer was the murderer.

Davis escorted the two detectives to the restaurant, but they fared even worse there. The head waiter was adamant that he had not seen anyone fitting Mrs Hart's description, or that of a man with a black goatee beard.

'I'm obliged to you for your help, Mr Davis,' said Hardcastle, as he and Marriott took their leave of the hotel manager. But he was disappointed that this particular lead had come to naught.

From the White Hart Hotel, Hardcastle and Marriott made their way to the General Post Office, a few yards along the High Street.

'I want to see the postmaster,' Hardcastle announced, once he had introduced himself to a clerk.

'Certainly, sir.'

Moments later a man in a black jacket and striped trousers appeared. 'My name's Rogers, Inspector. I'm the head post-master. What can I do for you?'

Hardcastle explained his involvement in Victoria Hart's murder, and produced the telegram that she had received at the theatre. 'Would that have been sent from this office, Mr Rogers?'

Rogers donned a pair of horn-rimmed glasses and studied the telegram. 'Yes, it was, Inspector. It was received here at eleven minutes past four in the afternoon of the twenty-fourth of December.'

'Would it be possible to discover which member of your staff accepted it?'

'I very much doubt it, Inspector. Apart from the fact that we were very busy on Christmas Eve, I can tell from the code on this – ' Rogers flourished the telegram – 'that it was telephoned to this office.'

'Is there any way of discovering where that telephone was?'

'I'm afraid not, Inspector. Unfortunately, it could have been sent from anywhere in the country. In all probability, the sender went into a shop that has public telephone facil-ities. You might have seen the blue signs that read, "You may telephone from here." All the sender would have had to do is write his message on the appropriate form, pay the correct fee, and the shopkeeper would've sent the message.'

'Bugger it!' said Hardcastle.

'Quite so, Inspector,' said Rogers with a smile.

Arthur Courtney, the senior partner of the firm of solicitors in Chancery Lane that handled the Harts' affairs, was at least sixty-five years old. He adhered to the fashion of his generation, a mode of dress that in his view conformed to the requirements of his profession: a winged collar, tailed morning coat and striped trousers.

'Do take a seat, gentlemen. Coffee will be along in just a moment,' he said before seating himself behind a huge mahogany partners' desk, inlaid with red leather. 'I under-stand from Detective Sergeant Marriott's telephone call that you are investigating the murder of Mrs Hart, Inspector. Lamentable business, most regrettable.'

'Show Mr Courtney the letters, Marriott,' said Hardcastle.

Courtney took the letters, laid them on his desk and clipped on a pair of gold-rimmed pince-nez. 'Where did these come from, Inspector?' he asked, a puzzled frown on his face.

'They were found in Mrs Hart's theatrical digs in Windsor, sir. They appear to have come from an admirer, and four of them were delivered by hand at the stage door of the various theatres at which she was appearing.'

'How very interesting.' Courtney took several minutes reading each of the missives with great care. 'I think there is something you should see, Inspector,' he said, crossing the room to a Perry's fire-resistant safe, and taking out a bundle of letters. 'You'd better have a look at these. In my opinion, they are written in the same hand as those you found at Windsor.'

Hardcastle glanced at the letters and looked up. 'May I ask where you got these from, sir?'

'From Mrs Hart,' said Courtney, seating himself behind his desk again.

'But why did she give them to you?'

'If you read them, I think you will understand, Inspector. Mrs Hart explained to me that, as an actress, she was often the object of unwelcome attention from undesirable persons, but that they usually ceased when her revue moved on to another town. She was quite candid about the show in which she took part, and explained that she wore an extremely scanty and revealing garment. In fact, I went to see the show at her invitation, when she was appearing at the London Palladium. Last March, I think it was.' Courtney smoothed a hand across his desktop. 'But, of course, her apparel on stage is no reason why she should have been the victim of . . . ' He paused for a moment. 'Unwarranted harassment is, I suppose, the best way of describing it. But I suggest you read them before we continue this discussion. Ah, the coffee,' he added, as a severe looking woman entered with a tray. 'Thank you, Mrs Dobbs.' The woman placed the coffee on Courtney's desk and departed without having spoken a word.

Like the letters in Hardcastle's possession, some of those produced by Courtney had passed through the Royal Mail, postmarked Kingston upon Thames, whereas others were unstamped and, quite possibly, had been delivered by hand.

When Hardcastle had finished reading them, he glanced up. 'These are worse than the seven we found. This one –' he held it up – 'delivered to the Empire Theatre, Leicester Square, two months or so before her murder, still addresses her as *Miss* Hart, and the writer repeats that he doesn't believe her to be married. He goes on to say, as in the others, that she's merely trying to put him off. But he finishes by saying that if he can't have her, he'll make sure that no one else does.'

'I found that one particularly disturbing, Inspector,' exclaimed Courtney.

'It's more than that, sir,' said Hardcastle. 'I reckon we could convince a stipe that that's an offence under section sixteen of the Offences against the Person Act of 1861.'

'What, threats to kill or murder, you mean? Do you think that the evidence of one anonymous letter is sufficient to secure a conviction?'

But Hardcastle had no such qualms. 'Well, how do you interpret the statement "making sure that no one else will have her," eh, sir?'

'I have to admit that my area of expertise is more concerned with wills, probate, trusts and the occasional property conveyance, Inspector. However, Mrs Hart handed them to me and sought my advice.'

'Did you not think of handing these letters to the police, sir?' asked Hardcastle, a slightly censorious tone in his voice. But he drew back from suggesting that had the solicitor taken some action, Victoria Hart might still be alive.

'But we didn't know who the man was, Inspector,' protested Courtney. 'I suggested that I kept those – ' he gestured at the letters – 'and advised Mrs Hart that once the man had been identified, an injunction against him would be sought. I have to say, however, that I was unaware of the existence of the letters that you seized from her Windsor address, and Mrs Hart didn't mention them. I can't think why she didn't give me those too. I suppose it was because I had told her to keep any *future* correspondence she received from the man.'

Marriott, however, agreed with his DDI. 'Threatening to murder is worth a run, I suppose, sir,' he said to him, recalling how, in the past, Hardcastle's persuasive testimony had secured convictions in cases with less evidence than that contained in the letter delivered to the Leicester Square Empire. 'But we've got to find him first.'

Courtney gave a grim laugh. 'As Sergeant Marriott says, Inspector, you've got to find the fellow first.'

'Oh, we will, sir, we will.' Hardcastle briskly rubbed his hands together. 'As a matter of interest, did Mrs Hart say whether she had mentioned these letters to her husband?'

'I asked her that, Inspector, but she said she didn't want to worry him. He's at sea with the Royal Navy, you see.'

'Yes, I know,' said Hardcastle. 'I've already spoken to him, and the letters we found came as a bit of a shock when I showed them to him.'

'Yes, they would have done, I imagine.'

'However, sir, I have a favour to ask.' Hardcastle gazed briefly at a Spy cartoon of someone called Mr Justice Darling that hung on the wall behind the solicitor.

'And what is that, Inspector?'

'I was wondering if you'd be prepared to put a notice in the newspapers to the effect that the late Mrs Hart had left a sum of money in her will for her anonymous admirer, and that he could collect that sum from your office on a given date.'

'Good heavens!' Courtney frowned. 'That sounds most unethical, Inspector.'

'Might be for you, sir, but not for me. I have a duty to arrest the man who murdered Mrs Hart, and bring him to justice. Whatever it takes. As the Chief Magistrate once said, "I'm not interested in the manner in which the prisoner was brought before the court. He's here, and that's that."'

'But how would such a stratagem help?' Courtney appeared genuinely to be baffled, and dismayed, by Hardcastle's suggestion.

'Because Sergeant Marriott and me would be here on the date you select, and we'd feel his collar, sir, that's what.'

But still Courtney was doubtful. 'I'm not sure that the Law Society would approve of such a ruse, Inspector.'

'Then I shouldn't tell 'em, if I was you, sir,' said Hardcastle. 'I certainly shan't.'

Eight

After leaving Arthur Courtney's chambers in Chancery Lane, Hardcastle surprised Marriott by turning left once they reached Fleet Street. 'Seeing as how it's New Year's Eve, Marriott,' he said, 'I'll stand you a bite of lunch at the Cheshire Cheese in Wine Office Court.'

'Very kind of you, sir.' Marriott had never regarded Hardcastle as the most generous of men, and could not remember the last time he had bought a drink for his sergeant. Or, for that matter, anyone else.

When they reached the famous public house, Hardcastle led the way in, and he and Marriott pushed their way through a crowd that consisted mainly of journalists from the nearby newspaper offices. One or two of the reporters recognized Hardcastle and wished him a prosperous New Year. One even ventured to ask how he was getting on with the Victoria Hart murder, but received short shrift.

'Charles Dickens used to sit there,' said Hardcastle, extending a forefinger as he embarked on another of his historical anecdotes. 'Between the bar and the fireplace.' He paused to warm his hands at the blazing log fire. 'Very shrewd man was Dickens, even though he was a reporter.' The DDI had no great liking for the press. 'Apart from when he was making fun of the police.' He ordered two pints of best bitter, and to Marriott's further amazement, paid for it.

'D'you mean like Inspector Bucket in *Bleak House*, sir?' asked Marriott, taking a sip of his beer. 'Or his account in *Household Words* of meeting a couple of detectives?'

Hardcastle shot a sharp glance at his sergeant. 'I never took you for much of a reader, Marriott.'

'I like a good book occasionally, sir, but generally speaking, I don't have much time to get into it,' said Marriott, and received another sharp glance.

After a filling lunch of steak and kidney pudding and mashed potatoes, followed by plum duff, for all of which Hardcastle settled the bill, the two detectives walked back to Fleet Street.

'I don't think we can do much till Monday, Marriott,' said Hardcastle, standing on the kerb and peering up and down the street in search of a cab, 'and I don't see much point in going back to Windsor before we hear if Courtney's agreed to help us feel the collar of Victoria Hart's letter-writer.'

'D'you think he'll turn up if Mr Courtney does set the trap, sir?'

'I've a feeling in my bones he will, Marriott,' said Hardcastle, and then offered the sergeant the benefit of his long experience as a detective. 'There's very few people in this world what can resist the promise of a few sovereigns when they're dangled in front of their nose.' He took a ten-shilling note from his wallet and handed it to his sergeant. 'Buy Mrs Marriott a box of chocolates, and get something for the children, seeing as how I buggered up their Christmas.'

'That's very kind of you, sir.' Marriott was astounded by this latest example of the DDI's uncharacteristic goodwill, and pocketed the note. 'But it wasn't really your fault.' Today was turning out to be full of surprises.

Hardcastle grunted an acknowledgement, almost as if embarrassed by his own generosity. 'And wish your good lady a Happy New Year an' all,' he said gruffly. 'See you at the nick at eight o'clock on Monday morning.' And with that he clambered into a taxi and directed the driver to New Scotland Yard.

Later that afternoon, Arthur Courtney telephoned Hardcastle at Cannon Row police station and told him that, not without some reservations, he had arranged for an entry to be inserted in all the following day's leading London newspapers.

'I've requested that the gentleman who proposed marriage to the late Victoria Hart, the actress, in numerous letters, should attend my office at ten o'clock in the forenoon of Monday the fourth of January when he will hear something to his advantage.'

Hardcastle laughed. 'I'm much obliged to you, sir,' he said, 'but if I have my way, the only advantage he'll have is a rope round his neck.'

It was a comment that did little to comfort Mr Courtney. 'I suppose there's no chance that you could intercept this man on his way in, rather than actually in my chambers, is there, Inspector?'

'I'll try, Mr Courtney, although I can't promise.' But optimist though he was, Hardcastle secretly agreed with Marriott that there was little chance of the mysterious letter-writer turning up. If he had murdered Victoria Hart, he would not go within miles of the solicitor's office.

Curiously enough though, George Joseph Smith, the 'Brides-in-the-Bath' murderer, was arrested exactly one month hence as a result of a similar deception.

The DDI crossed the corridor to the detectives' office. 'Catto.'

'Sir?' Catto leaped to his feet and made towards the door, colliding with the corner of a desk as he did so.

'The cab that's used for observations and the like.'

'Sir?'

'Get hold of it from whoever keeps the thing, and tell 'em I want it here by eight o'clock on Monday morning. And if you have any trouble, tell 'em to see me.'

'Very good, sir,' said Catto, and turned away.

'I haven't finished yet,' barked Hardcastle. 'On Monday morning, you'll drive me and Sergeant Marriott to Chancery Lane where we hope to lay hands on the bugger what's been sending threatening letters to the late Mrs Victoria Hart.'

'Very good, sir,' said Catto again.

'I suppose you can drive, can you?' asked Hardcastle.

'Yes, sir.'

'And Catto . . . '

'Yes, sir?'

'Don't be late, Catto.'

It was five o'clock when Marriott let himself into his police quarters in Regency Street.

'Whatever are you doing home this early, Charlie?' The delighted Lorna almost ran to meet her husband, closely followed by the Marriotts' two small children, James and Doreen.

'Ernie Hardcastle's let me off the hook till Monday.'

'That's wonderful.' Lorna laughed. 'Is he sickening for something?' she asked, expressing mock concern. She knew only too well how much of a taskmaster was her husband's boss.

'I have to admit to wondering that myself, love,' said Marriott, 'because he stood me lunch in the Cheshire Cheese, and when we were leaving, he gave me ten bob to get you a box of chocolates, and something for the little ones.' He opened a carrier bag to reveal three brown-paper parcels, each carefully tied with string.

'Well, who'd've thought it?' said the astounded Lorna, putting a hand to her mouth.

James, the Marriotts' five-year-old, clutched at his father's overcoat. 'What have you got for me, Daddy? What is it?' he demanded breathlessly.

'Just hold on, young Jimmy, and wait until I've got my hat and coat off. Anyway, you had presents at Christmas, less than a week ago. I'm not sure you deserve any more.'

'Stop teasing him, Charlie,' said a laughing Lorna. She laughed easily. 'Get your things off and I'll make a pot of tea.'

'Let the children open their presents first, love,' said Marriott, 'or they'll burst with excitement.'

The family adjourned to the sitting room and sat around the blazing fire.

'Where's mine?' demanded James, hopping from one foot to another with excitement.

'Ladies first,' said his father with mock severity, and handed a parcel to the three-year-old Doreen.

The little girl hastily tore off the wrapping. 'Ooh! Look, look, Mummy,' she squealed. 'Box. Box.' The child looked at her mother. 'What's it do?' she asked, a look of grave concentration on her face.

Lorna removed the lid from the box. 'It's a dolls' wardrobe, pet,' she said. 'Those two cardboard dolls are for dressing up in all these lovely frocks and coats and things.'

Marriott finally yielded and handed over the present he had bought for his son.

The boy carefully unwrapped the parcel and gazed with wonderment at what it contained. 'It's a lorry, Daddy.'

'I know it is, Jimmy,' said Marriott. 'I bought it for you. And if you wind it up, it'll go all by itself.'

'It's got little coal sacks on the back and a blanket thing to go over them,' said the delighted boy.

The excited children retreated to a corner of the room and began to play with their gifts.

'I never thought that Mr Hardcastle would be responsible for keeping our children quiet, Charlie,' said Lorna.

'And this is for you, love,' said Marriott, handing his wife a parcel containing a huge box of chocolates. 'And he said to wish you a happy New Year.'

Lorna unwrapped the package, and rested the box on her lap. 'I don't think I've ever had one this large,' she said, tracing her fingers lightly over the embossed Rowntree name on the lid. 'I shall be putting on weight.' She looked up. 'Are you sure you got all these things for ten shillings, Charlie?'

Marriott laughed. 'I went to Selfridge's, that new store in Oxford Street.'

'It's not all that new,' said Lorna. 'It must have been open a good five years now.'

'The children's presents were three bob each,' whispered Marriott, 'but I'm not going to tell you what the chocolates cost. Just let's say there are a few pennies left over.'

It was past seven o'clock by the time Hardcastle opened the front door of his house in Kennington Road.

'I thought you'd gone forever, Ernie,' said Alice, 'and I

suppose you'll be wanting supper now you *are* here.' She was sitting by the fire darning a sock, a needlework basket open on the floor beside her.

'There's no hurry, Lally,' said Hardcastle, using, as he occasionally did, the diminutive for his wife's name. 'I think right now a whisky'd go down well.' He walked through to the kitchen and took a bottle of The Famous Grouse from a cupboard. 'Can I get you anything, love?' he called.

'A drop of sherry and lemonade wouldn't go amiss,' said Alice.

Hardcastle carried the drinks through to the sitting room and settled in his armchair. But then he leaned forward, seeing for the first time a small cloth doll on the arm of his wife's chair. 'What on earth's that?' The doll had been made in a striking resemblance of Kaiser Wilhelm.

'It's a pin cushion,' said Alice, and plunged her darning needle into the doll at about where its heart would have been. 'I suppose you'll be off again first thing tomorrow,' she said mildly. She was accustomed to the hours demanded of a senior detective officer.

'No, I've given myself the weekend off.'

'Are you sure they can spare you, Ernie?' asked Alice in a mocking tone of voice. 'The criminals will have a field day.'

'Where are the girls?' Hardcastle ignored his wife's scornful comment.

'Maud's upstairs reading some medical book. This week she wants to be a doctor.'

'That's an incentive to stay healthy, if ever there was,' muttered Hardcastle.

'You're too hard on the girls, Ernie,' cautioned their mother.

'And where's Kitty?'

'Kitty's off with her latest boyfriend. They're determined to see in the New Year together.'

'I'm not sure I approve of that,' said Hardcastle.

'Well, you weren't here to disapprove of it, were you? I don't know if you realize it, Ernest Hardcastle, but running this house and feeding the family single-handed isn't easy.'

'Who is this fellow that Kitty's gone out with?' Hardcastle was determined not to be drawn into a discussion about the demands of the Metropolitan Police, and the strains it put on the family.

'It's the young copper who came here with that message for you on Christmas Day.'

'Well, he didn't waste any time, I must say. How did that come about?'

'He's posted to this beat for the month, and he sort of bumped into Kitty, so she said, when she left the house on Boxing Day morning.' Alice smiled. 'He invited her out for a walk that evening, and they've been seeing each other every day since.'

'Sort of bumped into her one morning?' queried Hardcastle sceptically. 'Pull the other one! I'll bet he was hanging about just waiting for her. Lucky not to have been caught by the section sergeant.'

'I seem to remember a certain young PC Hardcastle doing much the same thing many years ago,' said Alice crushingly.

'What's his name, this lad?'

'Roderick Graves, but he's called Roddy. You needn't worry though, Ernie. I've warned Kitty against marrying a policeman.'

Hardcastle picked up the *Daily Mail*, shook it and made a pretence of studying the front page.

Although he would rather have gone to bed, Hardcastle had been persuaded, reluctantly, to see in the New Year with Alice, their daughter Maud and their son Walter. Kitty kept her promise of greeting the New Year with her latest beau, and did not come home until almost one o'clock in the morning.

'And where have you been, young lady?' demanded her father.

'Celebrating the New Year in Trafalgar Square, Pa.'

'I'm not sure I approve of young girls staying out half the night,' said Hardcastle, trying to inject a censorious tone into his voice. But he knew that he was wasting his time.

His attempts at disciplining this wayward young woman usually ended in failure.

'I was quite safe, Pa. I was with a policeman.' Having advanced that irrefutable defence, Kitty skipped across the room and planted a kiss on her father's cheek. 'A happy New Year, Pa.'

'Who was this fellow?' asked Hardcastle, even though his wife had told him. But knowing the capricious Kitty as he did, she might already have abandoned that suitor in favour of another.

'Roddy Graves. He was the policeman who called with the message on Christmas Day. He speaks very highly of you, Pa.'

'He'd be foolish not to,' muttered Hardcastle, and went to bed.

To nobody's surprise, Hardcastle was in his office promptly at eight o'clock on the Monday morning. He had spent a miserable weekend mooning about the house, and occasionally stirring himself to do one of the odd jobs that Alice had stored up for him.

But now, back in his natural habitat, Hardcastle stood on the threshold of the CID office and gazed around. He was greeted by a chorus of 'Happy New Years' from the detectives, and grunted a suitable response. 'Where's Catto?' he asked.

'In the station yard, making sure the observation cab's ready for the road, sir,' said DC Watkins.

'I should hope so,' grumbled Hardcastle. 'Marriott, come in the office.'

DS Marriott followed his chief into the DDI's office. 'Yes, sir? By the way, sir, Lorna and the children asked me to thank you for their gifts.'

Hardcastle mumbled an embarrassed acknowledgement, before continuing with the matter in hand. 'What we'll do, Marriott, is to get Catto to drive us to Chancery Lane, well in advance of ten o'clock. We'll park up outside Courtney's chambers and see if we can catch this letter-writing bugger on his way in. Then we'll feel his collar.'

'If he turns up, sir.'

'You're a right Job's comforter, Marriott, d'you know that?'

'Yes, sir,' said Marriott with a grin.

As Hardcastle had said earlier, the promise of a few sovereigns is hard to resist. And his prediction proved to be correct.

At one minute to ten, the watching detectives were rewarded with the sight of a man striding towards the cab in which they were sitting. And he fitted the description given by the two stage-door keepers exactly: some five foot eight in height, and a black goatee beard. This morning, he was elegantly attired in a single-breasted Chesterfield overcoat with a velvet collar, and a Homburg hat. A silk cravat peeped out at the neck, and box-cloth spats covered his calf-leather shoes. In his right hand, he swung a malacca cane.

'Looks a bit of a swell, don't he, Marriott?' said Hardcastle, and alighted from the cab with surprising agility for a man of his size. 'You stay here, Catto, and keep the door open.'

The DDI tapped his suspect on the shoulder, just as the man was about to enter Courtney's chambers. 'Excuse me.'

The man stopped. 'Yes? What d'you want.' He gazed at Hardcastle as though he were a beggar about to solicit a farthing for a cup of tea.

'I'm a police officer,' said Hardcastle.

'Are you really?' The tone was condescending. 'How dare you touch me like that.'

'What's your name?'

'I am the Duke of Clarence and you'll address me as "Your Grace".'

'I don't think so,' said Hardcastle, 'and I'm arresting you on suspicion of sending written threats to murder.' And with that the DDI took hold of the man's arm as a token of apprehension.

Marriott was horrified. 'Is this wise, sir?' he whispered. He knew that Hardcastle often took chances, but arresting a duke without a shred of evidence that he was the one who had written to Victoria Hart, seemed like professional suicide.

'Take your hands off me,' protested the duke. 'You'll pay for this with your career, my man,' he shouted.

'Now, now,' said Hardcastle mildly, 'don't make a spectacle of yourself, there's a good gentleman.' He pushed the struggling man towards the open door of the 'observation' cab.

The prisoner, still protesting vociferously, was placed in the interview room near the front door of the police station. Hardcastle had wisely deprived him of his walking stick, fearing that he might lash out with it.

'I demand to know your name,' shouted the duke. 'You may rest assured that I shall complain to Sir Edward Henry, who happens to be a close personal friend of mine.'

'The Commissioner must have thousands of friends,' said Hardcastle in a stage whisper to Marriott. 'Practically everyone we nick these days seems to know him.' And addressing his prisoner, said, 'Turn out your pockets.'

'I shall do no such thing.'

'Search him, Marriott,' said Hardcastle. 'And you give him a hand,' he said to Catto, who had accompanied the group into the interview room.

Catto stood behind the prisoner and placed his arm around the man's neck, restraining him.

'No need to strangle the bugger, Catto,' observed Hardcastle mildly.

When Marriott, still concerned about the outcome of arresting a duke, had finished, he had recovered a gold pocket watch, a wallet containing several banknotes, some silver and copper in loose change, a handkerchief and a quantity of correspondence.

'Aha!' exclaimed Hardcastle, reaching for the letters. He spent several minutes examining them before handing them to Marriott without comment.

'These are in the same hand as the ones sent to our victim, sir, and in similar vein,' said Marriott, when he had finished reading them. He was careful not to mention Victoria Hart's name. 'And these are addressed to an actress appearing at the Lewisham Hippodrome.'

Hardcastle next examined the wallet. 'So,' he said, 'you're Godfrey Knight.'

'I am the Duke of Clarence,' insisted the prisoner. 'I am a son of the late Queen Victoria, and you may rest assured that my nephew the King will hear of the disgraceful abuse of authority which you have today perpetrated upon my person.'

'How old are you?' asked Hardcastle casually. 'Forty at the most, I should think.' The 'duke' remained silent. 'That means that the late queen – by then a widow – would have been about fifty-five when you were born. I don't think so.'

Knight confined himself to sneering.

'Where were you on Christmas Eve, Mr Knight?' asked Marriott.

Knight regarded Marriott as though he were a piece of rat-infested cheese. 'Be quiet,' he said haughtily.

Hardcastle thumped the table loudly. 'I'm fed up with you,' he said, as Knight started back in alarm. 'And any minute now, I'm likely to take you along to a cell and knock seven bells out of you. Now, answer my sergeant's question.'

'If you must know,' said the chastened Knight, 'I was at Sandringham. I always spend Christmas with the royal family, of which, I would remind you, I am a member.'

Hardcastle stood up, exasperated. 'Put him in a cell, Marriott, and tell the station officer to keep a close eye on him. I don't want him topping himself. At least, not until we find out if he's the man we want. And then telephone Mr Courtney, thank him for his help and tell him that we've got the man we were looking for.'

When Marriott and Catto had left with their prisoner, Hardcastle went upstairs. Looking into the detectives' office, he crooked a finger at Detective Sergeant Wood.

'Yes, sir,' said Wood.

'Get across to the records office a bit *jildi*, Wood, and see what you can dig up on a Godfrey Knight, who's calling himself the Duke of Clarence. And I don't want no rubbish about him having been a suspect in the Whitechapel murders neither.' The Duke of Clarence's name had been one of several put forward by a fanciful press as being the true identity of Jack the Ripper.

'I thought as much, Marriott,' said Hardcastle as he looked up from studying the file that Wood had brought back from the records office. 'He's well known. It's all here.' He jabbed a finger at the docket. 'Goes about calling himself by all sorts of names, usually titled ones, including the Duke of Clarence. It also says here that he makes a habit of frequenting theatres, and writing harassing letters to actresses.'

'Is there an address on there for him, sir?'

'There is, m'boy,' said the delighted Hardcastle. 'One-nine-seven Ewell Road, Surbiton.'

'But the postmarks were Kingston, sir.'

'That'll be because mail posted in Surbiton will most likely go to the Kingston sorting office, Marriott. It's only a couple of miles away from where our Duke of Clarence lives.' Hardcastle laughed, glanced at his hunter, briefly wound it and dropped it back into his waistcoat pocket. 'We'll go and have a look at his "palace".'

'As a matter of interest, sir, how did you know he wasn't really the Duke of Clarence?'

'The Duke of Clarence – eldest son of King Edward the Seventh – died in eighteen-ninety-two,' said Hardcastle, surprising Marriott yet again with his knowledge of history, 'and the title died out. Anyway, if he'd really been a royal duke he'd've insisted on being called "Your Royal Highness", not "Your Grace". It's only non-royal dukes that are called "Your Grace".' The DDI chuckled. 'Of course, Marriott, it was just his bad luck having his collar felt by an A Division officer. Pick up all sorts of useful informa-tion when you've got Buck House on your toby.'

Nine

The house in Ewell Road, Surbiton, was a white double-fronted residence, rising two storeys high above a basement. It was immaculate; the paintwork was in pristine condition, and the front garden tended to perfection.

'This drum'll have cost a few hundred sovs,' remarked Hardcastle, as he and Marriott mounted the flight of steps.

'Good afternoon, sir.' A young girl opened one of a pair of front doors. Dressed in a black woollen stuff dress, muslin apron and frilly cap, she was clearly the maid.

'I'd like to speak to the lady of the house,' said Hardcastle.

'Who shall I say it is, sir?'

'We're police officers.'

'If you care to wait, sir, I'll see if the mistress is at home.' The maid showed the two detectives into a black-and-white temple-tiled hall, and disappeared through a door on the left.

'That's a bit gruesome, sir,' said Marriott, gazing at a large painting depicting a surgeon undertaking what appeared to be an autopsy. There were candles in the background, but the horrifically dominant part of the picture was a torch of flaming wood and tallow stuck into the cadaver's anatomy.

'I don't reckon he'll live,' commented Hardcastle cynically. 'What is it our medical friends say: the operation was a success, but the patient died?'

The maid returned. 'The mistress is in the drawing room, sir,' she said. 'This way, please.' And she opened the door of the room from which she had just emerged.

The two officers followed the maid around a four-leaf painted screen, positioned to stop draughts from the hall.

'The gentlemen from the police, ma'am,' said the maid.

'Perhaps you'd bring some tea, Skinner.'

'Yes, ma'am,' said the maid, and bobbed a brief curtsey.

The woman of the house was seated in an armchair beside a roaring fire, a rosewood pole-screen guarding her face from the flames. She wore a peach-coloured frock with a brown net overdress. A tired, drawn look around her eyes belied her age, which was probably about thirty-five.

'Good afternoon, gentlemen. Are you from the local police station?'

'No, ma'am,' said Hardcastle. 'We're attached to New Scotland Yard.' And he introduced himself and Marriott.

'Do please sit down.' The woman had evinced no surprise at the arrival of the police; indeed it was almost as if she had been expecting them. Her response to Hardcastle's next statement proved that she was.

'I understand that a Mr Godfrey Knight lives here, ma'am.'

'Yes, he does. He's my husband. I'm Hilda Knight.' She turned the panel of the pole-screen, and looked sadly into the fire, extending a hand towards it, warming herself. 'What's happened to him this time?' she asked, now staring directly at Hardcastle, a challenging expression on her face.

'I arrested him this morning, Mrs Knight.'

'I see. And what has he done now?'

'At the moment, I'm contemplating a charge of making written threats to murder, ma'am.' But since interviewing Godfrey Knight, Hardcastle had been forced to reconsider that course of action.

'He's not well, you know, Inspector,' continued Mrs Knight. 'In fact, he's been ill for some time.' She spoke listlessly.

'What form does this illness take, ma'am?'

'The family doctor referred him to a specialist at the National Hospital in Queen Square who diagnosed it as paranoid schizophrenia.'

'Do you happen to recall the name of this specialist, ma'am?' asked Marriott.

'Yes, it was a Mr Wilcox. But why d'you ask?'

Hardcastle answered the question. 'It may be that I'll have to see him at some stage.'

'But these are only innocent delusions my husband suffers from.' Distractedly, Hilda Knight watched the maid as she entered the room with a tray of tea, and placed it on a small table near her mistress's left hand. Once again bobbing briefly, the girl left the room without a word. 'You'll take tea, Inspector?' she enquired. 'And you too, Sergeant?'

'That's very kind, ma'am, thank you,' murmured Hardcastle.

Mrs Knight busied herself pouring the tea and handing it round.

'Not so innocent on this occasion, I'm afraid.' Hardcastle picked up the thread of the conversation. 'Your husband wrote a string of letters to a young actress in which he proposed marriage to her, despite being told that she already had a husband.'

'I'm sorry to have to tell you that he's always doing that, but he means no harm by it. It's a fixation he has for actresses.' The woman seemed unconcerned that her husband had been seeking a wife when he had one already. But Hardcastle attributed that to Hilda Knight's understanding of her husband's mental condition.

'The actress in question was murdered on Christmas Eve . . . in Windsor, Mrs Knight,' said Hardcastle. 'And she was the actress who he'd threatened.'

'Oh my God!' Hilda Knight put a hand to her mouth. 'But surely you can't imagine . . . ' She paused, momentarily distraught at the thought that her husband was a murderer. Then with an expression of relief, she added, 'But it can't have been anything to do with Godfrey. He was here with me, all over Christmas. And my parents were here as well. Please, I implore you to ask them.'

'Perhaps you'd give me their details, ma'am,' said Marriott.

'Certainly. Anything to prove that Godfrey had nothing to do with such a dreadful business. It's Mr and Mrs Garson, and they live in Guildford.' She gave Marriott the address.

'What's going to happen to Godfrey now, Inspector? You must accept that he couldn't possibly have—'

Hardcastle raised his hand. 'I'm sure, from what you've told me, that he had nothing to do with this young woman's death, ma'am,' he said, although still unconvinced. 'However, it may be best if this here Mr Wilcox was consulted, so's the authorities can come to some solution that's acceptable to all parties, so to speak.'

'What sort of solution?' She looked keenly at Hardcastle.

'It's not up to me, ma'am. It'll be a matter for a magistrate.'

'He's an educated man, you know, Inspector,' said Mrs Knight wearily, as though she had been obliged to vouch for her husband's character many times before. 'He went to Marlborough and was making his way in the City: stocks and shares, and that sort of thing. He was doing very well until this schizophrenia took a hold. Since then, he seems to have gone to pieces. I doubt he'll be able to carry on as a stockbroker for very much longer. He was left a substantial sum of money when his father died, so we don't have any concerns in that regard. But then, about four years ago, he developed this terrible condition.'

'I thought he might have been connected to the medical profession,' commented Hardcastle.

'Whatever made you think that?'

'The painting in the hall, ma'am.'

'Oh, *that* awful picture,' exclaimed Mrs Knight. 'Godfrey bought it about two years ago, and he would sometimes sit in the hall gazing at it for hours. I want to get rid of it, but he won't hear of it. It quite concerned me that he'd become obsessed with death. I'm so desperately worried that his condition may deteriorate even further. He has this pathetic belief that he's connected to the royal family.'

'So I gathered,' said Hardcastle drily. 'He claimed to be the Duke of Clarence when we detained him this morning.'

'What are you going to do about Knight, sir?' asked Marriott, on their way back to London. 'It looks as though he's in the clear as far as Victoria Hart's death is concerned.'

'I have to admit that what he wrote in that letter, about making sure that no one else had Victoria Hart, is a bit thin for a charge, Marriott. Particularly now we know he's been under a specialist for these here delusions of his. I'll get him up before the beak as soon as possible, and suggest that he's put in the care of this Mr Wilcox for an assessment. What happens to him after that ain't none of our business. But it does mean that we've now got to start afresh looking for Mrs Hart's killer.'

When Hardcastle and Marriott returned to Cannon Row police station there were two pieces of news awaiting them. Neither of them good.

Detective Sergeant Wood had been waiting for the return of Hardcastle, and followed him into his office.

'Yes, Wood?'

'I received a telephone call from a Mr Courtney about half an hour ago, sir.'

'He's the Harts' solicitor. What did he want? The cost of them notices he put in the papers about our friend Knight, I suppose. I doubt the Commissioner'll be too happy at footing the bill for that.'

'No, sir. He wished you to know that HMS *Dauntless* was torpedoed and sunk off Portland Bill on New Year's Day. Five hundred and forty-seven souls were lost, among them Commander Hart, sir.'

Hardcastle nodded. 'I suppose it's for the best in his case,' he said, never emotional about sudden death. 'Did Courtney say anything about advising any next of kin?'

'No, sir,' said Wood. 'But the Admiralty will do that, won't they?'

'Not the point, Wood,' said Hardcastle. 'You see, Marriott – ' he turned to his senior sergeant – 'we told Hart about the death of his wife. And that was enough for official action on our part. What we don't know is whether the commander told Victoria's parents. If they're still alive. Have a word with Courtney and see if he knows who they are and where they live.'

'Right, sir.' Marriott made a brief note in his pocket book.

'And when you've done that, get a telegraph off to Guildford Constabulary and ask them to check with Mr and Mrs Garson. We need to make certain that they can account for Godfrey Knight's movements over Christmas. It could be that the refined Mrs Hilda Knight was spinning us a twist, and that the "Duke" is our man after all. It's only natural for a wife to spring to the defence of her husband, ain't it?'

'Yes, sir,' said Marriott, and turned to carry out Hardcastle's orders.

'You still here, Wood?' said Hardcastle, stating the obvious.

'There was another message, sir, from Windsor.'

'Oh? And what's happened there that they're suddenly all of a lather?'

'It's from the chief constable, sir.'

'Would be,' mumbled Hardcastle. 'Perhaps the King's enquiring about the murder.'

'It's to the effect that a Sergeant Sidney Phillips of the Royal Berkshire Regiment was found beaten to death in the drill hall in Windsor.'

'Well I'm buggered,' said Hardcastle. '*Marriott!*'

'Sir?' Marriott hastened back into the DDI's office.

'That recruiting-sergeant fellow, Phillips, has been topped in the drill hall.'

'Does that mean we'll be dealing with that as well as the Hart murder, sir?'

But before Hardcastle could reply, a detective sergeant from Central Office at the Yard entered his office.

'What is it?' asked Hardcastle, recognizing the officer as one of Detective Chief Inspector Ward's men.

'Message from Mr Ward, sir,' said the sergeant, proffering a sheet of paper.

'Well, that answers your question, Marriott,' said Hardcastle, once he had scanned the brief instruction. 'Seems the Chief Constable of Windsor sent the same message to the Commissioner, and Mr Ward directs that we investigate Phillips's murder an' all. It never bloody rains but it pours,' he added caustically. 'Wood?'

'Yes, sir?'

'You heard what I told Sergeant Marriott about telephoning Courtney, and telegraphing Guildford. You'll have to do it because Sergeant Marriott and me have got to skedaddle back to Windsor. And don't make a Mons of it.'

'What about the "duke", sir?' asked Marriott.

'Ah, yes.' Hardcastle glanced at his pocket watch before pondering the problem for a moment or two. 'We'll take him up to Bow Street court right now and hand him over to the beak. Let him sort it out.'

The Chief Metropolitan Magistrate at Bow Street police court had just risen for the day, but Hardcastle managed to catch him in his chambers.

'Is it urgent, Mr Hardcastle?' The magistrate did not seem very pleased at the DDI's request for a special hearing.

Hardcastle recounted fully the circumstances of Knight's arrest, and the result of his interview with the man's wife. He also explained that he had to return to Windsor immediately in order to investigate a second murder.

'Oh, very well, I'll deal with it here.' The magistrate was still unhappy at being delayed. 'I can't be bothered to go back into court.'

A few moments later, a constable, into whose charge Knight had been given, brought in the stockbroker.

'You are Godfrey Knight?' asked the magistrate.

'I am the Duke of Clarence, and I am addressed as "Your Grace" by nobodies like you,' said Knight, fixing the magistrate with a supercilious stare. He turned to the officer who was restraining him. 'Remove your hand, you common creature.'

It took but a second or two before the magistrate said, 'Godfrey Knight, you will be detained under the provisions of the various Mental Health Acts. I am remanding you to a suitable institution where you will be examined by qualified persons prior to appearing before the Justices in Lunacy.' He opened the drawer of his desk, took out a form and scribbled a few lines on it.

*　　*　　*

'When did this happen, Stone?' demanded Hardcastle.

'About half-past two this afternoon, sir,' said Stone, rising rapidly from behind DI Struthers's desk.

'Well, don't just stand there, man. Give me the details.'

'A young fellow went into the drill hall in Bolton Road – it doubles as a recruiting office, sir – at about half-past two, intent on joining the army. He was about to—'

'Where is this man?'

'Downstairs, sir.'

'Fetch him up here, then. I don't want to hear the bloody story second-hand.'

'Yes, sir.' Stone almost ran from the office. It seemed to him that in Hardcastle's eyes he could not do anything right. But he was not alone in thinking that; it was a feeling experienced by most of the DDI's subordinates.

'God Almighty, Marriott,' fumed Hardcastle. 'I wouldn't mind betting that even when a motor car had a man with a red flag walking in front of it this lot had a job catching up with it.'

Stone returned, followed by a youth of about eighteen. 'This is Robert Lines, sir.'

'Sit down, lad, and tell my sergeant where you live and where you work.'

The young man gave a Windsor address and revealed that he was a cellarman at a hotel in the centre of the town.

Hardcastle waited until Marriott had recorded these details and then said, 'Tell me about your attempt to join the army, Mr Lines.'

'I was hoping to join the Coldstream Guards, sir. My brother's a lance-sergeant in the second battalion, and he reckons it's the best regiment in the army.'

'I'm sure he's right, lad, but tell me what happened when you went to the drill hall.'

'It was about half-past two, sir. I had the afternoon off, being as how I'm on split shifts, and I'd been thinking about joining up for a long time, so off I went to the drill hall. It's a gloomy place and there was no lights. There was a table and chair in the centre of the room, but it seemed like there was no one there. I give a shout, but nobody come out of the office at the back.'

'Is that usual, Stone?' asked Hardcastle, turning to the Windsor sergeant.

'I think there's usually an officer there, sir. I understand that it requires an officer to swear in recruits.'

'Really? How come that Phillips managed it on his own at the Windsor Empire, then?'

'Well, he didn't really, sir. He took the names of them as volunteered, and told 'em to report to the drill hall at nine o'clock the next morning. He'd take 'em up to Victoria Barracks for a medical, and then bring 'em back to the drill hall to be sworn in. I think he sort of strongly hinted to them that they were already in the army, having volunteered, and that if they never turned up, they'd be run in as deserters.' Stone gave a crooked grin.

'Find out who this officer is, will you?' Hardcastle turned back to Lines. 'What happened next?'

'I went into the office through a door at the back, still looking for someone, and that's when I saw this body lying on the floor in a corner. I knew it was the recruiting sergeant, sir, because I'd seen him round the town. I thought he might've been drunk, but then I saw there was blood all over his head, and on the floor round him.' The white-faced Lines looked as though he was about to be sick. 'It was horrible, sir.'

'You'll see a lot worse than that if you finish up in Flanders, lad,' Hardcastle said flatly, although he had no greater knowledge of the conflict than he had read in the newspapers. 'So what did you do then?'

'I ran out and waited until I saw a copper, and told him.'

'Who was this constable, Stone?'

'PC 72 Snow, sir.' Stone had quickly learned that it was a very good idea to have answers to the questions he thought the London DDI might ask.

'I'll want to see him, straight after I've finished with Mr Lines here.' Turning back to the would-be recruit, Hardcastle asked, 'Did you see anyone near the drill hall? Or hear anything?'

'No, sir, nothing.' Lines paused. 'It was just like a normal day.'

'Have you taken a statement from this young man, Stone?' asked Hardcastle.

'No, sir, not as yet.'

For several seconds Hardcastle regarded Stone with a sour expression on his face, before turning to his own sergeant. 'Go next door and take a statement from him, Marriott.'

'Very good, sir,' said Marriott, doing his best to conceal a smile at DS Stone's obvious discomfort.

'Where's Phillips's body now, Stone?'

'Er, in the mortuary, sir.' The way in which Stone answered implied that there was nowhere else it could be.

'Has the pathologist examined it yet?'

'I'm not sure, sir.'

Hardcastle took out his pipe and began slowly to fill it. 'There's something you should understand while you're working with me, Stone,' he said mildly. 'I expect a detective sergeant to use his brains, and not wait to be told to do something that any detective, let alone a sergeant, should be doing off of his own bat, so to speak.'

'But, sir—' began Stone, who was standing lamely in front of the desk.

'I haven't finished yet. I want to know whether the pathologist has come to a conclusion about the cause of death. I want to view the scene, and if there's not a PC guarding it, I'll want to know why not. And I'll start by asking the chief constable, and then work my way upwards. I want to speak to this PC Snow and above all, I want to know how Phillips was killed. Got all that, have you?'

'Yes, sir.'

'Get on with it, then, and I want the answers *tout de suite*. Or sooner.'

'This is where the body was found by young Mr Lines, sir.' The chastened DS Stone indicated a large patch of blood on the floor of the drill hall, near a wooden filing cabinet.

Hardcastle tried the drawers of the cabinet. 'Locked,' he said. 'Who's got the key?'

'There was a key ring in Phillips's pocket, sir,' said Stone. 'There may be one on it that'll fit.'

'Yes, there may be. Find out.'

'Yes, sir.'

'And here, by the looks of it, we have the murder weapon.' Hardcastle knelt down and examined a thick chunk of metal partially obscured by the shadow cast by the filing cabinet. Some twelve inches in length, the metal bar was covered in blood.

'We left it there, sir,' said Stone hurriedly, 'because I thought you'd want to see the scene exactly as it was. Minus the body, of course.'

To Stone's discomfort, Hardcastle gave him a long pene-trating stare. But even if Stone had not discovered the weapon before, the DDI had to give him credit for making a quick recovery from what could have been further negli-gence on his part.

Hardcastle examined the weapon more closely. 'This is a window-sash weight, Marriott,' he said. 'We'll need to get it tested for fingerprints.'

'I wonder if the officer who does the swearing-in can shed any light on this, sir,' said Marriott.

'Yes, we'll have to have a word with him, a bit *tout de suite*.' Hardcastle turned to Stone. 'I think you'd better take urgent steps to find him, Stone.'

'Found out already, sir. He's a Captain Porteous, and he lives in the Grenadier Guards officers' mess at Victoria Barracks, sir. But he's not been back here since the body was found by Lines, because there's been a PC outside all the time.'

'In that case, Stone, get up to Victoria Barracks and tell Captain Porteous that I want to see him at the police station immediately. And if he shows any signs of reluctance, so to speak, feel his collar.'

'But he's an officer, sir.' Stone was aghast at the prospect of having to arrest a commissioned army officer.

'Exactly.' When the unhappy Stone had departed,

Hardcastle grinned at his own sergeant. 'Give it another five years and I reckon we'll have knocked him into shape, Marriott,' he said.

But it was as the two detectives turned to leave the room that Hardcastle saw that a quotation from the Bible had been scrawled in pencil on the distempered wall near the door: '*Vengeance is mine; I will repay, saith the Lord.*'

Ten

Hardcastle was agreeably surprised that within twenty minutes of his return to Windsor police headquarters, Detective Sergeant Stone arrived with an army officer.

'This is Captain Valentine Porteous, sir, the recruiting officer.'

'What dreadful news, er, Inspector,' said the army officer, his voice slurring. 'I've known what's-his-name, yes, Phillips, ever since the outbreak of war.' For some inexplicable reason, he giggled. 'This sergeant – ' he indicated Stone – 'tells me that Phillips has had his head bashed in with a sash weight. One expects that sort of thing in Flanders – er, not with sash weights, I don't mean – but not here in quiet little old Windsor, eh?' he mumbled.

Hardcastle came quickly to the conclusion that the army officer had been drinking quite heavily. A man in his late forties or thereabouts, he wore a battered cap and a creased uniform that was somewhat shabby. As for his Sam Browne belt and his shoes, they appeared not to have seen polish for quite some time. He was certainly not a good example to those he hoped to recruit.

'I don't recognize your regimental badge, Captain,' said Hardcastle, glancing at the bronzed device on Porteous's headdress, although in truth there were few that he *did* know. 'Please take a seat.'

'The Devonshire Regiment, Inspector, but I'm no longer available for active service. What with my age, a troublesome wound at the hands of the Boers at Spion Kop, and a Hun bullet at Mons, the powers-that-be assigned me to recruitment. What we call extra-regimental employment.

Should have retired really, but when this skirmish came along, I was kept on.'

'I'd be obliged if you'd account for your movements today, Captain Porteous.'

The army officer stared at Hardcastle. 'Are you thinking that I could have killed the poor fellow, Inspector?' he asked, with a measure of controlled indignation. But his pretence at outrage was spoiled when he hiccupped loudly.

'Well, did you?'

'Certainly not.'

'How have you spent your day, then?'

'I've been in the mess all day.'

That did not surprise Hardcastle. 'Not a recruiting day?' he asked, suspecting that Porteous took very little part in swelling the ranks of Kitchener's army.

'To be perfectly honest, Inspector, I leave – er, left – most of that to Sarn't Phillips. He was very good at persuading these youngsters to fight for King and Country. He'd get them to report to the drill hall at nine ack-emma the following day, and march them up to Victoria Barracks for the quack to give them the once over. Then he'd bring the buggers back, and I'd swear them in. Then off they'd go to Aldershot or wherever, don't you know.'

'And this morning, Captain?'

'There weren't any recruits this morning,' said Porteous. 'I'd given Phillips the weekend off, you see. Apart from Saturday morning after he'd collared another half dozen for the slaughter. He'd got them to volunteer on the Friday, d'you see. But we'd dealt with them by about eleven o'clock, and sent 'em off clutching the King's shilling and a railway warrant.'

'So you haven't been to the drill hall at all today?'

'No. I thought I'd made that clear.' Porteous stared glassy-eyed at Hardcastle, and began to wonder whether, in fact, he *had* made it clear.

'D'you read the Bible much, Captain?' asked Hardcastle in an offhand sort of way.

'The Bible? Good God Almighty no,' said Porteous, oblivious to the irony of that remark. 'When you've seen the killing that went on in South Africa, as I did, and what one saw at Mons, you've more or less given up on the existence of God.'

'Thank you, Captain Porteous, that'll be all. For the moment.'

'Well, you know where to find me, Inspector.' Porteous stood up. 'Now, I suppose, I'll have to find another sergeant from somewhere,' he mumbled, and staggering slightly, left the room.

Following Porteous's departure, Hardcastle sat in contemplative silence for a few moments. 'I'm not too happy about him, Marriott,' he said eventually.

'D'you think he might have had something to do with it, sir?'

'I somehow doubt it. If he's been in the mess all day, there'll be witnesses. But he's apprehensive about something, and he don't like talking to the police. He's been drinking all right, but perhaps not as much as he'd like us to believe.' The DDI pulled out his hunter and glanced at it. 'Damn near ten o'clock, Marriott. I think we'll call it a day and get back to the Horse and Groom. I could do with a wet, and that's not a bad drop of ale they serve there. Even if we do have to pay for it,' he added dismally.

The following morning, a telegraph arrived from Detective Sergeant Wood at Cannon Row. It told Hardcastle that the Guildford police had interviewed Mr and Mrs Garson, Hilda Knight's parents, and they confirmed that Godfrey Knight had remained at their daughter's Surbiton address all over Christmas.

'Well, that rules him out,' said Hardcastle, seemingly disappointed.

The telegraph also contained the information that Arthur Courtney, the Harts' solicitor, did not know whether Victoria Hart's parents had been told of her death. However, he supplied their address in London.

'Send a telegraph back to Wood . . . ' Hardcastle hesitated. 'No, on second thoughts, Marriott, address it to Detective Inspector Rhodes. Ask him to ensure that

Victoria's parents have been made aware of her death. Also get him to find out from the Admiralty where Commander Hart's people live. There could be some benefit from having a talk to both lots of parents. We might find out a bit more about Victoria Hart for a start. It's possible that she wasn't the pure little actress everyone seems to think she was. For all we know, she could've been a common tart.'

'D'you think so, sir?' Marriott finished noting down Hardcastle's instructions, and glanced up.

'You know me, Marriott,' said the DDI. 'Never take anything on face value. Particularly in a murder investigation. On your way down tell Stone to come in.'

'You wanted me, sir?' Stone, who now wore a permanent expression of harassment, appeared within seconds of Hardcastle's summons.

'Have Sergeant Phillips's next of kin been informed of his death, Stone?'

'Er, I'm not sure, sir.'

'Well, for Christ's sake find out, man. Do I have to do everything myself?'

Stone fled from the office, apprehensive that Hardcastle would bring his inadequacies to the chief constable's attention, as he had threatened to do. He returned almost immediately. 'Yes, sir. The late turn duty officer informed Mrs Phillips at approximately half-past three yesterday afternoon. He says she was very upset, sir.'

'Well, she would be.' Hardcastle thought about telling Stone that unnecessary information of that nature was not required in a formal report, but thought better of it. 'And another thing, Stone . . . '

'Sir?' Stone had the hunted look of a man who sensed that yet another rebuke was about to be delivered by this demanding Metropolitan officer.

'You told Captain Porteous that Phillips had been found with his head beaten in. And that a sash weight was the murder weapon.' It was a statement, not a question.

'Yes, sir. I thought that being Phillips's officer, like, he ought to know.'

'Well, for future reference, Stone, you do not take

responsibility for giving anyone that sort of information. I'm the investigating officer, and I'll decide who's told what and when. For all you know, Porteous might have been the one who killed Phillips, so you don't give the likes of him time to prepare their defence. Got that, have you?'

'Yes, sir.'

'Right, now bugger off and play with some paper or something.'

When Marriott returned, he found his chief in a mood of deep contemplation.

'I've sent the telegraph, sir.'

'What?' Hardcastle broke his reverie.

'The telegraph to Mr Rhodes about the Harts, sir.'

'Yes, good. I'm wondering, Marriott, if there's any connection between Victoria Hart and Sergeant Phillips both getting topped.'

'Something to do with the recruiting, you mean, sir?'

'Exactly, Marriott. I think we'll start by having a look at the records at the drill hall. Get hold of Stone, and we'll have a stroll up there. And tell him to bring the keys he found in Phillips's pocket.'

'What exactly are we looking for, sir?' asked Marriott, once the detectives had gained access to the filing cabinet at the drill hall.

'I don't know, Marriott,' said Hardcastle, for once admitting that he was uncertain about the direction the investigation ought to be taking. 'Clutching at straws, I suppose.'

'Should we be doing this without a warrant, sir?' asked Stone nervously. He still had to get the measure of the London DDI and, in view of their most recent exchange, feared he might never do so.

'We don't need a bloody warrant, Stone,' muttered Hardcastle. 'We're dealing with a murder here. Two murders now, of course. You ought to bone up on your law.'

'D'you think that Captain Porteous might be able to help, sir?' suggested Marriott.

'Not a hope in hell,' said Hardcastle curtly. 'He's probably as pissed as a rat most of the time.' He pulled a file from the top drawer of the cabinet. 'Ah, that's handy. This is a file marked Windsor Empire.' He flicked it open and found that the top sheet of paper comprised a list of names. Running his finger quickly down the column, he added them up. 'Fifty-three,' he said. 'Not a bad guess that Phillips made, when he said he'd recruited about sixty. Well, him and Victoria. The rest of the file is made up of the particulars of the recruits, each of 'em on what's called an attestation form.'

'I wonder why there's a separate file for the Windsor Empire, sir,' queried Marriott.

'No good asking me,' said Hardcastle. 'Perhaps the War Office runs some kind of reward scheme. Might have meant a few quid for Victoria Hart, or Sergeant Phillips.' He handed the file to Marriott. 'We'll hang on to this.'

'But what are we going to do with it, sir?'

'I haven't the faintest, Marriott. But I suppose we'd better get the bold Captain Porteous's OK to take it. The three of us don't want to get run in for nicking army property, do we?'

Stone didn't appear too happy about Hardcastle's last comment, but he had yet to realize that the London DDI occasionally made jokes. What he did not know was that even Hardcastle's own detectives had a problem with what passed for the DDI's sense of humour.

'If we're taking an interest in the men that Victoria helped to recruit, sir, shouldn't we be doing the other theatres as well? The ones where she gave a hand.' What Marriott did not say was that he thought Hardcastle was wasting his time.

'Yes. Which ones was they, Marriott?'

Unlike Stone, Marriott was always prepared for questions like that from his chief, and readily produced the names. 'The Palladium in Argyll Street, the Brighton Hippodrome, the Empire Leicester Square and the Theatre Royal in Margate, sir.'

Hardcastle nodded. 'Looks like we're going to be busy, Marriott,' he said. 'But there's one thing that puzzles me.'

'There *is*, sir?' Marriott knew how unusual it was for

Hardcastle to make such an admission, but he had to acknowledge that, so far, no motive was emerging for the murders of Victoria Hart and Sergeant Sidney Phillips.

'Why should Phillips's killer leave the weapon behind? He must've known that it's valuable evidence.'

'Not necessarily, sir.'

'Oh?' Hardcastle glanced enquiringly at his sergeant. 'What makes you say that, Marriott?'

'You're a skilled murder investigator, sir,' said Marriott, risking a touch of mild flattery. 'I doubt that our killer would be familiar with the way in which you can gather useful information from a bit of metal.'

'Yes, well of course that makes sense, Marriott,' said Hardcastle, accepting his sergeant's glib compliment as a genuine acknowledgement of his expertise. 'But we don't know where it came from, and I don't propose going all round Windsor enquiring if anyone's missing a sash weight. What's more, it don't tell us *why* he topped the two of 'em . . . if he did. Of course,' he went on, 'having written that bit from the Bible on the wall, he could be the sort of religious nut that Commander Hart mentioned. Murderers are queer folk, Marriott. For all we know, he might've taken exception to the outfit that Mrs Hart wore on stage and did her in because of it. On the other hand, it might've been a reaction to the suffragette movement. Surprising how those bloody amazons get up some people's noses. It could be, of course, that we're looking for a straightforward woman-hater. There's a name for them, but I can never remember it.'

'A misogynist, sir,' said Marriott.

'Yes, that's it.'

But secretly, Marriott thought that Hardcastle had never known the word.

Hardcastle made yet another of his unpredictable decisions, and announced that he and Marriott would return to London.

'I want to find out more about Victoria Hart, Marriott,' he said, when they arrived at Cannon Row. 'What was the address of her parents?'

'King's Avenue, Clapham, sir,' said Marriott promptly. As usual he had anticipated that a visit to the Lesters was what Hardcastle had in mind, and had the address to hand.

Putting his head round the door of Detective Inspector Rhodes's office, Hardcastle asked, 'You saw the Lesters, did you, Mr Rhodes?'

'I did, sir, as soon as I received your telegraph this morning,' said Rhodes as he stood up. 'They had indeed been informed of the murder by Commander Hart. Of course, they were desperately upset about their daughter – an only child, as it happens – and couldn't understand how it could have happened.'

'Very likely.' Hardcastle was never a man to show emotion about the death of someone whose murder he was investigating. '*It don't do to join in with other people's tears,*' he would say. 'Did Wood get an address for Commander Hart's parents?'

'Yes, sir. They live in Bath. The details are in a note on your desk.'

'What's this Lester man do for a living, Mr Rhodes?'

'He's a grocer, sir.'

'A grocer? Oh well, it takes all sorts, I suppose. Come, Marriott.'

The Lesters' large house was set back from the road and, to Hardcastle's surprise, there was a Rolls-Royce Silver Ghost on the drive.

'Blimey, Marriott, there must be more money than I thought in groceries. The bloke who owns the shop Mrs Hardcastle goes to, at the bottom of Kennington Road, has only got a bicycle. And that's got a basket on the front for deliveries. He told me once it cost him seven quid up Gamages. Mind you, it has got them pump-up tyres.'

'Perhaps Mr Rhodes got it wrong, sir,' ventured Marriott.

'I very much doubt it, Marriott,' said Hardcastle sharply, a comment that his sergeant took as a rebuke for criticizing a superior officer's competence.

A butler answered the door and after a short delay, showed the two policemen into a large drawing room.

'John Lester, Inspector.' The man shook hands with Hardcastle and Marriott, once the DDI had effected introductions. Lester was a tall, slim man, immaculate in evening dress, and had the appearance of someone yet to see his fiftieth birthday. His wife, whom he introduced as Flora Lester, was a real beauty and looked younger than one would expect of a woman who had given birth to a daughter twenty-five years ago. She glanced up from the sampler she was embroidering and afforded Hardcastle a wan smile.

'I'm sorry to have to trouble you again, sir,' said Hardcastle, 'and I hope I'm not intruding on your dinner.' He too was beginning to wonder if DI Rhodes had made a mistake about Lester's occupation. Not that he would say so to Marriott.

'Not at all, Inspector, not at all.'

'My Inspector Rhodes saw you this morning, I understand.'

'Yes, he did. In view of the fact that our son-in-law was lost at sea, I thought it extremely kind of the police to ensure that Flora and I had been told of Victoria's death.'

The room contained several upholstered armchairs and two padded sofas, the back of each protected by a fine linen antimacassar, and Lester invited the detectives to sit down.

'I have to tell you that there's been another murder in Windsor, sir.'

'Another?'

'Yes, sir. Yesterday afternoon, the recruiting sergeant with whom your daughter worked at the Windsor Empire was found battered to death at the drill hall.'

'Good grief! D'you think there may be some connection between those two awful events?'

'Maybe, sir. It's a possibility that I'm working on at the moment.'

'Would you care for a drink, Inspector?' asked Lester, suddenly remembering his responsibilities as the man of the house. 'I usually have a whisky at about this time.'

'That's very kind of you, sir. Thank you.'

Lester strode across the room and gave the bell-pull a sharp tug. A few moments later, the butler entered the room.

After receiving his instructions, the man returned with two decanters and several glasses on a silver salver, and poured whisky for the men and a sherry for Mrs Lester.

'Your good health, Inspector.' Lester raised his glass. 'So, how can I help you?'

Hardcastle was surprised at the man's composure, particularly in view of what Rhodes had said about the pair being 'desperately upset'. It seemed out of character for a man who had so recently suffered a double grievous loss. And with it, the DDI assumed, the chance of grand-children. But Hardcastle had to admit, if only to himself, that he sometimes saw suspicion where there were no grounds for it. It might have been, however, that Lester was of the calibre of man who would never display his grief in the presence of strangers.

'I was hoping you could tell me a bit more about your daughter, sir. All the police know at the moment is that she was an accomplished actress and singer.'

'Yes, she was.' For the first time since the arrival of the detectives, Flora Lester spoke. 'There was little doubt in our minds – ' she nodded towards her husband – 'that Victoria was cut out for the stage. We tried to dissuade her, thinking that it was a rather unsavoury profession for a refined young woman, but she wouldn't be talked out of it. It looks as though we were right, though.' For a moment the girl's mother looked sad, almost to the point of tears. 'She was a very strong-willed girl. D'you have daughters, Inspector?'

'Yes, ma'am, I do. Two. And one of them is extremely headstrong, so I know what you mean.'

'Well, I hope she doesn't share the same fate as Victoria,' said Flora Lester, and returned to her embroidery.

'Did you ever see her perform, sir?' Marriott asked.

'No, I'm afraid not, Sergeant. Business takes up a lot of my time, and my wife and I never got around to it. And now, I regret to say, we never shall.' Lester looked at Hardcastle. 'Did you by any chance see any of the plays she was in, Inspector?'

'No, sir. In fact, I'd never heard of her until this tragedy occurred. But I'm told she was extremely talented.'

Hardcastle was surprised that Lester had spoken of his daughter being in a play, but that enigma was resolved immediately.

'So I believe. Given that she was set on the stage as a career, we were rather pleased that she entered the classical theatre.'

Hardcastle was not sure whether Victoria Hart had deluded her parents, or whether they were attempting to delude themselves. 'She was a music-hall artiste, sir,' he said.

Lester laughed nervously. 'If you'll forgive me for saying so, Inspector, I think you must have made a mistake there.'

Hardcastle produced a programme he had obtained from the Windsor Empire, and handed it silently to Lester. On the cover was a photograph of Victoria Hart in the costume that she wore on stage.

As Lester studied the small pamphlet, his face expressed disbelief. 'I can't believe that our Victoria . . . ' He lapsed into silence, unable to find the words to express his shock at discovering that his daughter would allow herself to be seen in such a provocative outfit.

'Let me see, John,' said Flora Lester, holding out a hand. She took the programme and her face froze as she studied it. 'She looks like a whore,' she declared, but then a tear rolled down her cheek. 'I can't believe that she would have deceived us in this way.'

'She was top of the bill,' said Hardcastle, as though that might alleviate the Lesters' dismay, 'and was a great help in recruiting. I'm told that she rewarded every volunteer with a kiss.'

'Dressed like that?' Flora Lester handed the programme back to her husband. 'Did Kenneth know what she was doing, I wonder?' Despite seeing the photograph of her daughter, she somehow gave the impression that she thought Hardcastle to be lying.

'I spoke to the commander before he put to sea this last time,' said Hardcastle, 'and he told me that it was her performance at the Theatre Royal, Portsmouth, in nineteen-thirteen, that first attracted him to her. They were married shortly afterwards. June, I think he said.'

Lester shook his head in disbelief. 'I have to say that this has come as a terrible shock to us both, Inspector. We understood that she was appearing in productions like *The Importance of Being Earnest* or *The Rivals*. But that sort of thing – ' he returned the programme to Hardcastle – 'well, I would never have sanctioned . . . ' And once again, he lapsed into silence.

'Did your daughter have any gentlemen friends before her marriage to Commander Hart, sir?' asked Marriott, addressing his question to John Lester.

'She had quite a lot of admirers, yes. Young men were always calling at the house.' Lester's face maintained its bleak expression. 'There seemed to be a different one each week. But then she was a very attractive young woman. However, there was no one that I could imagine would wish to do her any harm, if that's what you're thinking, Sergeant.'

'She won't have seen a great deal of her husband, I imagine,' said Hardcastle. 'Especially since the war started.'

'It was not an ideal relationship, being married to a sailor,' said Lester. 'But it was a match made in heaven. One had only to see them together to realize that.' He looked wistfully across the room. 'And now they're both gone.'

The conversation went on in the same desultory fashion for the next quarter of an hour, but Hardcastle learned nothing that would assist him in discovering Victoria Hart's killer. It appeared that, apart from being strong-willed, the girl had similar interests to, and behaved much as, other young women in her social class. Until she became an actress, that is. There was no suggestion that she was in any way promiscuous and, in the circumstances, Hardcastle decided it would be tactless to question whether she might have been. He did not, though, preclude having to pose the question at some time in the future, once the Lesters had come to terms with the direction in which their late daughter's career had moved. He did wonder, however, whether she had taken to the stage to escape what she saw as a stifling home life.

'My Inspector Rhodes tells me you're a grocer, sir,' said

Hardcastle as Lester escorted him and Marriott to the front door.

'Calling myself a grocer is my little perversity, Inspector,' said Lester. 'In fact, I own a large number of grocery stores. I'm sure you must have seen a Lesters somewhere near where you live. Well, I hope you have.'

'Of course,' said Hardcastle, annoyed with himself for not having made the connection.

'Do call again if there's anything you think I may be able to help you with, Inspector,' said Lester. 'I have to say that I'm very pleased that whoever arranges these matters decided to put Scotland Yard in charge of getting to the bottom of this awful tragedy. Incidentally, I am connected to the telephone if you'd find it easier to speak to me in that way.' And he handed Hardcastle a pasteboard card.

'There's little point in returning to Windsor today, Marriott,' said Hardcastle, once they were back at Cannon Row. 'We'll spend the night at home and I'll meet you back here tomorrow morning.'

Eleven

Alice Hardcastle evinced no surprise at the return of her husband; she had been married to a policeman for too long to wonder when he would arrive and when he would go again. Sitting quietly by the fire in the parlour, she was busy with her self-imposed task of knitting socks and mufflers for the soldiers at the Front.

Hardcastle hung his hat and coat on the hooks by the mirror in the small hall, and looked around. Something was missing. Eventually he worked out what it was.

'Where's the cuckoo clock gone, Alice?'

'I've thrown it away, Ernie.'

'Whatever for? We've had that clock for over ten years. Had it gone wrong, or something?'

'No, but I read in the paper that most cuckoo clocks were made in Germany. I had a look at ours, and it was. So I threw it in the dustbin.' Alice put down her knitting.

'Good job we hadn't got a German piano,' observed Hardcastle drily.

'And another thing,' Alice said, warming to her subject. 'I was in Selfridge's yesterday.'

'Hope you didn't spend too much,' remarked Hardcastle.

Alice ignored that comment, one that her husband frequently made when she told him she had been shopping. 'They've taken all the German toys off the shelves.'

'What have they done that for?'

'They said that the German toy factories are making munitions now, so they're not going to sell any more German toys.'

'Don't see how that helps,' muttered Hardcastle, and helped himself to a glass of whisky.

'And because of the Germans the price of pepper has gone up to fivepence-ha'penny a quarter,' complained Alice.

'Don't buy any, then,' said Hardcastle.

'You'd soon complain if there wasn't any,' said Alice. 'And while you're here, Ernie, you can help me get these Christmas decorations down. It's Twelfth Night tonight.'

Having discovered that there was no one at Windsor competent in the science of fingerprints – at least to the level of his demanding standards – Hardcastle had brought the sash weight to London.

The result was disappointing. Detective Inspector Charles Stockley Collins, the Yard's fingerprint expert, examined the weapon used to kill Phillips, but could find no identifiable prints. 'He'll have worn gloves, Ernie,' Collins said.

'There's nothing else for it, Marriott,' said Hardcastle. 'We'll have to go round the theatres where Victoria Hart did her recruiting act, and see if we can find anything that might tie someone into her murder. Someone who Catto and Wilson never found out about.'

'It's Watkins, sir.'

'Who is?'

'The DC you called Wilson, sir.'

'Why does he keep changing his name, then?' demanded Hardcastle, making a lame attempt at a joke. He donned his bowler hat and Chesterfield overcoat, but having done so, hesitated in the doorway of his office. 'It might be that the army could give us a hand out with the theatres,' he said pensively, as he turned to face Marriott. 'On second thoughts, I think we'll walk down Whitehall and have a chat with that fellow who runs the military police.'

The assistant provost marshal of the army's London District had his office in the Palladian-style Horse Guards building, outside which were two mounted troopers. But since last August the colourful ceremonial uniforms that they wore in peacetime had been replaced by drab khaki. In unison, they raised their swords in salute as Hardcastle passed through the open gates. Accustomed to being mistaken for an army officer, Hardcastle solemnly raised his bowler hat in silent acknowledgement.

A sergeant of the Military Foot Police examined Hardcastle's warrant card. 'Very good, sir. I'll take you into the colonel straight away.'

The APM, Lieutenant Colonel Ralph Frobisher of the Sherwood Foresters, stood up and shook hands. 'And what can I do for the civil police, Inspector?' he asked.

'I'm investigating the murder of Sergeant Sidney Phillips of the Royal Berkshire Regiment, Colonel. He was the recruiting sergeant at Windsor.'

'I heard that he'd been killed, Inspector. It was reported to me as a matter of routine. I suppose you've heard about the other recruiting sergeant who was murdered.'

'Another one? No, I haven't,' said Hardcastle angrily. 'Where was this?'

'Here in London.' Frobisher reached for a docket in one of his filing trays. 'Yes, here we are. Panton Street. Apparently he'd just left the Empire Theatre in Leicester Square, and was on his way to catch a bus to Chelsea when he was struck from behind. I'm told that the blow fractured his skull, and he died instantly.'

'And when did this occur?' Hardcastle was furious that he had not heard of this murder from his own sources.

'According to the report I received from the police at Vine Street, it happened at about eleven-thirty in the evening of Saturday the seventeenth of October.' Frobisher glanced up. 'Did you not know about this, Inspector?'

'No, I bloody didn't,' growled Hardcastle, infuriated that the Vine Street police had told the military, but that the information had not reached him. 'And someone's going to be answering some pretty searching questions. It was in all yesterday's papers about Phillips's murder. You'd've thought someone would have got around to telling me, on account of the coincidence, so to speak. D'you have the name of this sergeant, Colonel?'

'Sergeant Mayhew of the Scots Guards, Inspector. He was a single man, quartered at Chelsea Barracks.'

Hardcastle gazed thoughtfully at Frobisher. 'I'm beginning

to wonder if there's a connection with recruiting, Colonel, because to get back to what I was saying just now, I'm also investigating the murder of an actress called Victoria Hart. Her body was found in Windsor Great Park early on Christmas Day, although we're satisfied that she was murdered some hours previously. Probably at about seven o'clock on Christmas Eve.'

'But I don't see what the actress had to do with it, Inspector,' said Frobisher.

'Victoria Hart took an active part in recruiting at the Windsor Empire,' began Hardcastle slowly, 'and at other theatres since the war began. In Windsor, she worked in company with Sergeant Phillips, and usually finished her act with some patriotic song. She promised each recruit a kiss if they signed on and, it seemed, they couldn't wait to flock on to the stage in their dozens.' He turned to his sergeant. 'Give me that list, Marriott.' He spent a second or two perusing the details. 'Thought so. The seventeenth of October last year was the last day that Victoria Hart was appearing at the Empire Theatre in Leicester Square, *and* she was helping with the recruiting drive there. There's got to be a link between all three murders.'

'How can I assist you, then, Inspector?'

'Would you be able to discover the names of those men who were enlisted at the theatres where Mrs Hart was appearing, Colonel?'

'That shouldn't be too difficult,' said Frobisher. 'If you can tell me the theatres concerned, I'll see what I can do. This music-hall campaign is quite a successful mode of recruitment, you know, and I have to say that the army is greatly indebted to those young actresses who help. We don't expect them to be murdered for doing it, though.'

'Those are the theatres, Colonel,' said Hardcastle, handing over the list he had been studying.

'Are these the only ones?' Frobisher fingered the sheet of paper and placed it squarely in the centre of his desk.

'They're the only ones I know of so far, but I shall make urgent enquiries as to any others,' said Hardcastle.

'Very well, I'll set the ball rolling, Inspector, and if you can let me have details of the other theatres . . . '

'As soon as I have them, Colonel, I'll send an officer down here with 'em *tout de suite*.'

'That list also shows which weeks Mrs Hart was at each theatre, sir,' explained Marriott to the colonel.

'I'll be in touch as soon as I get anything, Inspector,' said Frobisher. 'You're at the Yard, I take it?'

'No, at Cannon Row, Colonel.'

Still furious at what he perceived to be the incompetence of the neighbouring division's CID, Hardcastle returned to Cannon Row and immediately telephoned the divisional detective inspector of C Division at his headquarters in Vine Street.

He was further frustrated, however, to be told that the DDI would not be on duty until the following morning.

'Tell him I'll be coming to see him first thing tomorrow and not to leave the office till I get there,' thundered Hardcastle, and slammed the receiver so hard on to the pedestal telephone that the support broke off.

'Get someone to fix that bloody thing, Marriott, will you?' said the DDI.

'Yes, sir,' said Marriott, and promptly retreated to the detectives' office. He had encountered Hardcastle's fury before, and knew that it was best to keep out of his way on such occasions.

Hardcastle spent the remainder of the afternoon catching up on everything that had been happening at Cannon Row in his absence. Although his deputy, Detective Inspector Edgar Rhodes, was an able officer, Hardcastle was never willing to leave matters entirely to him, and always needed to satisfy himself that nothing had been overlooked or left to chance. As was his custom, he read through all the outstanding crime reports, made pencilled comments of criticism on most of them and even required some of them to be rewritten.

Finally, he decided to examine all the official duty diaries of his officers, paying particular attention to their claims for expenses. It was a course of action that alarmed his subordinates in no small measure; the DDI did not normally carry out such checks until the Friday of each week. And today was only Wednesday.

'After we've been to Vine Street in the morning, Marriott, we'll go back to Windsor. Better see what's been happening down there, I suppose. Probably time I had a chat with the pathologist. I'll see you here tomorrow, just in case anything's cropped up during the night.'

'Very good, sir.' Marriott could not foresee that anything was likely to crop up, but was glad of the chance to spend another night in his own bed.

The morning, however, brought a surprise.

'Good morning, sir.'

'Good morning, Mr Rhodes,' said Hardcastle.

'We've received a telegraph from Windsor, sir.'

'Have we now? Don't tell me there's been another murder.'

'No, sir,' said Rhodes, who never assumed that Hardcastle was joking. 'Floods.'

'Floods?'

'Yes, sir. Apparently there's been heavy rain and, as a result, the river at that point has broken its banks. It seems that most of Windsor's under water.' Rhodes flourished the telegraph message. 'It says here that Windsor Castle is marooned in the middle of a lake, and that Eton's playing fields are submerged.'

Hardcastle let out a bellow of laughter. 'If that don't cause the chief constable to get off his arse, Mr Rhodes, nothing will,' he said.

Rhodes permitted himself a brief smile. 'The chief constable suggests that it might be as well if you stayed in London till the floods have abated, sir.'

'Oh dear! What a disappointment,' said Hardcastle. Crossing the corridor to the detectives' office, he summoned Marriott. 'And now we're going to sort out the CID on C Division, Marriott. God knows what's happened to Vine Street nick since I left it.'

* * *

William Sullivan, the divisional detective inspector of C Division, had his office on the first floor of Vine Street's four-storeyed police station.

A colourful character – some described him as raffish – Sullivan was usually seen in a single-breasted suit that was way ahead of its fashion, and invariably affected a watered-silk waistcoat. Whenever he ventured out in winter, it was always in a fawn twill overcoat with a velvet collar. And summer or winter, he was never seen without a silver-topped malacca cane and a bowler hat which, in Hardcastle's opinion, had just too much of a curl to its brim. But the accessory that singled him out from any other detective was his monocle. It was an affectation that caused the local villains to dub him 'Posh Bill with the Piccadilly window'.

'My DI told me you were coming, Ernie. He reckoned you were in a bit of a lather about something.' Sullivan leaped up from behind his desk and shook hands with Hardcastle. 'So, what brings you here?'

'You bloody well do, Bill,' said Hardcastle. 'By the way, this here's DS Marriott.'

'Pleased to meet you, Skip,' said Sullivan, and opened the bottom drawer of his desk. 'Sit yourselves down. You'll have a drop of Scotch, won't you, Ernie?'

'That's the least you can offer me in the circumstances,' said Hardcastle.

Sullivan poured whisky for the two A Division detectives, and a glass for himself, before sitting down behind his desk. 'You sound as though you got out of the wrong side of the bed this morning, Ernie. What's eating you? Have a spat with the missus, did you?'

'Sergeant Mayhew of the Scots Guards.'

'That's my problem, not yours,' said Sullivan. 'Why d'you want to know about him? You got someone lined up for it?'

'Did you read about Sergeant Phillips's murder in the linen drapers, Bill? Got topped in Windsor last Monday.' The report had been on the front page of most of Tuesday's London dailies, with 'Hardcastle of the Yard' featuring prominently as the investigating officer.

'I think I did see something about that.'

'Well, why the hell didn't you let me know about Mayhew?'

'Didn't think it was relevant. D'you reckon there's a tie up, then?'

Hardcastle explained about the murder of Victoria Hart and the possibility of a connection between that and the murder of the two recruiting sergeants, Phillips and now Mayhew.

'So it would have been nice to have been told about your topping, Bill, seeing as how I'm struggling with a similar job out in the sticks.'

'Yeah, I see. You might have a point there, Ernie.'

'So tell me what you know.' Hardcastle drained his glass and pushed it across the desk for a refill. 'Nice drop of Scotch you've got there,' he said.

'The landlord of the Man in the Moon next door usually drops a bottle of single malt in. Likes to keep on the right side of the law.' Sullivan laughed, and poured liberal measures of whisky into all three glasses. 'You on this job with Mr Hardcastle, Skipper?' he asked Marriott.

'Yes, sir.'

'Well, you've got a good guv'nor there.' It was a blandishment that had no effect on Hardcastle. 'Now then, about Mayhew's topping, Ernie,' continued Sullivan. 'This was about half-past eleven on the night of Saturday the seventeenth of October last year. A tom was working Panton Street, and was about to pack it in, on account of it starting to rain, when she saw this heap on the footway. Least, that's how she described it in her statement: a heap. But on closer examination she saw it was a swaddy, and he'd had his head bashed in. She shouted blue murder and the PC on that beat came running. Nobody suspicious was seen in the vicinity. I've had enquiries made all over the parish, but nothing. The first thoughts were that Mayhew had welshed on a tom, and her pimp had done him for it – or she had – but I've had the squeeze put on the lot of 'em, and no one's peaching. Mind you, the attack was a bit vicious for a woman, even though some of them toms are strong lassies. To tell you the truth, Ernie, I'm right up a gum tree.'

'You ain't been trying hard enough, Bill. When I was a skipper here, the DDI we had then would have a body in the nick quicker than you can say Jack the Ripper.' But, despite being annoyed that Sullivan had not told him of Mayhew's murder, Hardcastle knew that random killings – and this had all the appearance of one – were among the most difficult to solve.

'Any trace of the murder weapon, Bill?'

'Not a glim. I had foot-duty men scour the area, but nothing. Pathologist's report said cause of death was being struck with a heavy implement of some sort, but you didn't have to be a doctor to work that out.'

'Like a sash weight?'

'Could've been. Why?'

'Because that's what Phillips was topped with, and the assailant left it at the scene.'

'Any dabs on it?'

'Nothing. I got Charlie Collins to give it the once over, but not a trace. He reckoned the killer must've worn gloves.' Hardcastle took another mouthful of whisky. 'When your PCs had a look round, I suppose they never came across anything written on a nearby wall, did they? We found a quote from the Bible at the drill hall where Phillips was topped: *Vengeance is mine; I will repay, saith the Lord.*'

'Hold on a moment, there was something.' Sullivan walked across to his office door and shouted for someone called Croft. 'This is DS Croft, my first-class,' he said when the sergeant appeared. 'This Mayhew job, Croft. Wasn't there something written on a wall near where the body was found?'

'Yes, there was, sir. But no one thought it had anything to do with the murder.'

'Well, what did it say, man?' asked Sullivan impatiently.

'It said: "Nemo me imp", sir, and was written in chalk. Don't mean anything to me. I've got an idea he was a circus strong man. The Great Nemo seems to ring a bell.'

'Thank you, Croft. Very helpful,' said Sullivan with a sour face. 'Mean anything to you, Ernie?' he asked once Croft had departed.

'No, Bill, not a thing.'

'The law-writer in *Bleak House* was called Nemo, sir,' volunteered Marriott.

'Ah yes, I'd forgotten you was a Dickens fan, Marriott,' said Hardcastle, 'but somehow I don't think he was hanging about in Panton Street chalking his name on a wall.'

'Well, Ernie,' said Sullivan, 'if you happen to feel someone's collar for the Mayhew job, I'll be extremely grateful.'

'How grateful?' asked Hardcastle archly.

Sullivan thought about that. 'How about treating you to a slap-up lunch at Kettner's?'

'You're all heart, Bill.' Hardcastle laughed. 'I thought for a minute it'd be somewhere where you'd've had to pay for it.'

'We'll walk back to the nick, Marriott,' said Hardcastle, as the two officers left Vine Street, 'and have a nose round in Panton Street.'

They cut through Regent Street and Jermyn Street, crossed Haymarket and finally turned into Panton Street.

'I see *Peg O' My Heart* is still running,' commented Hardcastle, as they passed the Comedy Theatre. 'I took Mrs H. to see that a while back. You ought to give Mrs Marriott a treat one night and take her. It's got that Laurette Taylor in it. She's very good.'

'The problem is getting someone to look after the children, sir.' In view of Hardcastle's fragile mood, Marriott thought it unwise to mention that working for the DDI meant that he very rarely got an evening off.

'Yes, I had the same problem a few years back,' said Hardcastle. 'Mind you, it only gets worse when they grow up. That Kitty of mine is a strong-willed young girl.' He pointed to a restaurant on the other side of the street. 'And beforehand you could take your missus in there. Stone's Chop House does some very good grub.' He stopped by a wall. 'This looks like it, Marriott. There's just a trace of chalk there, see? Can't read any of it now, but it must have been about here that Mayhew got his comeuppance.'

Hardcastle suddenly crossed the street, narrowly avoiding a youth on a bicycle who shouted some obscenity at him.

'I'll have you, you bloody urchin,' yelled Hardcastle.

'Up yours!' responded the youth before pedalling away furiously.

A waiter in a long white apron strode towards the detectives as they entered the restaurant. 'Table for two, sir?' he asked.

'I'm a police officer,' Hardcastle announced.

'Ah! Still looking into that murder, are you, guv'nor?'

'What d'you know about it?'

'Nothing really. I was on duty the night it happened, but I never saw nothing. First I knew of it was when I heard some tart screaming her head off. Next thing was police whistles going off, and suddenly the street's full of coppers.'

'But you didn't see anything? No one who might have done this? No one running away?'

'No, boss, but it was coming down cats and dogs. I shouldn't think anyone was out.'

'Well, at least two people were,' said Hardcastle. 'The bloke who got killed, and the bloke who killed him.'

Hardcastle eventually decided that they were wasting their time; it was a conclusion that Marriott had reached some time previously.

'And now, Marriott, we'll set about making some enquiries,' said Hardcastle, and led the way down Whitcomb Street to Trafalgar Square. But instead of making for Whitehall, the usual route back to the police station, he crossed the road, narrowly being missed by a cab, and started down Northumberland Avenue.

Twelve

'Blimey, you're becoming a bit of a regular, guv'nor.' The landlord of the Ship and Shovel public house in Craven Passage pushed two pints of bitter across the counter. 'On a case, are you? I saw from the linen drapers that you was down Windsor way. Bit of a juicy murder, you've got there, guv'nor. The missus pointed it out to me in the *Daily Mirror*, all about Hardcastle of the Yard. Didn't know you'd been transferred.'

'I get all over the place in my job,' said Hardcastle, making no attempt to pay. He never told a publican anything that he did not want passed on to the next customer; licensees were notorious gossips.

'Well, I hopes you catches him, whoever he is,' said the landlord, and moved away to serve a thirsty costermonger.

'I think that Master Savage might be able to give us a hand out with these here theatres, Marriott,' Hardcastle confided to his sergeant. 'If this show of his has been on the road for eighteen months, he should know what theatres our Victoria was at when she done her recruiting palaver.'

'D'you think he'll be at the Playhouse this early, sir?' asked Marriott, glancing at his watch. 'There's not usually a matinée on a Thursday.'

'One way of finding out,' said the DDI. He drained his glass and made for the door, leaving Marriott hurriedly to gulp down the remainder of his beer.

But a surprise awaited them when they reached the Playhouse Theatre: it was closed, and a sticker marked 'Cancelled' had been pasted over the posters advertising the *Beaux Belles*.

'Well, that's a turn-up, and no mistake,' said Hardcastle.

'Although after that dog's dinner of a performance we saw last week, it don't come as no wonder.' He walked round to the stage door and hammered loudly.

Eventually, a man peered out from behind the dirty pane of glass set in the door. Wearing an unbuttoned waistcoat over his collarless shirt, he was holding a half-eaten sandwich in one hand. 'Watcha want?' he demanded, mouthing the words.

By way of a reply, Hardcastle held up his warrant card, and within seconds the stage-door keeper was hurrying to admit him.

'Sorry, guv. Didn't know you was the law.'

'Who are you?' demanded Hardcastle.

'The name's Haddock, guv'nor. Henry Haddock.'

'I'm looking for Percy Savage, Mr Haddock,' said Hardcastle.

The stage-door keeper cackled loudly. 'You won't find him in a hurry, guv'nor. He's gone bottom up and scarpered.'

'When did this happen?'

'Last Saturday, guv. Four nights running before that, that Vera Cobb got the bird, and that was that. Come off in tears, she did. As for the escapologist, he never managed to escape. Probably still tied up here some place.' The man chortled at the thought. 'D'you know, guv, this house has got six hundred and twenty seats all up, an' no more than a couple of hundred of 'em was took all week. Mind you, the war's buggered things up a treat. We just ain't getting 'em in. They seem to have gone off variety a bit.'

'Any idea where Savage went?' asked Hardcastle, tiring of Haddock's dissertation on the decline of the music hall.

'Could be anywhere, guv,' said Haddock unhelpfully, and wiped his nose on the cuff of his shirt. 'Likely gone to ground. We've had debt collectors and process-servers round here looking for him ever since he took it on his heels.'

'Have you got that address in Pimlico that Savage reckons he was staying at, Marriott?' asked Hardcastle, when the two detectives were back in the street. He waved his umbrella at a cab. 'Not that we've got much hope of finding him, seeing as how matey back there reckons he's vamoosed.'

'It's Denbigh Street, sir.'

Having searched in vain for either a bell or a knocker, Hardcastle used the handle of his umbrella to rap loudly on the door of the big old house. But it was some time before a woman opened it and stared suspiciously at the two detectives.

'Yes?'

'I'm looking for Mr Savage,' said Hardcastle.

'Huh! Aren't we all, love? Owe you money an' all, does he?'

'Do I look like I came up the Clyde on a bicycle, missus?' retorted Hardcastle. 'I'm a police officer and it's important that I find him in connection with a murder I'm investigating.'

'You'd better come in,' said the woman, but once in the hall, stopped and turned to face the DDI. 'Done someone in, has he?' she asked, with a loud sniff. 'Wouldn't surprise me,' she continued. 'Bit too smarmy, for my liking, that one. Even though he's an actor. They're not all like him, you know. I had that Wilkie Bard in my rooms here one time. Now he was a real gent, he was. D'you know what he said to me once? "Here, Mrs Pack," he said, "here's a ticket to see my show down the Victoria Palace." Just after it opened, that was. The Vic, I mean. One of the best seats in the house, it was. Well, Wilkie comes on dressed as a charwoman and does one of his comic songs. Laugh? I nearly wet meself, dearie. And another one I had staying here—'

'I'm sure you've had all the best turns on the halls in here at one time or another, Mrs Pack,' said Hardcastle, managing, at last, to force a stop to the landlady's reminiscing, 'but it's Percy Savage I'm after.'

'Yes, well like I said, he's gone. But if you want to have a word with his leading lady, Vera Cobb, she's upstairs in her room.'

'Thank you,' said Hardcastle, wishing that Mrs Pack had mentioned that in the first place.

'Come into the parlour, and I'll fetch her down.' Mrs Pack paused on the threshold. 'Like a cup of tea, would you, dears?' she asked. She appeared to notice Marriott for the first time. 'You ought to be on the boards, love,' she said. 'Good-looking young man like you.'

'We don't have time for tea, thanks,' said Hardcastle, afraid that Mrs Pack would make it an excuse for further tales of the theatre.

A few minutes later, Vera Cobb entered the room. She was wearing a faded dressing gown that failed to disguise the fact that she was pregnant, and her hair hung in rat's-tails around her shoulders. It was obvious from her red, puffed eyes that she had been crying.

'I'm looking for Mr Savage,' said Hardcastle.

'Don't talk to me about Percy Savage,' exclaimed Vera heatedly. 'He's gone bust. I've not had any wages for a fort-night *and* he's left me with a bun in the oven.'

'Bit sudden, wasn't it?' remarked Hardcastle. 'Him going bust.'

'I should've seen it coming,' said Vera, collapsing into an armchair. 'The show's been rocky for a long time now, and when Vicky got done in that was the finish. I did my best to fill the gap, but the audiences weren't having it. They wanted Vicky and weren't going to have anyone else.'

'What's happened to Fanny Morris?' asked Marriott. 'The other girl we met at Mr and Mrs Armitage's.'

'She's trying her hand round the halls, solo, but I doubt she'll have much luck. She never had much of a voice, and her comic songs were . . . well, they weren't funny, if you know what I mean. But I wouldn't mind betting that wher-ever Fanny is, Percy's not far away.'

'And do you have any idea where she is?'

'She's got a room down Victoria way.' Vera wrinkled her brow as she tried to recall where her former friend had gone. 'Twenty-seven Allington Street, right behind the Victoria Palace, was the last address I had for her,' she said eventually. 'But I don't know if she's still there.'

'That party you had on the stage at the Windsor Empire

on Christmas Eve, Miss Cobb,' Marriott began, 'after the show was over.'

'What about it?'

'Was Savage really with you all evening?'

There was a distinct pause before Vera answered, and it seemed that even though Savage had left the girl penniless and pregnant, she still felt some loyalty towards him. But then she yielded in favour of the truth. 'No,' she said eventually, 'he wasn't.'

'Oh? And where was he?' asked Hardcastle, taking up the questioning again.

'He pushed off just after Vicky went,' said Vera. 'And he took Fanny with him.' And with that, she burst into tears.

'It strikes me that our Percy Savage is a bit of a penniless Casanova, Marriott,' said Hardcastle, as they approached the address in Allington Street.

'D'you reckon we'll find him here, sir?'

'If we don't, we'll have to go looking, Marriott. Considering what young Vera Cobb told us about him going missing just after Victoria left the theatre, I reckon he's back on my list for the topping. Might be a lady-killer in more ways than one.'

But the detectives did not have to go looking. To their surprise, a dishevelled Percy Savage answered the door. Gone was the nattily dressed showman they had interviewed in Windsor on Christmas Day. In his place was a man in thick grey flannel trousers held up by striped braces, and a shirt with a tear near the collarless neckband. His hair – no longer neatly pomaded – was in grave need of a barber.

'I want a word with you, Mr Savage,' said Hardcastle, using his forefinger to propel the unfortunate actor-manager back into the hall.

'I've done nothing wrong, Inspector,' wailed Savage, having recognized the two police officers instantly.

'I'll be the judge of that,' said Hardcastle, a comment that afforded Savage no comfort whatever.

'You'd better come in, then.'

It was a pointless invitation; Hardcastle was already in, whether Savage liked it or not.

'Right, my lad. Where were you on Christmas Eve between five o'clock in the afternoon and, say, midnight?'

'I told you before that I was—'

'What you told me before was a pack of lies, lad,' interrupted Hardcastle. 'And I don't take kindly to people who try to sell Ernie Hardcastle the pup.'

'But I was with—'

'I'll tell you who you was with, mister,' said Hardcastle, his temper rapidly shortening. 'You was with Fanny Morris, because I've just had a chat with Vera Cobb who, incidentally, tells me she's carrying your dustbin lid.'

'My *what*? What on earth are you talking about?' Savage was clearly bemused by Hardcastle's patter.

'Dustbin lid: kid,' explained the DDI. 'As in child, baby. Call it what you like, but she ain't best pleased with you.'

'What did she tell you about that night, then?' Savage rapidly steered the conversation away from the subject of Vera's pregnancy.

'She told me you left the theatre straight after Victoria Hart left.'

'Lies,' exclaimed Savage vehemently. 'That's just spite because she's trying to get her own back—'

'It's true,' said a voice from the doorway.

The three men turned to see a barefooted Fanny Morris, attired in a pink satin wrap.

'What's true, Miss Morris?' asked Hardcastle.

'Percy and I left the theatre just after Vicky received that telegram.'

'And where did the pair of you go?'

'We had dinner at the Manor Hotel in Datchet, and spent the night there. You can check if you like.'

'I shall, miss. Don't you worry about that.' Hardcastle did not doubt that Fanny was telling the truth, but decided to discomfit Savage a little further. 'I just hope he hasn't put you in the family way like he did Vera Cobb. I don't wonder you did a runner,' he continued, turning to Savage.

'But it seems you didn't run far enough, because Miss Cobb knows where you are.'

Fanny took a step closer to Savage. 'Is this true, Percy?' she demanded hotly. 'Have you and Vera been . . . ?'

'Well, I, er—'

It was all Savage had time to say before Fanny, bringing her hand up from near thigh level, struck him so violently across the face that he staggered back and fell on to a settee.

Hardcastle gazed at the prostrate, moaning Savage and then turned to Fanny. 'Perhaps you'd wait till I've finished talking to Mr Savage before you knock him about any more, miss,' he said mildly.

'I'll talk to you later, Percy Savage,' screamed Fanny. 'In the meantime, I'll be upstairs packing.' And deploying what little thespian talent she possessed, swept theatrically from the room, and slammed the door behind her.

'I think your lady friend's a bit upset with you, Savage, old cock,' observed Hardcastle. 'But now Sergeant Marriott here has some questions to put to you.'

Still half-lying on the settee, rubbing his face, Savage stared at Marriott. 'What now?' he asked. 'Haven't you done enough already?'

'I want a list of the theatres Victoria Hart appeared at since the war started, Mr Savage.'

Savage appeared surprised at the mildness of the request. 'I'll have to get those details for you,' he said. 'They're upstairs.'

'Then I suggest you go and get them,' said Marriott firmly.

'And don't go jumping out of no windows, Savage, because if you do, I'll come and find you,' said Hardcastle. 'If I have to search every hospital in London,' he added.

Savage was gone for quite some time, and Hardcastle was on the point of sending Marriott to find him, when the bankrupt actor-manager reappeared.

'You've been a long time,' observed Marriott.

'I had to find this,' said Savage, displaying a ledger.

'I thought for a minute you was trying to placate Miss Morris,' said Hardcastle. 'But knowing women as I do, you'd probably have been wasting your time.'

Apart from shooting a malicious glance at Hardcastle –
for whom he blamed his latest predicament – Savage did
not respond to the DDI's quip. Instead he sat down and
opened the ledger on his knees. 'What exactly d'you want,
Sergeant?' he asked.

'Names of the theatres, the dates and whether Mrs Hart
was engaged in a recruiting campaign there,' said Marriott.

Running his finger down the list, Savage began to read
out the details that Marriott had requested. Finally, he closed
the book and looked up. 'That's it,' he said.

'Only ten weeks of engagements since August last year?'
queried Marriott.

'Yes. There were quite a few weeks when we couldn't
get any bookings at all.'

'I don't wonder you went bust, then,' said Hardcastle.

'That was Vicky,' said Savage.

'What d'you mean, that was Vicky?'

'It was the last straw, her getting murdered. I'd arranged
to take the Playhouse Theatre for the first week after
Christmas. We'd put out the publicity in advance, and
everyone was expecting Victoria Hart to top the bill. A lot
of people in London had seen her before, and they loved
her. But when Vicky was killed, I had to replace her with
Vera, and it didn't go down too well. In fact, Vera got the
bird. It was plainly obvious that she wasn't as good as
Vicky, and the crowd took it out on her. In the end, they
were even throwing cabbages and tomatoes at her. The poor
kid came off in tears.'

'Yes, it happened when we saw the show,' said Hardcastle.
'And just to add to her anguish, you put her up the spout
as well. I heard your escapologist didn't escape either. Still
in chains at the Playhouse, struggling to get out, is he?'

'He was hopeless,' admitted Savage. 'I don't know why
I took him on.'

'Should have got Harry Houdini,' said Hardcastle. 'I saw
him once at the London Hippodrome.'

Savage scoffed. 'It would've cost me about a hundred and
twenty quid a week to book Houdini. Twenty was the most
I could come up with. And that was when I was flush. But

now I can't even pay the rent for the week we had at the Playhouse.'

'What are you going to do now?' asked Hardcastle.

'What d'you think I'm going to do, for God's sake? I've got creditors chasing me all over London.' Savage gave a hopeless shrug of his shoulders. 'I'm a song-and-dance man, and I'm trying to get a booking somewhere. Anywhere. But I'm afraid the *Beaux Belles* is finished for good.'

'If you happen to move house, Mr Savage, drop a note into Cannon Row police station, and let me know where you've gone,' said Hardcastle, without much hope that the actor-manager would comply. From what he knew of debtors, Savage would disappear like morning mist at the first sign of the sun. 'I might want to talk to you again.'

'That Savage ain't having a lot of luck,' commented Hardcastle, as he and Marriott made their way back to the police station. 'I wouldn't think it's a wise thing to do, welshing on theatre owners. And I wouldn't mind betting that young Vera Cobb'll be chasing him for money once her kid's born. That'll put paid to her warbling for a while, I wouldn't wonder, and I reckon she could turn a bit nasty once her dander's up.'

'Fancy a pint, sir?' asked Marriott as they approached the Red Lion on the corner of Derby Gate.

'You paying, Marriott?' asked Hardcastle.

'Yes, sir.'

'Good. I thought you'd never ask.'

It was five o'clock by the time Hardcastle and Marriott returned to Cannon Row.

'Catto!' shouted Hardcastle as he entered his office.

'Yes, sir?' A breathless Catto appeared on the threshold within seconds.

'Where's your jacket, Catto?'

'In the office, sir.' Catto pointed towards the room where the CID had their desks.

'Well, don't come in my office without your jacket on. I don't go and see the superintendent without my coat on, do I?'

'No, sir. Sorry, sir.'

'Right, now then. Sergeant Marriott here has got a list of theatres.'

'Yes, sir?' Catto sounded depressed, probably imagining that he was about to be sent on another round of tiresome, and undoubtedly fruitless, enquiries.

'Know where the assistant provost marshal's got his office, lad?'

'Er, the War Office, sir?'

'No, not the War Office, Catto. You know where them fancy swaddies sit on horses all day, halfway down Whitehall?'

'Yes, sir.'

'It's in there. Take the list that Sergeant Marriott'll give you, and hand it to Colonel Frobisher in person. No one else. Got that, have you?'

'Yes, sir.'

'And if them soldiers are a bit short-sighted, and should happen to salute you by holding their swords upright, be sure to raise your hat, or they'll likely cut your head off. And when you've done that, come back here and tell me you've done it. Got that?'

'Yes, sir.' Catto paused in the doorway. 'What shall I do if this Colonel Frobisher's not there, sir?'

'Use your initiative, lad,' said Hardcastle, and taking off his shoes, began to massage his feet.

Thirteen

Hardcastle and Marriott returned to Windsor on the Friday. Although the previous day's floods had subsided, they had not disappeared altogether. But the trains were able to run again, and the route from the railway station to St Leonard's Road was clear of water.

'Have you rescued the King yet, Stone?' Hardcastle enquired jocularly when he arrived at headquarters.

'The King, sir?' From the stunned expression on Detective Sergeant Stone's face, it was apparent he had yet to discover that what passed for Hardcastle's sense of humour was, at times, difficult to identify.

'I heard he'd been marooned in Windsor Castle by the floods.'

'Oh no, sir,' said Stone. 'He was at Buckingham Palace.'

'I'm only joking, Stone.' Hardcastle laughed. 'I knew he was at Buck House. As a matter of fact, I popped in. He was very interested to know how we were getting on down here with this murder.'

Stone's eyes opened wide. 'He *was*, sir?'

'Oh yes. I'm in there quite often. He lives on my toby, you see. His Majesty asked after you, too, Stone, and he wanted to know how Mr Struthers was getting on in hospital. Talking of which, how is the DI?'

For a moment or two Stone stared at Hardcastle with an incredulous expression on his face. 'Er, coming along all right, sir, so I'm told. Should be out in a day or two, but it'll be some time before he's back to duty.' The Windsor sergeant had taken Hardcastle's comments seriously, and now firmly believed that the London DDI was on intimate terms with the Sovereign.

Hardcastle's remarks did, however, have an amusing corollary. And it also demonstrated how quickly news travelled in a small police force. Later in the day, he met the chief constable in the corridor outside his office.

'Ah, Hardcastle.'

'Good afternoon, sir.'

'I understand that His Majesty was enquiring about the progress you're making in the murder of Victoria Hart and this Sergeant, er . . . '

'Phillips, sir.'

'Yes, Phillips.' The chief constable paused to flick cigarette ash from the lapel of his jacket. 'Do you often visit Buckingham Palace, Hardcastle?'

'Indeed, sir,' said Hardcastle. 'One of the problems of having Buck House in my bailiwick. I'm forever up and down The Mall.' The reality was that, as the senior detective on A Division, Hardcastle was obliged occasionally to pay duty visits to the inspector in charge of the Palace police. But he never got further than the police lodge alongside a patch of grass known as the Entrée.

Nevertheless, Hardcastle's evasive answers had left the chief constable believing the London officer to be far more influential than he actually was.

Having decided to trust Stone with a number of inconsequential enquiries, Hardcastle and Marriott returned to London for the weekend. Although it irked him to be unable to make progress in the two murders he was investigating, he knew that he had to be patient. Most important of all were the enquiries he had entrusted to the military policeman at Horse Guards.

The two detectives were back in London by midday, and Marriott was looking forward to, perhaps, the rest of the day off, and a weekend with his wife and family. But, thanks to another of Hardcastle's unforeseen ideas, it was to be much nearer midnight that day before the sergeant reached his quarters in Regency Street.

'As we've got a few hours to spare, Marriott,' said

Hardcastle, 'I think we'll go down to Bath and have a word with Commander Hart's parents.'

'But do we know they'll be there, sir?' Marriott was not at all pleased at this sudden decision on his DDI's part.

'One sure way of finding out, Marriott. Speak to them on the telephone. I'm sure you can get the number from one of them nice young ladies who answers when you pick the thing up. Tell 'em it's police business.'

Marriott returned to Hardcastle's office ten minutes later. 'They are there, sir, and willing to see us this evening,' he said, trying to keep the disappointment from his voice. 'It's a Captain Joshua Hart, a retired Royal Navy officer.'

'Find out the train times, did you?'

'Yes, sir.' Knowing that the question would be asked, Marriott had made a point of consulting a Bradshaw for details of the rail service to Bath.

It was gone six o'clock on the Friday evening before Hardcastle and Marriott reached the elegant town house that was home to the late Kenneth Hart's parents.

'I trust your journey wasn't too tiresome, Inspector,' boomed Captain Hart, as he led the way into the drawing room. He was a bluff, stocky man, probably sixty or so, and had a pointed beard and a flowing moustache; what the navy called 'a full set'.

'It could have been better, sir.' Hardcastle detested long train journeys, and found them irksome, no matter how fast or comfortable they were.

'This is my wife, Edith,' said Hart, indicating a slender woman in her late fifties who was sitting in an armchair, a woollen shawl clutched tightly around her shoulders. Edith Hart ignored the arrival of the police, and continued to read a copy of *The Lady* magazine. From the woman's frosty disregard, Hardcastle assumed that she did not much care for the police. 'Take a seat and tell me what you'd like to drink, Inspector. You too, Sergeant.'

'Thank you, sir. A whisky if you have it,' said Hardcastle, speaking for both of them.

'Should have some somewhere. Prefer a horse's neck

myself,' muttered Hart, and went into another room to dispense the drinks.

'I'm very sorry about your son, Mrs Hart,' murmured Hardcastle. He was none too good at commiserating with the bereaved, but felt he had to say something to fill the conversational void.

'Thank you,' said Edith Hart. 'We miss him terribly.' After which she lapsed once again into silence, and continued to read.

'There we are, Inspector,' said Hart, returning with the drinks on a silver salver. He noticed Hardcastle looking at it. 'Inscribed with the names of the officers of my last command. Given to me when I was paid off. Now then, tell me what I can do for you.'

'As my sergeant explained on the telephone, Captain Hart, I'm investigating the murder of your daughter-in-law, and also an army sergeant. Both these murders occurred in Windsor within ten days of each other.'

'Sounds a rum do. Think there's a connection, do you?' Hart took a cigarette case from his pocket and offered it to the policemen.

'No, thank you, sir,' said Hardcastle. 'I'm a pipe man.'

'Carry on, Inspector,' said Hart, lighting his cigarette. 'Seems a strange business you're investigating.'

'I think it might have something to do with recruiting, sir,' Hardcastle said eventually, after he had filled his pipe and got it alight. 'And I've since learned that another recruiting sergeant – a Scots Guardsman – was murdered in London last October.'

'But what does it all mean, Inspector?' Hart's expression was one of complete bafflement.

'The only connection is the late Victoria Hart. She was assisting both those sergeants to recruit for the army.'

Edith Hart at last set aside her magazine, and took a sudden interest in the conversation. 'Recruiting? How on earth was she doing that?' she asked in scandalized tones.

Hardcastle was not quite sure how much the Harts knew of Victoria's stage career, but it no longer mattered that they were about to discover something that was possibly unpalatable. And it so happened that they were to find it unpalatable.

'Victoria was a musical-hall song-and-dance artiste, as you probably know, ma'am. At the end of the performance, she would sing a patriotic song and appeal to men in the audience to enlist. Of course, they were encouraged by the scanty costume she wore, and the offer of a kiss for them as took the King's shilling.'

'Good God Almighty!' exclaimed Captain Hart. 'What d'you call a scanty costume?'

Hardcastle described the outfit that several people had seen Victoria wearing, and produced the programme bearing her photograph.

'Ye Gods and little fishes.' Hart appeared to be appalled by this revelation, but it may have been an outrage pretended for the benefit of his wife. He certainly studied the photograph of Victoria for longer than was really necessary before handing it to his wife. 'I had no idea that she was that sort of actress.'

'I knew that girl was no good for Kenneth,' said Edith Hart, returning the small booklet after a cursory glance at its cover. 'The first time he brought her home, I knew she was nothing but a common tart. Whatever possessed the boy to marry her mystifies me completely.' It was obvious that Victoria's mother-in-law had taken a violent dislike to the girl from the outset; Hardcastle's description of her behaviour and apparel, and the photograph, had merely served to confirm her view.

'Don't forget that she *was* an actress, Edith.' Hart spoke mildly. He did not seem to have taken as much of a dislike to his son's wife as Edith had, and was clearly trying to temper what his own wife was saying. In fact, the length of time he had taken looking at Victoria's picture seemed to indicate that he was secretly attracted by the girl's implied promiscuity.

'I don't see that that makes any difference, Josh. There are accepted standards of behaviour in society, you know, actress or not. And that outfit was most certainly not lady-like. I don't know why Kenneth couldn't have married into the service. There are plenty of presentable daughters of naval officers whom he could have married. And they understand what marriage to the Royal Navy involves.' Edith Hart glanced at Hardcastle. 'Her father was a grocer, you know,' she said disparagingly, as if that were the final condemnation. '*My* father was an admiral.'

'Really, ma'am?' It appeared that the woman was being deliberately condescending; she must have known that her late son's father-in-law was nigh on a millionaire. But Hardcastle wondered whether there was any more to be derived from Edith Hart's openly expressed dislike of Victoria, and determined to find out what he could. *Something between Joshua Hart and Victoria, perhaps?* 'Do you think that there might have been someone else who was romantically involved with her, Mrs Hart? After her marriage to your son, I mean.' It was a clumsily framed question, designed to discover if Victoria had been unfaithful to her husband, but it was the best that Hardcastle could do.

'I wouldn't be at all surprised, Inspector. Theatre folk are a raffish lot, and I've always suspected that actresses are a somewhat free and easy class of person.'

'What exactly d'you mean by that, ma'am?'

'Great Scott, Inspector, you're a policeman, you must know what I'm talking about. It's well known that an actress will jump into bed with any man who asks her. In my view, they're harlots, all of them; little better than prostitutes.'

'And d'you think that was the case with Victoria?'

But Edith Hart drew back from voicing a positive denunciation of the actress. 'Well, I wouldn't be at all surprised, Inspector. That girl was . . . ' She paused while she sought the right word. 'Coquettish, I suppose is the best way of describing her.'

'We've examined the records of her involvement in recruiting, ma'am,' said Marriott, 'and since the war broke out, she managed to persuade several hundred to enlist.'

'Yes, well the army falls for that sort of thing,' said Edith scathingly. 'I'll wager she didn't recruit anyone for the Royal Navy. The trouble with Victoria was that she had no respect.

I was her mother-in-law, after all, but she tended to treat
me as though I were her equal. She actually had the temerity
to address me as "Edith" on one occasion. Well, I soon put
her right on that. In my young day, a daughter-in-law knew
her place. Would speak only when she was spoken to, and
certainly wouldn't volunteer opinions of her own. She should
think herself lucky that she didn't have the mother-in-law
I had. Apart from anything else, it would never have
surprised me to learn that Victoria was tied up with this
suffragette movement.'

'We haven't come across anything to suggest that she
was a suffragette, Mrs Hart,' said Hardcastle.

'As far as you know.' The haughty manner of Edith's
response was such as to cast doubt on Hardcastle's detective ability. 'Those wretched amazons are very deceitful
people when it suits them. Politics is a man's business.
What do they want the vote for? I really don't know why
Kenneth couldn't have married that young Charlotte
Gibbons. She was a charming girl, *and* she was the daughter
of a baronet. Brought up in the right sort of society, you
see. But then Kenneth found this chorus girl, or whatever
she was, and before we knew where we were, he was
married to her.'

Hardcastle forbore from pointing out that it was not
uncommon for members of the aristocracy to marry
burlesque actresses known, in the 'Naughty Nineties', as
Gaiety Girls. He realized, however, that whatever he said,
Edith Hart would not be dissuaded from her poor opinion
of the late Victoria Hart, and he kept his counsel.

'Well, thank you for seeing me at such short notice, sir.'
Hardcastle and Marriott stood up. 'And thank you for the
whisky.'

Captain Hart escorted the two policemen out to the hall,
and was careful to close the drawing-room door behind
him.

'You mustn't take too much notice of what my wife has
been saying, Inspector. The truth of the matter is that she
has been hit very hard by Kenneth's death. Women are
perverse creatures, and I think she somehow blamed Victoria

for the boy's loss. Absolute nonsense, of course. If anyone's
to blame it was the skipper of that German submarine –
U24 it was – that sank the old *Dauntless*.'

'I quite understand, sir,' said Hardcastle.

'We don't know any of the details,' Hart continued. 'Only
the brief note from the Admiralty, but Edith has this bee in
her bonnet that, after Victoria's murder, Kenneth felt he had
nothing to live for, and made no attempt to save himself.
The *Dauntless*'s complement was seven hundred and eighty,
and, according to *The Times*, over two hundred of them
survived. But we shall never know.' Hart gave a sigh of
resignation as he opened the front door. 'I hope you don't
regard your journey as a wasted one, Inspector.'

'Not at all, sir,' said Hardcastle as he shook hands with
the retired naval officer. But once in the street, he said to
Marriott, 'Well, that was a bloody waste of time. That
woman certainly had it in for young Victoria.'

'I got the impression that she wouldn't have accepted
anyone her son married, sir,' said Marriott. 'Even when it
came to the baronet's daughter.'

'No, I reckon you're right about that, Marriott.'

'D'you think it's possible that Captain Hart was responsible for Victoria's death, sir?' ventured Marriott.

Hardcastle stopped, and turned to face his sergeant. 'Good
God, Marriott, what on earth makes you think that?'

'Well, sir, Mrs Hart didn't disguise her feelings about
Victoria, but supposing the captain had tried it on with her
and was spurned. She threatened to tell her husband
Kenneth, and Captain Hart topped her.'

'That's the most fanciful theory I've ever heard, Marriott,'
said Hardcastle dismissively. But it did not prevent him
from tucking it away in his mind and thinking about it.

It was very late when Hardcastle and Marriott arrived back
in London.

'Take a cab, Marriott,' said Hardcastle, 'and charge it
to expenses, otherwise I'll have Mrs Marriott after me
again.' He had not forgotten the bruising encounter he had
had with Lorna Marriott on Christmas Day. That did not

particularly worry him, but he knew from long experience
that a detective who had an unhappy home life was unlikely
to be an effective officer. And it was that that concerned
him, rather than Marriott's wife's view of the demands of
the Metropolitan Police.

'Thank you, sir.' Marriott was amazed at Hardcastle's
flouting of the regulations. Usually any of the detectives of
A Division who used a cab, even for duty purposes, was
subjected to an interrogation from the DDI about the avail-
ability of public transport, and why it had not been used.

'See you first thing on Monday morning at the nick.'
Hardcastle waved his umbrella at a cab, exercising his right
as Marriott's senior officer to take the first one to come
along.

When he arrived at his office at Cannon Row, early on the
Monday morning, Hardcastle was agreeably surprised to
find a message awaiting him from Colonel Frobisher.

'An orderly was here not ten minutes ago, sir,' said
Detective Inspector Rhodes, 'to tell you that Colonel
Frobisher has the information you want.'

Fourteen

'Seems these khaki policemen can get going when they have to, Marriott,' said Hardcastle, as the pair arrived at the APM's office at Horse Guards.

'I hope this will be of assistance, Inspector.' Frobisher proffered a manila folder containing several sheets of paper secured by a treasury tag through the top left-hand corner. 'They're the names of the men who enlisted following an appeal by your Mrs Hart when she was appearing at the theatres you mentioned.'

'I must say you didn't waste any time, Colonel. It was only last Thursday that you were given the list.'

'The murder of two recruiting sergeants is as much of interest to me as it is to you, Inspector,' said Frobisher. 'Now then, there are some two hundred names in that file, but God knows how you're going to sort the wheat from chaff.' He crossed to a window and closed it, shutting out a constant cacophony of shouted commands. 'That noise gets on your nerves after a while. They're drilling recruits on Horse Guards Parade. *With broomsticks.*' He shrugged. 'I just hope there'll be sufficient rifles for them when eventually they get to the Front.'

'I see the regiments these men joined are shown on here,' observed Hardcastle, naively believing that possession of that information would make it easier to find them.

Frobisher laughed bitterly. 'So they might be, Inspector, but heaven knows where they are now. Soldiers are sometimes transferred from one regiment to another overnight, just to fill dead men's boots. Literally. And, of course, some of those recruits – ' he gestured at the file Hardcastle was holding – 'will almost certainly be dead themselves by now.

Or at best, back home in hospital. Perhaps even discharged minus arms or legs.'

'I imagine this is asking a big favour, Colonel, but would it be possible to find out which of 'em are dead and which ain't?'

Frobisher pursed his lips. 'Much as I'd like to help, that's a pretty tall order. But we can eliminate some of them almost immediately. Many of them will still be under training at their depots, and others will have been earmarked for a commission and will be undergoing officer training.' Reaching for the lists of theatres that Catto had delivered the previous Thursday, he studied them anew. 'What exactly are you hoping to achieve by this exercise, Inspector?' he asked.

'A seeker after revenge,' said Hardcastle.

'Revenge?' echoed Frobisher. 'I'm sorry, I don't think I quite understand.'

'D'you mind if I smoke, Colonel?'

'Please do.'

Hardcastle spent a few silent moments filling his pipe and lighting it. 'I could be on the wrong track, but my thinking is that someone who was killed or maimed had a relative who blames the recruiters for what happened to their son, father or brother. Or even husband, I suppose. And decided to take it out on Victoria Hart and your two sergeants.'

'Good God!' exclaimed Frobisher. 'That's a bit extreme, surely?'

'I haven't yet come across a murder that's been committed for what you and me would regard as a logical reason, Colonel. Apart from anything else, I've got in mind the biblical quote what the killer of Sergeant Phillips left on the wall at the drill hall.'

'I haven't heard about that,' said Frobisher, leaning forward and displaying a spark of interest. 'What did it say?'

'What was it, Marriott? You're the reader.'

'"*Vengeance is mine; I will repay, saith the Lord.*" At least, sir, we believe it to be Phillips's killer who wrote it there,' said Marriott.

'If that's the case, you may well have a reason for thinking what you are thinking, Inspector. But how are you going to set about finding the killer?'

'Or killers,' commented Hardcastle.

'You think there might be more than one?' Frobisher raised his eyebrows.

'From what I've read in the *Daily Mail*, Colonel, there are a lot of soldiers getting themselves killed over there.'

'True, but surely it's stretching credulity somewhat to imagine that there may be more than one murderer, each of whom had the same motive.'

'Always think the impossible, Colonel, that's my motto,' said Hardcastle tartly. 'Anyway, you were saying that you might be able to cut this list down a bit.'

Frobisher drew a blank sheet of paper across the desk. 'Now if we say that training is about twelve weeks . . . ' He looked up. 'It varies, of course, depending on the regiment, and the demand for reinforcements made by the C-in-C of the British Expeditionary Force. But supposing we take twelve weeks as the minimum.' He glanced at his calendar, and began jotting down dates. A couple of minutes later he screwed the cap on to his fountain pen, and sighed. 'That doesn't seem to help much,' he said. 'Sergeant Mayhew was murdered on the seventeenth of October last year. That means that none of the recruits was out of training by then, so the chances of their having been in action is practically nil. I think you're on the wrong track, Inspector.'

'Isn't it possible that some of them were drafted a touch early, Colonel?' Hardcastle was loath to abandon his theory that some grieving relative had exacted revenge on those responsible for putting their loved one in the firing line.

Frobisher thought about that. 'I suppose so, Inspector,' he said, 'especially if they were recalled reservists, but I'd be disinclined to pin too much hope on finding your man. When you consider the number of men being sent to France, it'd be like looking for a needle in a haystack. There are boatloads leaving Southampton almost every day.'

'Maybe so, Colonel, but we have to go down every road till we come to a dead end. Then we go back to the crossroads and start again, in a manner of speaking. No one ever said our job was simple.'

While Hardcastle was talking, Frobisher was considering what the DDI had said about a draft being sent to join the BEF earlier than usual. 'I'll see what I can find out for you, but it'll not be easy. However, I'll see if I can persuade the powers-that-be to inject a sense of priority into the enquiries. I'll let you know as soon as I have anything for you.'

It was to be another two days before Lieutenant Colonel Frobisher sent a message to say that he had some information.

Hardcastle, however, could not bear to be idle, and although he knew it would be a waste of time, he and Marriott visited the four London theatres at which Victoria Hart had assisted in recruiting. But they learned little. Not unnaturally, the managers at each remembered the vivacious Victoria Hart, and recalled how successful she was in persuading those described by one manager as 'reluctant heroes' to volunteer.

The commissionaire at the Empire Theatre in Leicester Square, himself an old soldier, remembered the night that Sergeant Mayhew was murdered, but being some way from Panton Street, where the actual slaying had taken place, was unable to assist in furthering the police enquiries in any way.

'I suppose you've never heard of someone called Nemo, have you?' asked Hardcastle. At first, he had dismissed the weak suggestion put forward by Detective Sergeant Croft at Vine Street that Nemo might be a showman, but was now grasping at anything that could advance his moribund investigation. 'Like the Great Nemo, for instance?'

'What's that all about, then?' asked the commissionaire.

'It was chalked on a wall near where Sergeant Mayhew's body was found.'

The doorman frowned, as though doing his best to help. 'Don't mean nothing to me, sir. I ain't heard of any Great Nemo. Is that all it said? Just Nemo?'

'No, it said "Nemo me imp", whatever that's supposed to mean.'

'I was in the Grenadier Guards,' said the commission-aire.

'What's that got to do with anything?' asked Hardcastle, by now convinced that this ex-soldier in the fancy uniform just enjoyed having a chat with anyone prepared to stop and gossip awhile.

'Well, the Grenadiers always stood right of the line, next to the Scots Guards, see. The Coldstreamers wouldn't stand next to us because they reckoned they was the senior regi-ment, on account of being formed first. So they insisted on standing down the other end. They ain't senior, of course. They was General Monk's Regiment of Foot, you see, guv'nor. Cromwell's men, they was. But when Charles the Second come back, the crafty Coldstreamers marched up the Tower of London, laid down their arms and then picked 'em up again in the King's name. But the Grenadiers was already serving the King, so we reckoned that having been Monk's men never counted in seniority. Not as King's men.'

'Is all this getting anywhere?' demanded Hardcastle impa-tiently.

'Yeah. Well, the Coldstreamers' motto is *Nulli secundus.* Second to none. Cheeky buggers.'

'God Almighty!' exclaimed Hardcastle, as he and Marriott turned to go.

'But the Scots Guards' motto is *Nemo me impune lacessit*, see,' shouted the old Grenadier at Hardcastle's retreating back.

Hardcastle stopped and turned. 'Say that again.'

'*Nemo me impune lacessit*,' said the commissionaire, although his pronunciation of the Latin tag left much to be desired.

'What's that mean, then?' asked Hardcastle.

'Dunno for sure, guv'nor. A Jock I knew once reckoned it meant "Keep your hands to yourself", but he could've been spinning me a yarn.'

'How d'you know all this?'

'When I joined,' said the commissionaire, puffing out his chest so that his Boer War medal ribbons were more notice-able, 'we had to learn all our battle honours, who in our lot had got Victoria Crosses, and the names of the colonel and all the officers. And we had to learn the mottoes of the other two regiments.'

'But aren't there four Foot Guards regiments altogether?' put in Marriott.

'Yeah, you're right there, squire. The Irish Guards was formed in nineteen-hundred, but we ain't got used to having the Micks around yet.'

'Thanks very much,' said Hardcastle, and, to Marriott's astonishment, handed the commissionaire a shilling. 'Have a drink on me.'

'Gawd bless yer, guv'nor,' said the old soldier, adroitly pocketing the coin with one hand, and raising the forefinger of the other to the peak of his cap.

'What d'you make of that, sir?' asked Marriott, as he and Hardcastle strode away.

'If what our friend says is true, Marriott, it could mean that Mayhew was topped by another soldier. I don't reckon too many civvies would know what the Scots Guards' motto was.'

Colonel Frobisher seemed quite excited when Hardcastle and Marriott arrived at his office.

'I think I might have narrowed the field for you, Inspector.'

'That'd be a help,' murmured Hardcastle.

'The Fourth Battalion of the Royal Fusiliers got a dreadful mauling at Mons. It's a regular battalion, and was one of the first into the fray. I've discovered – it's a long shot, mind you – that there were recruits already in training, but that was cut short and they were sent across to make up the numbers of the depleted Fourth.'

'D'you know when, Colonel?'

Frobisher referred to a report. 'All I can tell you, Inspector, is that the recruiting sergeant who was with Victoria Hart at the Palladium was a Royal Fusilier, and some of the men he recruited went to the Tower of London and were then sent, almost immediately, to the Isle of Wight, the depot of the Fourth Battalion. Some of those recruits were killed at the Battle of the Marne.'

'When was that, Colonel?'

'It took place between the fifth and the tenth of September last year. But if you want to find out who they were, you'll have to speak to the regimental adjutant at the Tower.' Frobisher opened a small notebook. 'He's a dugout officer—'

'D'you mean he's something to do with digging trenches, sir?' asked Marriott.

'No, Sergeant. It's a piece of army slang. A dugout officer is one who had retired, but was called back for duty when the war started. That is to say, he's been dug out of retirement. Anyway,' said Frobisher, glancing back at his notebook, 'his name is Holmes—'

'That sounds like a good omen,' commented Hardcastle. 'His first name's not Sherlock, I suppose?'

Frobisher laughed. 'I'm afraid not, Inspector. Anyway, Major Holmes is the man to see. It'll save you traipsing down to the Isle of Wight.'

'I'll get up to the Tower immediately, Colonel, and many thanks for your help.'

'Perhaps you'd let me know the outcome, Inspector. In the meantime, I'll telephone Monty Holmes and tell you're on your way.'

Hardcastle paused in the doorway. 'One other thing, Colonel. Can you tell me the exact translation of this?'

Frobisher took the slip of paper and studied it. '*Nemo me impune lacessit*? Yes, it means "No one provokes me with impunity". It's the motto of the Scots Guards. They translate it loosely as: "Touch me not with impunity." Same thing, really. Why d'you ask?'

Hardcastle explained about the writing on the wall near where Sergeant Mayhew's body had been found.

'That's most interesting, Inspector. You know, of course, that Mayhew was a Scots Guardsman, and it looks as though the killer knew he was.'

'Which means that whoever topped him could've been a soldier, Colonel.'

'Or a Latin scholar,' said Frobisher drily. 'In view of what you've just told me about the quotation on the wall at the

Windsor drill hall, it looks as though your murderer is an educated man who selected suitable aphorisms for each occasion.'

'I hope he's got one in mind for when he meets the hangman,' muttered Hardcastle.

Frobisher smiled. 'To quote from John Aubrey, Inspector, how about: "To be hanged with the Bible under one arm and the Magna Carta under the other"?'

'Sounds good enough to me, Colonel,' said Hardcastle, who had never heard of John Aubrey.

'Colonel Frobisher telephoned me to say you were coming to see me, Inspector.' The officer who limped across the room was wearing his greatcoat, and leaning heavily on a walking stick. Despite Frobisher saying that Holmes was a 'dugout' officer, Hardcastle assumed that he had been wounded in action at some time. 'I'm not a hero,' Holmes said, noticing Hardcastle's glance. 'I was struck on the ankle by a golf ball at the weekend. Bloody painful it is, too.' He shook hands. 'Montague Holmes. What can I do for you? The APM tells me you're looking into the murder of a couple of recruiting sergeants and an actress. Is that right?'

As succinctly as possible, Hardcastle outlined the circumstances of the murders.

'Sounds interesting,' said Holmes. 'So what can I do to help?' he asked, screwing a monocle into his left eye. 'Incidentally, Colonel Frobisher mentioned that you're interested in our recruits, and I got my clerk to dig out some details.'

'I'm thinking that one of your men who was killed in action some time before the seventeenth of October last, might've had a relative who blamed one or other of the victims, Major.'

'Why that particular date, Inspector?'

'Because that was the date Sergeant Mayhew was topped.'

'Topped?' Holmes stared at Hardcastle, his monocle dropping from his eye.

'Murdered.'

'Ah, I see.' Holmes replaced his monocle, opened a thick

file and spent a few minutes studying it. 'Twenty-eight men were recruited to the Seventh before that date, Inspector.'

'The Seventh?' Now it was Hardcastle's turn to be puzzled. 'Colonel Frobisher mentioned the Fourth.'

'The Royal Fusiliers are the Seventh of Foot, the City of London Regiment, Inspector. We're known colloquially as "The Shiny Seventh".'

'I see,' said Hardcastle, who did not really see at all. He took the list of theatres from his pocket, and checked the names. 'Do you know which of them was recruited at either the Palladium or the Shepherds Bush Empire, Major?'

'No, I'm afraid not, Inspector. We only have the names of the towns where they were attested. So many men are being recruited at the moment that, to be frank, we don't really care where they joined up. I don't think that Kitchener realized, when he started this campaign, just how over-whelming would be the response.' Holmes glanced at the list again. 'However, according to this – ' he tapped the file – 'ten of them have already been reported killed in action, or missing believed killed.'

'Would it be possible to have a list of those men, Major?'

'Certainly.' Holmes crossed to a door on the far side of his office, and called for a sergeant.

'Yes, sir?'

'Sarn't Stevens, get someone to make a copy of this list,' said Holmes, handing the sergeant the file. 'And make it a bit *jildi*. The inspector's waiting.'

'Very good, sir.'

'Shouldn't be too long, Inspector.' Holmes pulled his greatcoat more firmly around himself, and rubbed his hands together. 'People imagine that it's terribly romantic being stationed at the Tower of London, you know. But I'll tell you this, Inspector, it's as cold as bloody charity.'

Some ten minutes passed, during which the conversation turned, inevitably, to the war. Finally, Sergeant Stevens returned and handed Hardcastle a copy of the list containing the names and civilian addresses of the ten dead or missing soldiers that Holmes had mentioned, together with their places of attestation.

'One other thing, Major,' said Hardcastle. 'I'm told that the recruiting sergeant at the Palladium last August was in the Royal Fusiliers.'

Holmes found a page in a large book and scanned it. 'That's correct.'

'I think he might be in some danger, Major. Given that two other recruiting sergeants have been murdered. I wondered if perhaps . . . '

Holmes shut the book. 'Too late, Inspector. He was drafted to the Fourth Battalion shortly afterwards and was killed at the Marne.'

Fifteen

'Have a go at these lists, Marriott.' Hardcastle settled himself in his office chair and shuffled through the sheets of paper. 'We've got the names that Savage gave us of the theatres Victoria Hart appeared at, and we've got the one that Colonel Frobisher got for us. And now Major Holmes has given us the details of them fusiliers what's dead or missing. If we can find the common denominator, we might be getting a bit nearer to finding out who did for young Victoria.' He put his pipe in the ashtray. 'After what Edith Hart was saying about her, I'm almost tempted to put her on the list of suspects,' he said with a chuckle. But he was still thinking about what Marriott had said about the possibility that Captain Joshua Hart had attempted to begin an affair with his daughter-in-law. With fatal results.

'Yes, Victoria's mother-in-law didn't much care for our soubrette, did she, sir?'

Hardcastle shot a sharp glance in his sergeant's direction. 'Don't get clever with me, Marriott,' he said.

Marriott took the lists and retreated to his own office. The calculations proved to be simple, and he returned to the DDI within ten minutes.

'You done already, Marriott?'

'Yes, sir.'

'Better take the weight off your plates, then, and tell me all about it.'

Marriott sat down. 'It was quite easy really, sir. Out of the ten soldiers either killed or missing, three were recruited in Birmingham, two at the Willesden Hippodrome, one at the Finsbury Park Empire and one at the Palace Theatre of Varieties in Leicester. Victoria Hart wasn't at any of the last three, but she was certainly at the Birmingham Empire, but between the twenty-fourth and twenty-ninth of August. Those men were recruited on the fourteenth, so I reckon that leaves them out. Apart from which, according to Savage, she didn't take any part in recruiting in Birmingham. That leaves the Palladium in Argyll Street.'

'Ah! The Palladium. What about the Palladium, Marriott?'

'Three of the dead men on Major Holmes's list were recruited there during the week Mrs Hart was handing out kisses to anyone who was prepared to—'

'Die for King and Country,' interrupted Hardcastle, cynically completing Marriott's sentence for him. 'Got the names there, have you?'

'Yes, sir. Harry Ogden, Tom Briggs and a Cyril Tilley, sir. The first two were eighteen when they were killed, and Tilley was nineteen.'

'If they were killed, Marriott. They might just be missing.'

'I reckon they're a goner, sir. According to my brother-in-law in the Middlesex Regiment, it's very unusual for a missing man to turn up. He reckons that once the war's over, there'll be thousands of men who were never found. He told me that he's seen men blown to pieces when a shell from one of those German seventy-seven howitzers lands even as far away as twenty yards from them. Usually they never find any remains.'

'You're a real Job's comforter, you are, Marriott,' commented Hardcastle. 'However, have you got the addresses of their next of kin?'

'I've certainly got the addresses they gave when they signed on, sir, but whether those are their real addresses or whether they made them up isn't known. What's more, they sometimes put up their age when they sign on, and if they don't want their folks to know, they give a false address.'

'So it's possible that their people wouldn't even know they're dead,' said Hardcastle. 'I'll tell you this much, Marriott: this country will never be the same after this war's over.'

'If they don't know they're dead, sir, that rules out the vengeance theory.'

'True, Marriott,' said Hardcastle thoughtfully. 'So, if my thinking's correct, it's only the ones who've been told that we should be looking at.'

The address provided by Tom Briggs when he enlisted was in Tansey Road, Poplar, in London's East End. The dead soldier's next of kin had been recorded by the military as Joseph and Fanny Briggs. But that record proved, in part, to be out of date.

Although it was a mean, terraced house, the windows were sparklingly clean, the curtains recently washed and the doorstep freshly whitened with soapstone.

The woman who answered the door was probably no more than forty, but her careworn face gave the impression of a woman much older. Her hair, prematurely grey, was drawn back into a tight bun.

'Yes?' She wiped her chapped hands on her apron, and looked suspiciously at the two policemen.

'Mrs Fanny Briggs, is it?' enquired Hardcastle as he raised his hat.

'Yes.'

'We're police officers, Mrs Briggs.'

'Oh no, not again.' Mrs Briggs, her face draining of colour, clutched at the doorpost for support.

For a moment Hardcastle thought the woman was about to faint. Stepping across the threshold, he took hold of her arm. 'There's nothing to worry about, Mrs Briggs, I can promise you.'

Fanny Briggs recovered slightly at that assurance. 'I thought for a minute you'd come to tell me that Eddie had been killed,' she said.

'Who's Eddie?'

'My son. My other son.'

'No, it's not about Eddie.'

'Tom was killed at the Marne last September,' said Mrs Briggs listlessly, 'and my husband at Mons in August. Joe had only been back a couple of weeks.'

'Joe was your husband, was he?' queried Hardcastle.

'He was a reservist in the Royal Fusiliers. Got called

back the minute the war started. He'd been working on the trams for the last three years. A driver, he was.' Suddenly realizing that this conversation was being conducted on the doorstep, Mrs Briggs belatedly invited the detectives in.

The sitting room was neat and tidy, although sparsely furnished with poor quality chairs. Even though it was winter, there was no fire in the grate, just a carefully folded piece of newspaper shaped like a fan.

'Well, if you haven't come to tell me about Eddie, what are you here for?' asked Mrs Briggs.

Hardcastle, now in something of a quandary, was loath to question Fanny Briggs about the murders. She had lost her husband and a son, admittedly both before the murder of Sergeant Mayhew. However, in the DDI's view, she would not have been capable either of Mayhew's brutal murder, or those of Victoria Hart and Sidney Phillips. But perhaps her surviving son, Eddie, had wrought vengeance for the death of his father and brother.

'Where is your son Eddie, Mrs Briggs?'

'In Belgium, at a place called Ypres, I believe. I haven't seen him since the war started. He joined up straight away – in August last year – and went over within weeks. He writes to me whenever he can, and he says it's quite safe where he is.'

This was clearly not the time to tell Mrs Briggs that Ypres was one of the most vulnerable places on the Western Front, and that since the end of last October it had been pounded constantly by German artillery on the Messines Ridge.

It was Marriott who stepped in. 'We're sorry to have bothered you, Mrs Briggs. We didn't know that your son Tom had been killed. Please accept our condolences.'

'What did you want him for, anyway?' Fanny Briggs's face creased into a frown.

'We're trying to trace another young man who was recruited at the Palladium Theatre the same night as your son. We thought Tom might've been able to help.'

'He's beyond helping anyone now,' said Tom's widowed mother sadly, but did not ask what it was that the police thought her late son could assist them with.

'We'll see ourselves out, Mrs Briggs,' said Hardcastle, 'and I'm sorry to have disturbed you. I hope that Eddie comes home safe and sound when this dreadful war's over.'

But Eddie did not come home. He remained in Ypres, and was killed the following May by masonry falling from the ruined Cloth Hall when it was struck by yet another shell. All in all, it proved to be an unlucky family. In 1917, the house in Tansey Road, Poplar, received a direct hit from a landmine dropped from a German Gotha bomber. The house was completely wrecked, as were the houses on either side of it. Mrs Fanny Briggs was one of the dead.

'Well, we didn't have much luck there,' remarked Hardcastle, as he and Marriott strolled down Tansey Road. 'But if anyone had cause to be upset with the army, it was Mrs Briggs.' He stopped to fill his pipe. 'I think we'll call it a day, Marriott. Go home and see your lady wife.'

'Thank you, sir.'

'And give Mrs Marriott my regards.'

The following morning, they travelled south of the river. This time they made for Cyril Tilley's address in Robsart Street, Stockwell.

'Yes?' The man who answered the door had one arm.

'Mr Tilley?'

'That's me. Fred Tilley. Who are you?'

'Police,' said Hardcastle.

'Well, whatever it is, I never done it,' said Tilley, with a dry, humourless laugh. 'Or maybe you've found me other arm.'

'We want to talk to you about when your son Cyril was recruited, Mr Tilley.'

'Waste of bloody time, that is. He's dead. But I s'pose you'd better come in.' Tilley showed them into a parlour very similar to the one at Poplar in which they had been the previous day.

'I've been told that he joined up one night at the Palladium in Argyll Street.'

'S'right.' Tilley waved at a dilapidated settee, a mute invitation for the policemen to sit down.

But Hardcastle and Marriott remained standing.

'Always round the music halls, was Cyril. Dunno what he saw in 'em, personally. I think he fancied being an actor hisself. But he'd seen that girl who pranced around the stage wearing next to nothing. She was called . . . ' Tilley furrowed his brow. 'S'no good, I can't remember.'

'Victoria Hart,' said Marriott.

'That's the one. I reckon he had a crush on her. Went to see her whenever he could. Any road, he was up the Palladium back in August, not a week after the war started. When he come home, he was full of it. There was some recruiting sergeant on the stage at the end of the show, and that there Victoria what's-her-name offered to give a kiss to anyone what signed up. Well, when it come to pretty girls, our Cyril's brains just flew out the window, so up he went, gets a kiss and that was that. All of a sudden, he finds hisself in the Kate Carney, and up the Tower of London before you can say knife.'

'Yes, we know about that, Mr Tilley.'

'Well, if that's the case, what you here for? He was killed last September at the Battle of the Marne. Done for my Dolly, did that. Hardly been out of bed since. The doctor reckons it's called nervous something. Nervous ability, would it be?'

'Nervous debility,' volunteered Marriott.

'Yeah, that's it. So I have to do the best I can, only having one arm.'

'Was Cyril your only son, Mr Tilley?'

'Yes. Now it's just me and the missus.'

'Were you in the war, Mr Tilley?' asked Marriott, nodding at Tilley's empty sleeve.

'In the wars, more like. Me own fault really. Come home from the boozer pissed, and got hit by a tram. Never saw it. Ain't worked since. Anyway, me skin-an'-blister comes over from Lewisham when she can, and gives a hand out. But you still ain't told me what you want.'

Once again, Marriott came to Hardcastle's rescue, and gave the same fictitious reason for their visit as they had given Mrs Briggs.

'I think we're on a bit of a wild-goose chase, Marriott,' Hardcastle said, as they turned out of Robsart Street into Stockwell Road. 'There's no way that Tilley could've strangled Victoria Hart, not with one arm missing. The pathologist reckoned that there were the marks of two hands round her throat.'

The visit to Acton was even more frustrating than the previous two.

The house in Dordrecht Road was of the sort that one would expect to be occupied by middle-income clerks; perhaps those who worked for solicitors or in a bank.

A tall man in shirtsleeves came to the door. Looking quizzically at the two men standing on the step, he asked, 'Have you come from the water board about the leak?'

'No, sir, we're police officers,' said Hardcastle.

'Good heavens, what's happened?'

'Are you by any chance Mr Ogden?'

'No, my name's Campbell. Jack Campbell. You'd better come in.'

'I'm Divisional Detective Inspector Hardcastle of Scotland Yard, Mr Campbell.' For a moment, the DDI thought that, at last, he might have arrived at the right place. But only if the Campbells had a son who had joined the army under the name of Ogden.

The sitting room was in chaos. Like the hall, there were tea chests everywhere, and there were no curtains at the windows.

'You'll have to excuse the mess,' said Campbell, 'but we only moved in yesterday.'

'Jack . . . ' A woman entered the room. Nearly as tall as her husband, she had long jet-black hair that lent her a slightly Latin appearance. 'Oh, I'm sorry, I didn't realize we had company.' She gazed enquiringly at the two detectives.

'This is my wife, Florence,' said Campbell, and turning to his wife, explained, 'These gentlemen are police officers, Flo.'

'Oh God, it's not about Murray, is it?' A sudden expression of grave concern crossed the woman's face.

'No, dear, they're looking for someone called Ogden.' Campbell turned to address Hardcastle. 'Our son Murray is a captain with the Eleventh Hussars, somewhere on the Western Front.'

'I'll make some tea. We could do with a break,' said Florence Campbell, and retired from the room.

'Is Captain Campbell your only son, sir?'

'Yes, why d'you ask?'

'We're looking for the relatives of a soldier called Harry Ogden, a private in the Royal Fusiliers. This was the address Ogden gave when he enlisted last August. At the Palladium in Argyll Street.'

'At the Palladium?' Campbell sounded surprised.

'Yes, sir. There have been quite a few recruiting campaigns taking place in theatres all over the country.'

'I see. I didn't know that. I suppose you want to tell them that this unfortunate young man's been killed.' Campbell shook his head wearily. 'This futile war is going to take all my son's generation, you know, Inspector,' he said.

'I imagine they've already been informed that Ogden was killed last September at the Battle of the Marne.'

'Then what . . . ? I don't understand.'

'As a matter of fact, we're investigating two cases of murder, Mr Campbell.'

'Good heavens! What, here in London?'

'No, both at Windsor, sir, although we think there may be a connection with another one that took place in London. I needn't weary you with the details, but it's important that we find the relatives of Private Ogden. Have you heard of anyone called Ogden?'

'No, I'm sorry. The name doesn't mean anything to me.'

Mrs Campbell returned with a tray of tea and a plate of biscuits. 'I'm sorry about the mess,' she said, 'but my husband probably told you we only moved in yesterday. If you'd like to shift those books from the settee, you're welcome to sit down.'

Hardcastle smiled. 'We're all right standing, Mrs Campbell. We do a lot of it in our line of business.'

Florence Campbell poured the tea and handed round cups.

'The inspector was just saying that he's investigating two murders in Windsor, Flo. And another in London.'

'Good heavens, how exciting. D'you know who did them?' asked Mrs Campbell, sipping genteelly at her tea. 'No, of course you don't. What a silly question. You wouldn't be here if you had.' She smiled sweetly at the detectives. 'So why *are* you here?'

'I was just explaining to your husband, ma'am, that we wish to interview the relatives of Private Harry Ogden in connection with these murders.'

'My word! D'you think they might have done them?'

'We don't know, but that's why we're making enquiries.'

'Have you heard of anyone called Ogden, Mrs Campbell?' Marriott looked around for somewhere to put his teacup, eventually settling for a windowsill.

'No, never. What makes you think they might have been here?'

'It was the address young Ogden gave when he joined the army,' Hardcastle explained again. 'What was the name of the people you bought this house from, Mr Campbell?'

'We haven't bought it, Inspector. We're renting it. I'm deputy manager at Dean's Bank in The Vale. But I doubt I shall be here for very long. I'm hoping to secure a manager's post in Birmingham very shortly. But in answer to your question, no, I don't know who the previous occupants were. Perhaps the letting agents will be able to tell you. They're called Jeffreys and they have offices in The Vale, just along from my bank.'

'I have a nasty feeling that we've backed the wrong horse, Marriott. Unless we have bit of luck at this here Jeffreys place, I think we'll have to knock it on the head and start all over again.'

Hardcastle's pessimistic mood persisted as he and Marriott made their way to the letting agents that Jack Campbell had mentioned.

A young man rose from behind a desk and beamed at the two policemen, doubtless believing them to be prospective clients. Hardcastle wondered why he was not in the army.

'May I help you, sir?' The young assistant asked unctuously, revolving his hands around each other as if washing them.

'I'm a police officer.'

'Oh!' The young man's welcoming smile vanished instantly, and he went red in the face. Hardcastle considered the possibility that he might be up to no good. Either fraud or embezzlement crossed his mind.

'I've just left the house in Dordrecht Road that you let to a Mr and Mrs Campbell,' said Hardcastle.

'Ah yes, a very desirable property,' said the assistant, recovering as his professionalism came to the fore again.

'Who were the previous occupants?'

'I'm not sure that I can divulge—'

'Well, lad, you'd better get hold of someone with a bit of authority who can "divulge", as you put it. Because I don't have time to waste on tuppenny-ha'penny clerks.'

The youth hastened away to return with an older man in a black jacket and striped trousers.

'I'm the manager, and I understand from my assistant that you're from the police.' The man donned a pair of pince-nez, and peered down his nose.

'That's so,' said Hardcastle, 'and I'd be obliged if you'd furnish me with the name and present address of the people who occupied the house in Dordrecht Road that's been occupied since yesterday by Mr and Mrs Campbell.'

'I'm afraid that I am unable to release privileged information of that sort without the consent of the client for whom we act,' said the manager in a voice loud and haughty enough to let his staff know that he was not to be browbeaten, even by the police. 'I suppose you'd have to get some sort of warrant. But that's your business.'

'Indeed it is,' said Hardcastle, 'and I forgot to mention that anyone obstructing a Scotland Yard divisional detective inspector investigating the murder of two members of His Majesty's Forces is likely to run into serious trouble with the Defence of the Realm Act. And, as you will undoubtedly know, those cases are only tried at the Old Bailey.' He had no idea whether the manager's prevarication would constitute such an offence, but neither did the manager.

'I shan't keep you a moment, officer.' The thoroughly cowed manager scurried away at an even faster rate than his assistant had done minutes previously. The assistant, now safely behind his desk, watched the manager's craven capitulation with some degree of carefully concealed amusement.

'As if we haven't got enough to contend with,' muttered Hardcastle, 'we have to put up with petty jacks-in-office like him.'

The manager returned almost as soon as he had gone, and thrust a piece of paper into Hardcastle's hand. 'This is the name of the last tenant, Inspector, but I can't tell you where he is now. The rent was fully paid up, you see, so his whereabouts are of no further interest.'

Hardcastle stared in disbelief at the name on the piece of paper. 'Well I'm buggered,' he said.

On the far side of the office, a lady typist coughed affectedly.

Sixteen

It was on the very edge of the Forêt de Brugny, some ten to twelve miles south-west of the River Marne in France, that the soldier saw the corporal of the Military Mounted Police, and ducked behind some bushes.

But the provost corporal, easily distinguished by his blue cap cover, had seen the soldier first. Reining in his horse, he opened his webbing holster, and withdrew his revolver.

'Come out of there with your hands in the air, laddie.' And just to encourage him, the corporal fired a round over the soldier's head.

Slowly the man emerged, his hands held high. His uniform was ragged and mud-stained, and he had at least three days' growth of beard. But he had no rifle, no bayonet and no cap. In fact, he had no equipment at all. The only indication of his regiment was the tarnished brass bar, one on each epaulette, bearing the letters RF.

'And where d'you think you're going?' Still pointing his revolver at the man, the corporal leaned forward slightly, holding on to the pommel for support.

'I don't know.'

'I don't know, *Corporal*!' insisted the policeman. 'And stand up properly when you talk to an NCO.' He jerked his revolver up and down to emphasize his order.

The soldier drew himself into some semblance of attention. 'I've lost my memory, Corporal. I don't know what I'm doing.'

The corporal let out a derisive laugh. 'Tell me the old, old story, son. Let's have your paybook, then.'

'I've lost it, Corporal.'

'What mob are you in, then?'

'Royal Fusiliers, Corporal.' In view of the regimental insignia on the soldier's uniform, there was no denying it. 'Fourth Battalion.'

'Lost memory be-buggered. You remembered that easily enough. The Fourth RFs are bloody miles away from here. I know what you are, son, you're a gutless, shirking, skulking bloody deserter, aren't you? I've seen a few in my time, an' I recognize 'em instantly.'

The young soldier gazed at his questioner with a forlorn expression on his face. He knew what was going to happen next.

'What's your number, rank and name, son?'

'12473 Private Ogden H., Corporal.'

'Well, my son, you're under arrest.'

It was the end of a desperate attempt to escape the din of constant, mind-numbing shelling, the appalling conditions of trench warfare, the rats that brought disease and pestilence and the horror of seeing men blown to pieces. And the ever-present dread of death or serious injury.

It was that unspeakable hell that brought many soldiers to the brink of losing their reason . . . and beyond. But these brutalized men had found different ways of dealing with such torture. Many shrugged, and cynically put into song a verse, penned by an anonymous soldier, that included the lines: *The bells of Hell go ting-a-ling-a-ling. Death where is thy sting-a-ling-a-ling.* Others advised their comrades that it was 'unlucky to be killed on a Friday', an ironic phrase that became more common as the war progressed. Some soldiers drank to excess, when they could get hold of alcohol; some committed suicide, either with their own weapons or by making a mad frontal assault on the enemy's front-line machine guns. A few shot off trigger fingers, only to be sent to the rear with a label marked with the ominous letters SIW – self-inflicted wound – to face a court martial. But a few, either through cowardice, or because their minds had gone, deserted.

Harry Ogden had chosen the latter course. When the Battle of the Marne was at its most intense, he simply walked away from the ration party of which he was a member, and disappeared into the darkness. Seconds later, the ration party, a lance-corporal and the remaining three men, were blown to smithereens by a 5.9-inch shell fired from a German howitzer known to the troops as a Jack Johnson, so nicknamed after the famous American black boxer. All the members of the ration party were listed as killed in action, there being no remains sufficient to enable the authorities positively to identify them. It was assumed that Ogden was among the dead.

For the first six days, Ogden travelled by night, sustaining himself with a few hard-tack biscuits and a tin of Tommy Tickler's plum-and-apple jam that he had filched from the rations he had been carrying. He became adept at avoiding the military police, and anyone else in authority, and once hurriedly threw himself into a ditch just as a general passed by in a staff car.

On the seventh day of his absence from his battalion, Ogden had the good fortune to call at a remote farmhouse occupied by a young widow – she was but twenty years of age – who gave him shelter and food. The woman, Monique Sochard, was attempting to run the family farm single-handed following the death of her husband Antoine in the opening stages of the war.

Although Ogden knew nothing of farming – he was a London boy, born and bred – he helped Monique with the heavier work in exchange for his sanctuary and his keep. And he learned how to milk a cow. In the course of the relationship, Ogden picked up a smattering of French, and Monique learned a few words of English.

Not only was the woman unconcerned that he was a deserter, she actually applauded his decision to escape from the madness of war. And to support Ogden's actions, she provided him with her dead husband's civilian clothing, and obligingly hid him in the loft every time British soldiers called at the farmhouse in search of food.

Over the weeks, it was inevitable that the relationship between the two young people developed to the point where it became intimate. And it was that that caused Ogden to stay longer than he should have done, despite the risk to his liberty.

Not long after his arrival at the farm, he had rigged up a rudimentary shower in an outhouse attached to one of the barns. Although the water was cold – and seemed colder because it was winter – it served to remove most of the grime of a day's work. In any case, it was better than anything he had enjoyed in the front line.

Harry Ogden assumed that what happened on that particular day had happened by accident, but he was unfamiliar with the ways of passionate women.

Having finished mucking out the stable of the one horse that the farm had been allowed to keep, he went into the barn. Believing Monique to be in the kitchen preparing supper – as she always did at that time – he stripped off his clothing and entered the outhouse.

Only to find that a naked Monique was emerging from beneath the shower's icy needlepoints of water.

Far from emitting a scream and seizing a towel, as the best novelettes would have one believe, she gazed brazenly at the equally naked Ogden, carefully appraising his strong, young body. It was Ogden, a virgin, who was embarrassed by the encounter.

Monique, deprived of a man's affections for over a month – a long time for the young farmer's widow – took immediate command of the opportunity she had so cunningly engineered. Smiling, she walked towards the young soldier and put her arms around him, claiming that she needed warming. Supper was forgotten, and Harry Ogden was introduced to the delights of the girl's frenzied lovemaking.

From that day on, Harry Ogden and Monique Sochard shared a bed.

But finally, despite Monique's pleading that he should stay until the war was over, Ogden decided to continue what he had set out to do. Had he known that he was already officially dead, he might have been tempted to stay forever. Early one morning, he began a journey that he hoped would eventually take him to the coast, where he would look for the skipper of a vessel willing to take him to England.

Three days later, he was arrested, bitterly regretting having donned his uniform again on leaving Monique Sochard's bed.

'I don't bloody believe it,' fumed Hardcastle. Apart from muttering the oath that had offended the lady typist, he had purposely not displayed any excitement at the name on the slip of paper that the letting agent had given him. In fact, he had said something about it not helping. But once clear of the agent's office he had revealed the name to Marriott.

'Captain Valentine Porteous, the recruiting officer from Windsor, Marriott. Would you believe that?'

'D'you mean he was the previous occupant of the house in Dordrecht Road, sir?' Marriott was as stunned by the information as his chief. 'But what connection had he got with Harry Ogden?'

'That is something we're going to have to find out, Marriott. But knowing how successful we've been so far in tracking down the killer, it's possible that Ogden just plucked a name out of thin air. Probably smokes Ogden tobacco, and thought that would do.'

'Bit of a coincidence, though, isn't it, sir?'

'Too much of one, Marriott. On the other hand, it's possible that Ogden lived in Dordrecht Road, but at a different number, and knowing that Porteous was an army officer, put his address down as some sort of joke.'

'Funny sort of joke,' commented Marriott. 'Shall I check with the town hall, sir? See if they've got a record of anyone called Ogden living nearby?'

'Don't you do it, Marriott. Get Catto off his arse and send him.'

Much to Marriott's chagrin, Hardcastle decided that an immediate return to Windsor was called for, and the pair arrived there at seven o'clock that evening.

Making immediately for the office occupied by Detective Sergeant Stone, Hardcastle demanded to know the outcome of the enquiries that he had entrusted to the Windsor officer.

'I called at the officers' mess at Victoria Barracks, sir,'

said Stone, 'and ascertained that, as far as could be verified, Captain Porteous was in the mess most of the day that Sergeant Phillips had been murdered.'

'*Most* of the day?' snorted Hardcastle. 'Fat lot of good that is, Stone.'

At lunchtime the following day, and after the usual rigmarole that had to be gone through in order to gain access to a barracks in time of war, Hardcastle and Marriott were eventually escorted to the officers' mess.

'Can I help you?' A major had been passing the door as the two policemen entered.

'I'm looking for Captain Porteous, Major. I'm Divisional Detective Inspector Hardcastle of Scotland Yard.'

The major laughed. 'Oh, don't tell me you're after him too.' But before Hardcastle could respond, the major added, 'You'd better have a word with the officer who's standing in for him. Come this way, Inspector.'

There were about ten officers in the anteroom, sitting around drinking and reading newspapers or magazines.

The major led them to a table near the bar. 'This is Captain Vernon Toogood,' he said, indicating a young man with a black eye-patch, whose uniform bore the collar badges of the Grenadier Guards. 'Vernon, this is an inspector from Scotland Yard. He's looking for Val Porteous.'

'Aren't we all?' said Toogood, smiling as he rose to his feet and shook hands. 'Sit down, Inspector, and let me get you a drink. You too, er . . . ?'

'Detective Sergeant Marriott, sir.'

'What's your poison, gentlemen?'

Once the trio was settled, each with a pint of beer in front of him, Hardcastle explained that he needed to see Captain Porteous urgently.

'It's a funny old business, Inspector,' began Toogood, 'but late yesterday afternoon, Porteous received a telephone call, here in the mess. Whatever it was about seemed to disturb him greatly. However, as he's always in the mess in the evening – and wasn't on this occasion – I went to his room. And, lo and behold, he'd vamoosed. I had a quick look round, and although he'd left some military kit, all his personal belongings had gone.'

'Was there any indication *why* he'd left, Captain?'

'Not a word, old boy. I didn't quite know what to do about it, so I had a word with my commanding officer, and he got in touch with the military police immediately. I've no idea what happened after that.'

'Is the CO here now?' asked Hardcastle.

'Indeed he is,' said Toogood. 'Come with me.' He led them to a table in the far corner of the room where a lieutenant colonel of the Grenadier Guards was seated.

Seeing that Toogood was accompanied by two strangers, the colonel folded his copy of *The Times*, and stood up. 'Got some more recruits for us, Vernon?' he asked jocularly.

'These gentlemen are from Scotland Yard, Colonel. Inspector Hardcastle and Sergeant Marriott. They're looking for Val Porteous.'

'Sit down, gentlemen, sit down. I suppose that Vernon told you that Porteous has disappeared in rather odd circumstances. "Conduct unbecoming an officer and a gentleman," eh? Especially in time of war, I can tell you. The authorities take a very poor view of such behaviour.'

'Captain Toogood told me that you contacted the military police, Colonel,' said Hardcastle.

'Certainly. I spoke to the assistant provost marshal of London District on the telephone.'

'That would be Colonel Frobisher.'

The colonel raised his eyebrows. 'D'you know him, then? Yes, I suppose you would, being from the Yard,' he said, answering his own question. 'Well, Ralph Frobisher took a few details and said that he'd look into it. That's all I can tell you, I'm afraid. The recruiting's none of my damned business, of course, but in the meantime I asked Vernon here to look after it until either Porteous returns, or a replacement is found. It's not a very strenuous job, is it, Vernon? Just swearing in a few chaps every so often, and he'll be able to combine it quite easily with his job here.' The colonel paused and laughed. 'What, actually, is your job here, Vernon?'

'I'm the transport officer, Colonel.' Vernon laughed too; he knew that the CO knew what his job was, but he also knew the colonel's predilection for lame witticisms.

'One other thing, Captain Toogood . . . ' said Hardcastle. 'What time did Captain Porteous receive this telephone call?'

'It must have been about half-past five, I suppose.'

'I reckon it was that bloody letting agent who telephoned Porteous, Marriott,' said Hardcastle, 'and told him that we were taking an interest in him. I knew Porteous was dodgy.'

It was on New Year's Eve 1914 that Private Harry Ogden of the Royal Fusiliers was arraigned before a field general court martial.

There was none of the ceremonial of a peacetime court; it was conducted in a ruined barn a mile or two behind the front line.

Ogden was charged with cowardice in the face of the enemy, and being a deserter while on active service. They were the only two counts on the indictment, and each carried the death penalty.

Three officers, a major, a captain and a lieutenant, all from his own battalion, were appointed to sit in judgement on him. Seated in a row behind a blanket-covered army table, they peered closely at the prisoner as he was marched in by the battalion's provost sergeant.

The proceedings did not take long. The damning evidence of the police corporal who had arrested him sealed Ogden's fate. The court quickly decided that the young soldier's offences were exacerbated by the fact that he had deserted the previous September, during the Battle of the Marne, and furthermore had avoided capture for over three months. How he had managed to remain at large for so long, and where he had hidden during that time, was of no interest to the court, and they did not seek to question him about it.

A second lieutenant with two months' active service – he had been commissioned after Ogden absented himself – was selected to act as the defending officer.

The subaltern, who six months previously had been a school prefect, gravely informed the court that Ogden was little more than a boy. He was, the officer pointed out, only seventeen at the time of his enlistment, but had put up his age. He portrayed it as an act of patriotism. As much as the officer's limited experience allowed him to make an impassioned plea in mitigation, he described the hell of the trenches, the nearness of instant death and the effect of constant shelling. The members of the court listened throughout with stony expressions.

At the end of it all – and it took but twenty minutes – the hapless Private Harry Ogden was sentenced to die by firing squad. Sobbing and screaming, he was half dragged, half carried from the courtroom. Uppermost in his mind was that he would never again enjoy the carnal pleasures to which Monique Sochard had introduced him.

Four days later, the remnants of the battalion were drawn up in a hollow square, the lone figure of Ogden at its centre, to hear that Field Marshal Sir John French, the Commander-in-Chief, had confirmed the sentence.

At four-thirty the following morning, accompanied by the chaplain and escorted by regimental policemen, Ogden was taken from his cell to a nearby railway embankment where a stake had been placed in the ground. A sergeant secured the prisoner to the wooden post with rope, and then blindfolded him. The medical officer placed a small piece of white cloth over Ogden's heart and stood back, allowing the chaplain to intone a few pointless words of comfort in the condemned man's ear.

Finally, a lieutenant dropped his handkerchief and a volley of rifle fire ended Private Harry Ogden's days on earth.

Hardcastle and Marriott returned to London on the afternoon of Friday the fifteenth of January, intent upon seeing the APM at the earliest opportunity. But that interview was destined to be delayed until the following Monday.

Hardcastle entered his office at Cannon Row police station, and was joined immediately by Detective Inspector Rhodes.

'Two things, sir,' said Rhodes.

'And they are, Mr Rhodes?' Hardcastle took off his coat and hat, and hung them on the hatstand.

'Firstly, sir, Catto made enquiries at the Acton town hall, and could find no trace of anyone called Ogden living in Dordrecht Road. Secondly, I received a telephone call yesterday from a Mr Campbell, also of Dordrecht Road. He says that you saw him earlier the previous day. Enquiries re Ogden?' Rhodes looked up from his notes.

'That's correct, Mr Rhodes. What did Mr Campbell have to say?'

'He said that this morning, sir, a letter was delivered to his house, addressed to a Mr Ogden.'

'Did he say what was in the letter?'

'No, sir, he didn't open it. But in view of the fact that the envelope was marked "War Office", and it was addressed to this Ogden, about whom Mr Campbell said you'd been making enquiries, he thought he should inform you. In the circumstances, I deemed it necessary to have possession taken of it, and I sent Watkins to Acton to seize it.' Rhodes handed over the letter.

'I'm much obliged, Mr Rhodes. Thank you.' Hardcastle took the letter from the envelope. 'I thought they just sent a printed form for this sort of thing,' he said. Putting on his glasses, he read aloud the contents, which surprisingly were longer than the usual notification of a death in action:

Dear Sir

It is my painful duty to inform you that a report has been received from the Headquarters of the British Expeditionary Force notifying the death of No 12473 Private Harry Ogden, 4th Royal Fusiliers, which occurred on Tuesday 5th January 1915, and not as previously notified on Tuesday 8th September 1914. I am further directed to express the sympathy of the Army Council at your loss. The cause of death was killed in action.

I am, sir, your obedient servant . . .

Hardcastle replaced the letter in its envelope and laid it on his desk. 'Well, I don't know what the hell that means, Marriott, but I'm hoping that Colonel Frobisher can shed some light on it when we see him on Monday.'

Seventeen

'Sorry I was unable to see you before today, Inspector,' said Frobisher on the Monday morning, 'but I had to take some of my chaps down to Southampton over the weekend to sort out a bit of trouble that promised to develop into a mutiny. A couple of dozen hotheads decided to confront the commanding officer with their grievances. Not a good idea.'

'I wanted to see you about Captain Porteous . . . and other matters, Colonel.' Hardcastle was not much interested in the reasons for the APM's absence from London, other than it had delayed his enquiry by two days.

'I thought that might be what you wanted to discuss.' Frobisher unlocked a desk drawer and took out a file. 'Damned funny business, Porteous disappearing like that, but I don't suppose I can tell you any more about it than you know already.'

Hardcastle told Frobisher of his visit to Victoria Barracks, and the outcome of his enquiries there, such as it was, and about his visit to Dordrecht Road in search of Harry Ogden. Finally, he produced the letter that Detective Inspector Rhodes had ordered to be seized from the Campbells.

Frobisher read the letter. 'I know about this,' he said, tapping the stark missive with his forefinger. 'Ogden was executed by firing squad on the fifth of January for desertion and cowardice. I get reports of all field general courts martial resulting in capital punishment that concern regiments whose headquarters are in London District.'

'Executed?' exclaimed Hardcastle. 'But it says there – ' he waved a hand at the letter – 'that Ogden was killed in action.'

'They always put that when a soldier is shot as a result of a court-martial sentence, Inspector. It tends to soften the blow as far as the next of kin are concerned. Of course, it comes out in the end, so I don't know why they bother.'

'Is that so?' Hardcastle scoffed. 'But if they executed him, how come they got the date wrong? At least, that's the way I read that letter.'

Frobisher told Hardcastle about the ration party that had been annihilated by a shell, and the assumption, on the part of the battalion commanding officer, that Ogden had been one of the dead. And that it was not until Ogden was arrested that the error had been discovered.

'But what has any of this to do with Captain Porteous, sir?' Marriott, who was trying to record the details of this exchange in some cogent form, addressed his question to Frobisher.

'It seems that Captain Porteous was Harry Ogden's father, Sergeant,' said Frobisher.

'His father?' exclaimed Hardcastle. 'But how the hell was that discovered?'

'By accident, apparently,' said Frobisher. 'After Ogden was executed, his personal effects were searched prior to their despatch to the next of kin; standard practice, of course. His platoon commander found a birth certificate in the name of Harry Porteous, in which his father was shown as Valentine Porteous, an army officer. Incidentally, Ogden, or Porteous, was only seventeen at the time of his execution.'

'And did they send these personal effects to Captain Porteous?'

'I somehow doubt it in view of the confusion over Ogden's real identity. I dare say they were hoping to get a reply to that – ' Frobisher gestured at the letter – 'before actually sending the stuff.'

'But why should he have changed his name from Porteous to Ogden?' Hardcastle was having some difficulty in absorbing this latest turn of events.

'A lot of men enlist under an assumed name, Inspector,' said Frobisher. 'There are many reasons: sometimes a man

will have deserted previously, and then will rejoin the
Colours in a different regiment and under a different name.'
He smiled. 'God knows why they want to re-enlist, but
there it is. Inexplicably drawn to the military life, I suppose.'
He gave a hollow laugh. 'Then again, some youngsters do
it because they've put up their age, and are afraid that their
parents will try to get them out again, once their true age
is known.'

'And that's probably why he did it,' commented
Hardcastle. 'Although I don't know why he should have
bothered. I'd've thought his father, being an officer in the
Devonshire Regiment, would've been proud to have a son
who was doing his bit, so to speak.'

'What made you think that Captain Porteous was in the
Devonshire Regiment, Inspector?' Frobisher raised an
eyebrow.

'He told me he was, Colonel. I interviewed him at
Windsor, the same day that Sergeant Phillips was murdered.'

'Well, I can assure you he wasn't in the Devonshires. When
his absence was reported, I drew his personal file.' Frobisher
took another docket from his desk drawer. 'Porteous was in
the Army Ordnance Corps. Did you not recognize his cap
badge?' He paused. 'No, I suppose you wouldn't have done.
Not really your field of expertise, is it?'

'No, I took his word for it, being an officer and a gent,
like.' Hardcastle at once determined that, if he were to have
much more contact with the army, he would make a study
of military insignia. 'He also told me he fought the Boers
and was wounded at Mons.'

Frobisher laughed. 'He wasn't in either place, Inspector.
But it looks as though he was borrowing the Devonshires'
glory when he mentioned South Africa and Mons.' He
forbore from mentioning medal ribbons; if Hardcastle could
not recognize cap badges, he was unlikely to identify
campaign ribbons. 'I think Porteous's record of service was
the reason why his son preferred to use a different name.
Captain Porteous had a somewhat chequered career, you
see.'

'That comes as no surprise,' said Hardcastle.

The APM referred to the file again. 'He was commissioned from the Royal Military College, Sandhurst, in eighteen-eighty-seven, and gazetted to the Connaught Rangers. It took him twelve years to get his captaincy, and he was probably lucky to get it at all. Reading between the lines of Porteous's confidential reports, I don't think his commanding officer was too impressed by him. To be fair, he probably took against him because he wasn't Irish and, according to Porteous's record, he was a Roman Catholic to boot. In any event, it's fairly unusual for an Englishman to be commissioned into an Irish regiment. Anyway, whatever the reason, Porteous was, shall we say, *persuaded* to apply for a secondment to the Military Provost Staff Corps.' He looked up with an arch smile on his face.

'What are they when they're at home?' asked Hardcastle, becoming more confused by the moment.

'They run military prisons, Inspector.'

'So Porteous was a sort of warder, was he?'

'Not quite,' said Frobisher with a laugh. 'He was actually the officer commanding one wing of the detention barracks at Aldershot. But in nineteen-oh-two he got into trouble there. It turned out that Porteous was something of a petty martinet, and would personally inflict quite serious injury on prisoners who didn't shape up to his standards. Apparently he had a penchant for beating them violently with his walking stick.'

'But don't you have regulations about that sort of thing?' asked Hardcastle. 'Didn't the army do anything about it?'

'Regrettably, it seems not, Inspector, but there was worse to come. According to information I've lately acquired, Porteous was responsible for the death of a prisoner whom he had beaten virtually to death.'

'Why wasn't he charged with murder?' Hardcastle had great difficulty in believing that army discipline was so lax.

'I'm sorry to say that it was hushed up,' said Frobisher, 'but Porteous was dismissed his post,' he added, as though that was punishment enough. 'And as the Connaught Rangers' commanding officer refused to have him back, he was transferred to the Army Ordnance Corps. Since then he has been employed on any sort of odd job that comes up, the latest being recruiting officer at Windsor. Between you and me, Inspector, they didn't dare send him on active service. With his reputation he would very likely have got a bullet in the back from one of his own. And I imagine that his son was afraid that if he enlisted under his real name of Porteous, a connection with his father would be made sooner or later. And that could've made the boy's life a misery. The army's quite a small family – well, it used to be – and word soon gets round.'

'It looks as though I'm going to have to have another word with the bold Captain Porteous,' said Hardcastle.

'If you find him before I do, Inspector, perhaps you'd let me know.'

'Oh, I'll find the bugger, Colonel, you can rest assured of that.'

'Everything all right, Wood?' asked Hardcastle, when he and Marriott returned to Cannon Row.

'Yes, sir. Just one item that might interest you.'

'Oh, and what's that?'

'The PC on five beat arrested a bloke for drunk and disorderly, and begging. At about nine o'clock this morning in St James's Park. The station officer said that the prisoner's asking for you.'

'Really? His name's not Porteous, is it?'

'No, sir, Percy Savage.'

Hardcastle laughed. 'Well, he can bugger off, Wood. Tell the station officer to charge him.' But then he paused. 'On second thoughts, I will have a word with him.' And he and Marriott descended to the front office of the police station.

'All correct, sir.' The station officer, a sergeant, young for his rank, stood up as Hardcastle swept in.

'Open up Savage's cell, Skip.'

'Yes, sir.' The sergeant took a large bunch of keys from a hook on the wall, and led the way into the cell passage. Sliding open the wicket in one of the doors, he peered in. 'Seems to be asleep, sir.'

'Well, I'll soon wake the bugger up,' said Hardcastle. 'Open the door.'

Savage woke up in alarm at the noise made by the door crashing back against the wall of the cell. Recognizing Hardcastle, the prisoner swung his feet on to the floor and stood up. 'Hello, Inspector,' he said nervously, his fingers twitching at the lapels of his jacket.

'You look in a bit of a state, Savage,' commented the DDI. The bankrupt actor-manager was indeed a sorry sight. The suit he wore was threadbare and torn in places, and it was apparent that he had not shaved for several days. Savage's overall appearance was not helped by the fact that the station officer had deprived him of his collar and tie, and bootlaces. It was a constant fear of officers in charge of police stations that one of the prisoners in their custody might commit suicide.

'I was wondering if you could do anything for me, Inspector.'

Hardcastle laughed. 'Really? Like what?'

'I can't possibly go to prison.' Savage spoke in wheedling tones.

'Have you been threatening the prisoner with Dartmoor, Sergeant?' asked Hardcastle, smiling as he turned to the station officer.

'Good heavens, no, sir,' said the sergeant, and grinned.

'What makes you think you'll finish up in stir, then, Savage? If drunk and begging is all you've been nicked for, I doubt you'll get banged up. Unless you can't pay the fine.'

'Well, I can't. I'm on my beam ends, Inspector, and that's a fact.' To emphasize his poverty, Savage pulled out the linings of his trouser pockets to show that they were empty. 'And I've got creditors chasing me all over London.'

'Did this prisoner have any money on him when he was searched, Skipper?' asked Hardcastle.

'No, sir, not a bean,' said the station officer.

'There's nothing I can do for you, my lad,' said Hardcastle, turning to face Savage again. 'You got yourself nicked and you'll have to take the consequences.'

'But if I get fined, and can't pay, I'll finish up inside.' Savage paused. 'So, I was wondering if—'

'I hope you're not trying to tap me for a few quid, Savage. Tantamount to interfering with justice that'd be.' Hardcastle turned to his sergeant. 'Perverting the course, don't you think, Marriott?'

'No doubt about it, sir.' But Marriott knew that anyone attempting to borrow money from his DDI – for whatever reason – stood no chance at all.

'The recruiting officer at Windsor was called Captain Porteous, Savage,' said Hardcastle. 'He was Sergeant Phillips's boss, so to speak.'

'What about him, Inspector?'

'Did you ever see him with Victoria Hart?'

'I don't know.'

'What d'you mean, you don't know?'

'I don't know a Captain Porteous. I've no idea what he looks like.'

'A bloody great help you are,' said Hardcastle dismissively, and turned on his heel, almost colliding with Marriott.

It was perhaps unfortunate for a certain Major Andrew Duncan of the Royal Fusiliers that neither the army nor the police had associated the deaths of two recruiting sergeants in the United Kingdom with the execution of Private Harry Ogden.

Anyway, a world war was being waged, and such comparatively trivial matters as the death of Sergeant Mayhew and Sergeant Phillips in London and Windsor respectively did not warrant widespread concern among the military. Particularly when in France and Belgium men were dying in their thousands. Furthermore, some three days prior to Major Duncan's demise, some twenty people had been killed in a Zeppelin raid on the Norfolk coast.

It was not until Monday the twenty-fifth of January that Hardcastle received a telephone call from Lieutenant Colonel Frobisher that signalled the beginning of the end of the DDI's murder investigation.

* * *

'I don't know whether this will have any bearing on your enquiry, Inspector,' began Frobisher, once Hardcastle and Marriott were seated, once again, in the APM's office at Horse Guards, 'but I've had a routine signal from the Provost Marshal of the British Expeditionary Force.' The colonel's face bore a grave expression.

'About Porteous, Colonel?'

'No, but it's a curious coincidence if it's not. The PM of the BEF reports that Major Andrew Duncan of the Royal Fusiliers has been murdered.'

'I should think quite a few people have been topped over there,' observed Hardcastle drily. 'But I don't see the relevance of this particular murder unless you're suggesting it's got some bearing on the ones I'm investigating.'

'I'm afraid that you'll have to be the judge of that, Inspector,' said Frobisher, 'but let me outline the facts for you. On Friday last – the twenty-second – the Fourth Battalion of the Royal Fusiliers were in rest in a village just south of the River Marne. At about eleven ack-emma, a soldier purporting to be a sarn't-major of the Military Foot Police arrived and asked to see Major Duncan, on his own, regarding an urgent and secret matter. As the visitor was a military police warrant officer, the major acceded to his request immediately. And in private.'

'But I still don't see what this has to do—'

Frobisher raised a hand. 'If you'll let me finish, Inspector, I think you'll be interested. Once this sarn't-major was shown into Duncan's quarters, he drew his revolver and shot the major dead. At the sound of the shot, Duncan's own sarn't-major rushed in, and he too was shot, but fortunately was only wounded in the leg. He called out the alarm, and other soldiers then rushed in. A scuffle ensued, but eventually they overpowered the military policeman.' The colonel paused for quite a few seconds. 'Except that he was an impostor, not a military policeman.'

'This is all very interesting, Colonel,' said Hardcastle, 'but I still don't see what it has to do with me or my investigation.'

Frobisher leaned back in his chair and linked his hands

across the buckle of his Sam Browne belt. 'Major Duncan
was the president of the field general court martial that
sentenced Private Harry Ogden to death, Inspector.'

'Well I'm buggered,' said Hardcastle.

'Exactly so, Inspector,' said Frobisher, smiling for the
first time since the DDI's arrival.

'You say this military policeman was an impostor. What
grounds d'you have for saying that?'

'Once the man was overpowered, the details in his
paybook were passed immediately to the brigade provost
marshal. Within a very short space of time, the brigade PM
discovered that those particulars were false. What I mean
to say is that although it was a genuine document, it did
not relate to the bogus military policeman. In fact the
paybook belonged to a Company Sarn't-Major Crawford
of the Essex Regiment who'd reported it lost or stolen some
months ago. Significantly perhaps, the buttons on the
detained man's uniform were also those of the Essex
Regiment, but the shoulder titles had been removed.
However, he did have military police headdress and wore
an MP brassard.'

'D'you think it's Porteous, Colonel?' asked Marriott.

'I don't know. No one at Four Battalion RF knows
Porteous by sight. And this bogus policeman refuses to say
who he really is. Apart from now claiming that he is
Crawford. But we know that's not true; Crawford has been
interviewed. So we're in a quandary. Porteous's original
commanding officer – the Connaught Rangers colonel – is
dead, and so, of course, is Sergeant Phillips, the recruiting
sergeant at Windsor.'

'Hold on, Colonel,' said Hardcastle. 'If you think I'm
going over to France on the off-chance of identifying this
man, you can think again. God Almighty, Mrs Hardcastle
would have a blue fit. And so, I should imagine, would my
Commissioner.'

Frobisher laughed. 'There's no suggestion that you'd be
asked to go to France, Inspector. The man, who has still
not been identified, is being brought to the Tower of
London.'

'Very appropriate,' murmured Hardcastle. 'But why there?'

'As you know, it's the regimental headquarters of the Royal Fusiliers, Major Duncan's regiment. Anyway, it's a convenient place for the prisoner to be interrogated, and for you to have a look at him. And if it turns out to be Porteous, you'll obviously have first claim on him. If you think he's your murderer, that is, and I assume you do.'

'But if it's Porteous, where would he have got hold of an Essex Regiment uniform, and why?' Hardcastle had earlier come to the conclusion that he would never understand the army.

'He's in the Ordnance Corps, Inspector. It's the corps responsible for issuing uniform.'

'Did this Major Duncan preside over any other courts martial, sir?' enquired Marriott. 'It could be that the murder of Major Duncan is connected to another case rather than Ogden's. Something to do with the Essex Regiment, perhaps?'

'That, of course, is a strong possibility, Sergeant. So far, we don't know the answer to that question, but urgent enquiries are being made to find out if Duncan was involved in any other courts martial.'

'And when is this soldier likely to arrive here, Colonel?' asked Hardcastle.

'Tomorrow morning, Inspector. He's being brought overnight from Le Havre to Southampton. Should be firmly ensconced in the Tower by lunchtime.'

Major Montague Holmes, regimental adjutant of the Royal Fusiliers, was still wearing his greatcoat when Frobisher and the two civil policemen arrived at the Tower of London.

'Excuse my dress, Colonel,' said Holmes, 'but it's bloody freezing in this place. There's damn' all exciting about being stationed at the Tower. By the bye, have you heard the news?'

'What news?'

'HMS *Lion* sank the *Blücher* yesterday. Admiral Beatty

seemed to think the Huns were going to have another go
at shelling Scarborough and Hartlepool.'

'Splendid news indeed,' said Frobisher. 'However, Monty,
to get back to our reason for being here, has this fellow
said anything?'

'Not a word, Colonel, apart from asking for a Bible.
D'you want to see him?'

'Yes, and so do these gentlemen who, I believe, you've
met before.'

'Indeed I have,' said Holmes, shaking hands with
Hardcastle and Marriott. 'D'you want this chap brought up
here, Colonel, or will you see him in his cell?'

Frobisher turned to Hardcastle. 'Which would you prefer,
Inspector?'

'I'll see him in his peter, Colonel.'

'In his where?' Holmes, unfamiliar with the argot of the
civil police, raised his eyebrows. Although it was his second
meeting with Hardcastle, he had yet to gauge the man.

'It's criminal slang for a prison cell,' explained Hardcastle.
'With a name like yours, Major Holmes, I'd've thought
you'd've known that.'

'You'll learn a lot about the underworld from Mr
Hardcastle, Monty,' said Frobisher with a chuckle.

Holmes led the three policemen through a series of dank
passageways, down a flight of stone steps and into an icy
cold cellar, the walls of which were running with conden-
sation.

A regimental police sergeant leaped to his feet and saluted
at the sight of Frobisher and Holmes. 'Sah!' he screamed
for no good reason.

'Let these gentlemen into the unknown soldier's cell,
Sarn't,' said Holmes. 'They want a word with him.'

'Sah!' screamed the sergeant once more, and seized a
bunch of keys.

The cell, unlike any in police stations, was a window-
less, stone-flagged cavern with bars from floor to ceiling,
in the centre of which was a gate. Inside, the figure of a
soldier – his face to the wall – lay on a wooden plank that
served as a bed, its single blanket folded neatly on a bolster.

'I'll leave you to it, Colonel,' said Holmes. 'The RP sergeant will get someone to show you the way back to my office.'

'Sah!' yelled the sergeant. It appeared to be the limit of his military vocabulary.

There was a great rattling of old-fashioned keys, and eventually the sergeant swung open the heavy barred gate.

Eighteen

Hardcastle was first into the cell, closely followed by Marriott and Frobisher.

'Porteous!' shouted the DDI, taking a wild guess that he might at last have found the man he believed to be responsible for the deaths of Victoria Hart and Sergeant Phillips. And possibly that of Sergeant Mayhew.

The soldier stirred, turned and sat up. 'What? What is it?' Having been woken from a deep sleep, he had answered to his true name.

Hardcastle stared at the man, clad now in canvas fatigues. 'But you're not Captain Porteous,' he exclaimed in surprise.

'Never said I was, now did I?' The soldier's surly response was delivered with an Irish accent.

'On your feet, soldier. Officer present,' screamed the regimental police sergeant from the corridor outside the cell.

'Go to hell, you wee spalpeen.' The prisoner, facing a murder charge, was unconcerned at minor disciplinary infringements, and replied scathingly.

'I won't tell you again, soldier. Stand up.' The RP sergeant went red in the face and puffed out his chest at such insubordination.

'And what'll you be thinking of doing if I don't? Stamping your foot, is it?'

Hardcastle turned to face the APM. 'I'd appreciate it if I might be permitted to have a word with this man without interruption, Colonel,' he said mildly.

'Yes, of course.' Frobisher was not as affronted by the prisoner's indiscipline as the sergeant. 'Just get back to your duties, Sergeant,' he said sharply. 'I'll send for you if I need you.'

'Sah!' screamed the sergeant predictably.

'Your name is Porteous?' said Hardcastle.

'So it is. That's what I answered to.'

'Well, as you're clearly not Captain Valentine Porteous, who are you?'

With a shrug, and a sigh of resignation, the soldier stood up. He took a half-smoked cigarette from his pocket. 'Anyone got a light?' he asked.

Hardcastle handed over a box of matches, and waited while the soldier lit his cigarette. 'I'm Divisional Detective Inspector Hardcastle of Scotland Yard.'

'Now there's a thing. I thought I'd be meeting you sooner or later, Inspector. I'm Company Sarn't-Major Clarence Porteous of the Essex Regiment.'

'How old are you?'

'Twenty-seven. Why?'

'Bit young for a sergeant-major, aren't you?'

'It might come as news to you, Inspector, but we're losing men hand over fist across the water. Promotion comes a hell of a lot faster these days than it did in peacetime. And I should know. I joined the Essex in nineteen-oh-five, and it took me nine years to make lance-corporal. On the first of January nineteen-fourteen, so it was. Then this lot started and here I am a sarn't-major.'

'And does Captain Valentine Porteous, of the Army Ordnance Corps, happen to be your father, Mr Porteous?' Although Hardcastle might not be too good at recognizing army cap badges, he had learned that warrant officers were addressed as 'mister', and saw no reason not to do so now.

'Yes, and a right double-dyed bastard he is, too.'

'Have you any idea where he is now?'

'Recruiting more poor sods for the carnage, I suppose. Still down at Windsor as far as I know. Why, what d'you want with him?'

'He's gone absent without leave, Sarn't-Major,' said Frobisher from behind Hardcastle.

Porteous let out a guffaw of laughter. 'Well, bugger me, sir. If that don't take the biscuit, nothing does. Fancy my old man going on the run. Makes you laugh, doesn't it? All that crap about officers and gentlemen he used to go on about.'

Hardcastle turned and took Frobisher's arm, steering him out of the cell. 'With your permission, Colonel,' he said quietly, 'I should like to have Sergeant-Major Porteous transferred to Cannon Row. I suspect very strongly that he's the man I need to talk to about the murder of Victoria Hart and Sergeants Mayhew and Phillips.'

'There is somewhat of a procedural problem here, Inspector,' said Frobisher thoughtfully, 'given that he's in custody for the murder of Major Duncan. Of course, if you were to arrest Sarn't-Major Porteous for murder . . . '

'I'd rather not do that, Colonel. Not yet, anyway.' Hardcastle gave a grim laugh. 'You see, I don't have any evidence. There's no doubt in my mind, at least from what you've told me, that he's guilty of murdering Major Duncan, but I'm not sure he was responsible for the others. It may even have been his father. After all, he's the one who's run, and I can't think of a good reason for him having legged it if he didn't do the toppings. Apart from anything else, Sergeant-Major Porteous was in France when his collar was felt, so to speak.'

Frobisher ran a hand round his chin. 'All right, Inspector,' he said eventually. 'I'll have an escort deliver him to your police station as soon as possible.'

Lieutenant Colonel Frobisher was as good as his word. At five o'clock that same evening, Porteous arrived at Cannon Row police station in the custody of two military police warrant officers. After a great deal of form-filling, and a bit of inter-service badinage, the prisoner was handed over to the civil police in the person of the station officer.

Thirty minutes later, Porteous was facing Hardcastle and Marriott in the interview room near the front of the station. Now that he was wearing uniform, it was apparent that Clarence Porteous was a very handsome man, with a full head of dark hair and twinkling brown eyes. But that did not interest Hardcastle as much as the man's stature. He was six foot tall and well built, and would have been quite capable of strangling Victoria Hart and carrying her body into Windsor Great Park.

'I must say your cells are a bloody sight more comfortable than them up at the Tower, Inspector. But what I want to know is why I'm here.'

Hardcastle had no intention of launching into too early an interrogation about the two murders he was investigating, and the one that 'Posh Bill' Sullivan at Vine Street was dealing with. 'Why aren't you commissioned, Mr Porteous?' he began. 'I understand that your father went to Sandhurst. Why didn't you?'

'I s'pose you haven't got a fag, have you?'

'Give the sergeant-major one of your cigarettes, Marriott,' said Hardcastle.

With an inward sigh, Marriott tossed the soldier a cigarette and slid a box of matches across the scarred table.

'Because I was born the wrong side of the blanket, Inspector,' said Porteous, once he had lit his cigarette, 'and they're not too keen on bastards at Sandhurst. At least, not as gentlemen cadets. They'd probably have taken me on as a drill instructor, though.'

'And I suppose your father didn't want to marry your mother,' suggested Hardcastle.

'Couldn't,' said Porteous succinctly. 'He was only nineteen when he put my ma up the spout. King's Regulations – well, it was Queen's Regs then – doesn't allow an officer to get married under the age of twenty-six. At least, not without the colonel's say-so, and the colonel he had in that Irish mob hated the old man's guts. So that was it. I finished up with a birth certificate that showed just the place of birth – Sligo – and the name of my mother, Mary Cullen, who died when I was sixteen. But where it had a space for the name of my father, there was a bloody great blank.'

'So how come you took the name of Porteous?'

'My mother told me who he was. A dashing young officer in the Connaught Rangers, she told me. So after she went to her grave – consumption and bloody starvation, so it was – I tracked the bastard down. We had a stand-up row, and I told him what I thought of him. Then I buggered off and joined the army. But I wish I'd changed my name. After I took the King's shilling, I found out about him beating a young swaddy to death at Aldershot. So anyone who asked me if I was related, I told 'em not bloody likely.'

'Why did you murder Major Duncan?'

'What's that got to do with you? It's a military matter.'

'Just interested,' said Hardcastle.

'Because that bastard sentenced my half-brother to death, the poor little sod.'

'You're talking about Harry Ogden of the Royal Fusiliers, I suppose.'

'That's him.'

'How did you find out that Major Duncan presided over that court martial?'

'Court martial?' exclaimed Porteous disgustedly. 'Bloody kangaroo court, so it was. But it's not difficult to find these things out when you're in the Kate Carney, Inspector,' he said, without revealing exactly how he had discovered Duncan's role in the death of Harry Ogden.

'And what about Victoria Hart?'

'What about her?'

'Why did you kill her?' Hardcastle posed the question tentatively, not really expecting a positive reply.

But Porteous was shrewd enough to know that he would undoubtedly be hanged for the murder of Major Duncan, so there was no point in denying his part in the other deaths. After all, he thought to himself, they can only hang you once.

'I didn't mean to kill her. I just wanted to talk to her about Harry. I wanted to know what sort of woman it was who could persuade young fellows like Harry to join up. I suppose it was because she danced about the stage practically bloody naked, and promised young kids a kiss if they joined up. Poor little bugger had no idea what he was getting into. Didn't know what it was like over there.' Porteous stared unseeing beyond Hardcastle as he visualized the brutal deaths of so many young men, cut down in the prime of their lives. And in his mind's ear, he still heard the constant, deafening thunder of the guns, and the rattle of enemy Maxims. 'All because some stupid bastard shot some bloody archduke in Sarajevo, and our clever sods of politicians decided the only answer was to go to war over it.' He glanced at Marriott. 'Can you spare me another fag, Sarge?'

Marriott gave Porteous another cigarette.

'You see, Inspector,' Porteous continued, 'Harry was my half-brother. After my father was made captain, he married an actress called Eliza Ogden, who was appearing at the Aldershot Hippodrome. The fleapit, the swaddies call it. She was Harry's mother, but she buggered off a couple of years after he was born.' He gave a caustic laugh. 'Ran away with a circus tightrope-walker. Mind you, she was quite a bit younger than the old man, so I heard tell. But it didn't half put his nose out of joint. Not the sort of thing one cares to mention in the jolly old mess, eh what?' he added, affecting an officer-like drawl.

'Did you send Victoria Hart a telegram last Christmas Eve, Mr Porteous?'

'I did that. I found out she was married to a naval commander, a bloke called Kenneth. So I signed it K in the hope she'd think I was him.'

'How did you find that out?'

'I sweet-talked one of the girls in the show. Picked her up one night, and bought her a sherry and lemonade, and she told me all I wanted to know. Surprising what a touch of the blarney can do.'

'Who was this girl?' Hardcastle was furious that it might have been either Vera Cobb or Fanny Morris. If that were the case, he would have a very sharp word with whoever of them had failed to tell him about this meeting.

'No idea, Inspector. I think she said her name was Elsie something, but I can't remember. The upshot was that I sent Victoria a telegram, pretending to be her old man, and asking her to meet me. And, bugger me, she did an' all.' Porteous grinned at the recollection.

'And what happened next?' Hardcastle knew that the pathologist had estimated that Victoria's time of death was about seven o'clock, and was surprised that Porteous had somehow managed to keep the music-hall artiste engaged for nearly two hours before killing her. Even though Porteous was not her husband, and had tricked her into the meeting.

'I sent the telegram asking her to meet me at the White Hart in Windsor. And there she was, sitting in the foyer. Funnily enough, she didn't seem at all annoyed when she found out I wasn't her old man. So I told her that she'd recruited Harry, and that he'd been killed in action. I thought it was better than telling her the poor wee sod had been shot at dawn. She said how sorry she was to hear it. I told her that I didn't want to hold her up, because she was bound to have another appointment.'

'What did she say to that, Mr Porteous?'

'She told me not to worry, and that she had all the time in the world. Anyway, I asked her to come for a drink because I wanted to talk to her about Harry. They don't let women in the bar at the White Hart, so I took her to a pub. She was very sympathetic, and said how sorry she was. But as we left the pub—'

'What time was that?' asked Hardcastle.

'Must have been about quarter past six,' said Porteous. 'Anyway, we left the pub and I was about to thank her for listening when she asked me to take her for a walk. She linked her arm through mine and said something about how much she liked soldiers, and that was why she helped with recruiting.'

'And this was all quite voluntary, was it?' asked Hardcastle suspiciously.

'Voluntary? Heavens, man, she was desperate keen to go for a walk, so she was. Perhaps it was the Irish in me that appealed to her.' Porteous smiled. 'It's surprising what a bit of Irish charm will do to a colleen.'

Hardcastle was surprised at that, and did not believe it. A woman who was apparently excited by the prospect of meeting her husband that evening, suddenly decided that she wanted to go for a walk with a soldier she had only just met. It seemed to indicate an entirely different side to Victoria Hart's character than his enquiries had revealed. Except, perhaps, for the view expressed by the girl's mother-in-law.

'Go on, Mr Porteous.'

'She was a smashing girl. Very friendly, and willing to listen. Well, we walked for quite a way, and finished up in Windsor Great Park, just inside like. But it was then that she started a come-on.'

'In what way?'

'She stopped under an oak tree, and pulled open the fur coat she was wearing. She pulled it right back and put her hands on her hips and I saw she was wearing the costume she wore in the show. There was hardly anything of it. Then she pushed out one of her legs, all in black silk they were. She smiled, and asked me what I thought of her. She must've been bloody freezing in that outfit for the weather was desperate cold. Then she came up real close and started to run her hands all over me. Completely shameless, so she was.'

'Weren't you interested in a woman who was offering herself like that, Mr Porteous?' Hardcastle sounded surprised.

'She was nothing but a common whore, Inspector.' Porteous put on a good show of sounding scandalized. 'But that apart, I remembered what happened to my dear mother, God rest her soul. After my old man had put her up the spout, he just abandoned her – and me – and went on his way rejoicing. Well, I was brought up in the Catholic faith, and I was not going to repeat the sins of my father, and I told her so.'

'Was she annoyed?'

'Holy Mary, Mother of God! Annoyed? She started accusing me of not knowing what to do with a woman when I was offered one on a plate. She was really shouting by then, and said if I didn't satisfy her, she'd accuse me of raping her, so I might as well take what was on offer. I was afraid someone would hear her, and take her word for it. Well, I couldn't let that happen.' Porteous sighed, and leaned back in the hard wooden chair on which he was sitting. 'So I put my hands round her neck to try and shut her up. But then she collapsed at my feet. I bent down to pick her up, but she was dead.'

'So you ran away,' said Hardcastle.

Porteous gave a derisive laugh. 'Well, what would you have done, Inspector?' he asked.

Hardcastle was surprised at how easily Porteous's confession had come, but he suspected that the sergeant-major was well aware that he would be unable to avoid the death penalty for the murder of Major Duncan. And any more murders he admitted to would make no difference. But he had not believed a word of Porteous's tale, and assumed that he was trying to justify having killed a woman.

'And Sergeant Mayhew of the Scots Guards?' The DDI threw in the name casually, and began to fill his pipe.

'He was the sergeant who actually recruited Harry. At the Empire Theatre, Leicester Square. That was different. He was in the army, and he knew what was going on across the water. He was in a cushy billet, and didn't care who he sent to his death. So in my book, he deserved to die. I followed him from the theatre and done him in Panton Street.' Porteous spoke in matter-of-fact tones, but Hardcastle assumed that a man fresh from the Front was no stranger to violent death.

'And did you write "Nemo me imp" on the wall?'

Porteous laughed. 'Yeah, but I never had time to finish it because some colleen turned the corner of the street. The bastard was in the Scots Guards. It's their motto, see.'

'So I've heard,' said Hardcastle drily. 'What did you hit him with?'

'An iron bar,' said Porteous laconically. 'And then I chucked it over a wall somewhere. I don't know where it was, because I'd been running for a bit. You see, I thought Harry was already dead by then. I'd called on the old man in Acton, and he showed me the letter he'd had from the Tower of London notifying him of Harry's death. But it all turned out to be a mistake. Harry had gone on the run, but they thought he was dead. Then I heard from a sarn't-major in the Shiny Seventh that Harry'd been shot at dawn for running.'

'But your half-brother enlisted as Harry Ogden, not

Porteous, so how did you and your father know it was him?'

'Didn't take much working out,' said Porteous. 'His first name was Harry, and the address was the same. And, like I said, Ogden was his mother's maiden name.'

Hardcastle glanced across at Marriott, writing furiously as he sought to get Porteous's account down on paper.

'Why, then, did you kill Sergeant Phillips?'

'He saw me.'

'When did he see you?'

'Just as I was leaving the White Hart with Victoria. I couldn't risk him telling you lot that he'd seen a sarn't-major from the Essex with her, could I? Wouldn't have taken you clever buggers long to track me down. I knew who Phillips was because I'd seen the show the night before. Mind you, he was pissed at the time, but I couldn't take a chance.'

'And the quotation from the Bible?'

'Seemed right,' said Porteous. 'I told you I was brought up a Roman Catholic, and I went to a Catholic school. Well, the nuns there rammed the Bible down your throat, all day and every day. I thought that that quote was just about right.'

'There's one thing that puzzles me in all this, Mr Porteous,' said Hardcastle.

'What's that?'

'According to the assistant provost marshal, your battalion was in action down near Armentières. How come you were in this country?'

Porteous laughed. 'Easy, Inspector. I deserted at the beginning of last October, just after we heard about Harry's death. Except he wasn't dead. Not then, any road.'

'If you were a deserter, what were you doing walking about the streets of Windsor in uniform? Weren't you afraid you'd be challenged?'

Porteous scoffed at the suggestion. 'And who's going to question a sarn't-major, Inspector? It was just the same when I went back to France to do Major Bloody Duncan. If you're a sarn't-major, you just walk on the boat down Southampton Docks. No one asks any questions.'

'But supposing your father had seen you in Windsor. Taking a bit of a chance, wasn't it?'

'Fuck him,' said Porteous. 'I'd've done him an' all.'

Six weeks later, Company Sergeant-Major Clarence Porteous was hanged at Pentonville Prison for the murders of Sergeant Frank Mayhew, Victoria Hart, Sergeant Sidney Phillips and Major Andrew Duncan.

Porteous's defence counsel had tried very hard to prove that his client came within the scope of *The Rules in McNaghten's Case* that allowed for a verdict of 'guilty but insane', and its consequent confinement in Broadmoor Criminal Lunatic Asylum. But the Old Bailey judge had dismissed any hope of that, rightly or wrongly telling the jury that, in his view, four such premeditated murders, spread over a period of three months, could not possibly have been the work of a madman. Rather, the judge continued, they had been the work of a calculating murderer. As for Porteous's claim that the death of Victoria Hart had been an accident, he dismissed that out of hand.

The following day, when Hardcastle had returned to Windsor to submit his final report, he met the chief constable in the corridor outside his office, and informed him of the result. Without breaking step, the chief merely nodded, and commented that he was 'pleased'.

A week after Clarence Porteous's execution, Hardcastle received a letter of thanks from John Lester, Victoria's father. He wrote that he and his wife had followed the trial, and could not possibly believe that their daughter had behaved in the way that Porteous's counsel had described.

Although Hardcastle never discovered what Edith Hart thought about it all, he was prepared to hazard a guess.

But the DDI himself was never quite sure about Victoria Hart. Did she have an affair with Percy Savage, despite the actor-manager's denials? Did she have other, undiscovered, romantic liaisons? Was her appearance on stage in a revealing costume, and her willingness to kiss recruits, deliberately provocative? Or was it just part of an actress's professional alter ego?

And then there was the question of the telegram purporting to be from her husband. Even though the deception would have been apparent to her the moment she set eyes on Clarence Porteous, she went willingly with him to a public house knowing that she was wearing only that skimpy outfit beneath her coat.

In the end, Hardcastle wondered if there was perhaps a scintilla of truth in the story the sergeant-major had told about his meeting with the girl.

It was an enigma, but the solution went with her to her grave.

Some days later, a Southend-on-Sea landlady took an early morning cup of tea to one of her 'paying guests', only to find that he had shot himself with a service revolver.

The landlady believed the dead man to have been a travelling salesman, but he was later identified as Captain Valentine Porteous of the Army Ordnance Corps. A note found next to the body spoke of Porteous's shame at having two sons each of whom had been executed.

Screwed up in Valentine Porteous's left hand was a pencilled letter dated 4th January 1915:

> Dear Dad
>   This will be the last letter you ever get from me because they are going to shoot me in the morning. They said I deserted, but I couldn't stand it any longer. I'm sorry to have brought disgrace on you, especially as you're an officer. If you ever meet mother again, please tell her I died a hero.
> God bless you.
> Your loving son,
> Harry

Near the man's right hand was a cutting from the *Morning Post* that reported the hanging of Clarence Porteous, and described in some detail the crimes for which he had been executed.

It appeared, however, that there was another reason for Valentine Porteous's suicide. Shortly after his disappearance from Victoria Barracks, an audit of officers' mess funds had been conducted, prior to the handover to the new treasurer.

Being mess treasurer is a thankless task, and the other officers had been extremely grateful when Porteous volunteered to take it on. But their gratitude had turned to fury when it was discovered that several hundred pounds were missing.

That, of course, was a matter for the military police, but when Lieutenant Colonel Frobisher told the DDI about it, he laughed.

'I knew there was something not quite right about him, the first time I saw him,' commented Hardcastle, certain that the letting agent had telephoned Porteous to say that the police were making enquiries about him. If that had been the case, Porteous must have believed that his embezzlement had already been discovered.

In September 1915 the Widow Sochard gave birth to a son at a remote farmhouse not far from the River Marne. It was an event that caused eyebrows to be raised among those of her friends who possessed some knowledge of mathematics. Nearly twenty-five years later – on the 16th of May 1940, to be precise – Harry Sochard was among the many French soldiers to die in the opening stages of the German invasion of France.